KING

OF THE

UNSIGHTLY

BELLE BRIAR

MAY YOU
FIND
HUMOR

*To my friends and family who told me
I couldn't quit even if I tried.*

TRIGGER WARNINGS

Profanity
Alcohol Abuse
Depiction of Cheating
Anxiety
Physical Abuse
Kidnapping
Torture
Violence
Blood and Gore
Harassment
Murder
Death
Dismemberment/Beheading

IN YOUR
DARKEST
MOMENTS
LIKE
ADELINE.

CONTENTS

1
WITCHING HOUR AND WHISKEY

All I wanted to do was relax in my crummy apartment, binge-watch my cliché romance movies, and cry my eyes out after my horrible breakup with Jared. Not deal with my mind's twisted idea of a bad omen.

Man, my hallucinations were out of control. No way that lady kicked down my door.

A muffled squeak fled my throat, and I nearly toppled over my dining room table as the lady materialized in a chair beside me. I lurched back, slid open my window, and scanned all the rusty cars crowding the parking lot.

Everything outside looked normal.

My sight fixed on the woman still leaning in the chair, and my breathing hitched; her long black fingernails clicking against the table sent shivers down my spine.

If this was a new type of foreplay, I was far from interested, and I *really* hoped Lucien didn't have the audacity to hire a stripper. The possibility wasn't entirely out of the question since he attempted something similar for my last birthday in hopes of raising my spirits. *Ridiculous.*

Her mouth curled into a crooked grin. "The name's Raagini, and we need to talk."

A small freckle on her left cheek disappeared into her smile lines as I gawked at her sheer confidence. "Yeaaah, okay." Wow. I finally hit rock bottom, even for me.

Her ebony hair bounced along with the tapping of her laced, black boots connecting with the tile floor; the thick layer of mud plastered on her soles chipped off with each tap.

She kicked her boot again and more mud fell, and I sighed in frustration. *A stripper would have the common courtesy to knock and not track dirt everywhere.*

This lady was so inconsiderate.

Raagini clapped her hands, and my concentration went back to her. "Soon you will be thrown into a war you don't understand. One Larisa started and you, sweetie, will have to end." She pulled out a lighter and popped it open, lighting a cigarette and taking a long drag before blowing it in my face. She met my gaze again with the cigarette between her tobacco-stained teeth, and I coughed at the secondhand smoke penetrating my lungs. "My, why are you acting so skittish? It's only a warning. I'm here because your mother's magic is fading, and her coven will stop at nothing to control the keys."

A thick layer of smoke permeated the air, and I waved my hand, blinking a few times to fully take in her presence.

What the hell was she even rambling on about?

She obliterated my front door, materialized in front of me, and babbled on about magic, keys, and my mother, and dared to judge me for acting a little skittish? Newsflash lady—any normal person would have kept screaming bloody murder. And I wasn't some coming-of-age preteen who recently found out about her dark past and was prophesied to save the world. No. I was a twenty-three-year-old woman eating premade sandwiches for dinner for god's sake, and who had more important things to worry about than a psychotic rant from a stranger—like my overdue rent.

Yeah, a stiff drink was needed after all this.

My throbbing temple threatened a migraine as I grounded myself back in reality. "Listen here, uh." I rubbed my forehead, and tried to remember the name she told me after she kicked down my door. "Rebel?"

"Raagini."

"Rigggggght. Well, I don't know if you've noticed but I don't have magic . . . and you're insane." I raised my voice and pointed to the hallway. "Now get the hell out of my apartment!"

Raagini threw her head back, slapped her knee, and cackled as if I said the funniest shit in the world. Her laughter died as she snatched the coffee mug in front of her and swirled it around. Her glare darkened as she smashed the cup against the wall, shattering it into tiny fragments. Her palm dripped blood as the artificial light reflected the pieces puncturing her open wound.

"This will be you if you don't learn to protect yourself."

She chanted under her breath, and the shards flew from the floor to her palm, reconstructing to their original form.

The cup fell to her hand, repaired like she didn't slam it against the wall. I pivoted slightly, my vision lingering on my jean jacket placed on the counter a couple of feet from where she sat.

Could I slip away while she entertained herself with cheap magic tricks? And did Lucien honestly think hiring a deranged magician would make me feel better? *Where was he, anyways?*

A hard lump formed in the back of my throat, and I swallowed. "Super cool." I scrambled to the counter, snatched the jacket, and shimmied into the black pants I left in the hallway when I thought my night would consist of movies, ice cream, and ugly crying, not some lady who got off on scaring the living shit out of me.

The door was still attached to the bottom hinge as I slid on my ankle boots and staggered out of my apartment.

"Now is not the time to run from your past, Adeline! The creatures next won't be as hospitable!"

"Sure thing, lady, and how about next time, you ring the fucking doorbell!" I yelled back. My muscles strained under the tension enveloping my body as I rushed down the hallway, not giving Raagini a second thought.

The elevator dinged as I flew past it to the twentieth-story emergency exit. I shouldn't take the stairs, but as a creature of habit, no way would I confine myself to such a tight, closed-off space. Elevators were a big no in my book, and I would rather be free and out of breath than trapped like a rat. It reminded me too much of the basement as a child.

My foster parents loved to spout nonsense like how it would cleanse me of all my sins if I stayed down there long enough. God, the Kelleys were complete psychopaths.

My hand was firmly pressed to the side of the wall as I shifted my weight and willed the thoughts of them away. My pace quickened as the loud thumps of my boots slamming against the steps rang in my ears.

I rounded the stairwell and my left shoulder collided with another, and I shrieked.

A wave of nausea washed over me. Raagini's sharp, piercing features now occupied my mind.

My frantic heart launched out of my chest, or at least on the verge of it when I spun to face who I crashed into.

Ah. It's not her. I emptied my breath and wiped the sweat dripping from my forehead.

"What's your problem?" the woman snarled.

I frowned at how her tattered navy blue hoodie hung loose over her shoulders as she glared at me. She passed over a needle to a gangly looking man with greasy hair. He slouched halfway over the railing; the stench of mouthwash and stale weed compelled my nose to wrinkle in revulsion.

Could I perhaps run into someone a little less aggressive, or was I asking too much?

The woman narrowed her eyes as I gave her a short shrug and continued my descent. I didn't need to apologize. I needed to get away from my apartment before Raagini appeared in front of me again.

A muffled *fuckin' psycho* echoed as I descended farther.

I chuckled between the sharp breaths stabbing my lungs. Any other day, I might have picked a fight with that lady, but not tonight.

Tonight . . . I reached my limit.

I pushed open the emergency door, avoiding the parking lot and the unwelcoming stares. The cool wind flailed against my skin as I bolted across the street, tripping over the sidewalk step and falling headfirst through a bush.

I grumbled and whacked it with my fists and took a deep breath before I regained my dignity and stood up. *Of course this would happen to me at the worst possible time.*

And even if I thought I had an ounce of magic, I would have turned my foster parents into toads or skipped town or maybe attempted to make money off scamming people. But I definitely wouldn't run from her if I did or let myself tumble into a bush like a clumsy idiot.

Hoping to god no one witnessed my minute of vulnerability, I trekked along the sidewalk. The dirt clung to my palms, and I patted them off on the sides of my pants. I lifted my head, and my stress evaporated as the gaudy sign embellished with silver wings sparkled in the moonlight above me.

I yanked my shirt down to appear less frumpy, and a murder of crows reflected in the tinted window of Hera's Palace, emerging from the dark alley behind me.

"For fuck's sake, let a girl breathe."

A couple walking hand in hand rounded the corner and shot me concerning looks. I waved, but it only creeped them out as they scurried faster and crossed the street.

Ouch. A little hurtful.

An obnoxious crow gilded past me and landed on the windowpane and craned its neck. "Is she dull, Gren?"

"She changed."

"She's hideous."

"I have doubts."

"Can't be."

"Definitely not."

"Quiet!" the one-eyed crow shouted. They hushed, immediately. He seemed like the one in charge and the one called Gren, seeing as they all settled their feathers and looked at him once he spoke again. "She is the one who has the key."

They all croaked and mimicked a *yes, yes* as if satisfied with Gren's answer, not that I cared. If I indulged in my hallucinations any further, it wouldn't do me any favors.

Disregarding their bickering, I pushed open the glass door and a sweet aroma of apples with a hint of oak and spice caressed my nose. In the corner, a pianist stroked the keys effortlessly as they swayed to the music. The ballad soared through the air, the heartbreak evident in each note.

From the crystal chandeliers to the dim lighting, I stuck out like a sore thumb. My outfit didn't match the aesthetic at all. People in formfitting suits and cocktail dresses occupied all the tables. I contemplated turning back when they skimmed me over. But I wouldn't let a few pompous-face assholes deter me. And I didn't have it in me to wait in the dark for a lift to Crest's, the place I frequented the most in Deanville.

So my options were . . . drink and get mean-mugged or sit in the alley and have a bunch of crows shit-talk me?

Obviously, I'd rather drink.

I passed a couple; the man sported a buttoned-up, all-black suit with a cerulean-blue tie and slicked-back hair, and the woman wore a slimming emerald dress adorned in silver jewels. Her long auburn hair rested in loose curls as she twirled a full glass of red wine. She looked me over, but surprisingly, without discontent. The man on the other hand, his look of disgust was palpable.

So I gave him what he wanted. *A show.*

I flashed him a smug grin and a wink, making damn sure he saw my *I Heart DILFs* shirt in all its glory. A glimpse of a smirk appeared on the woman's face, but she turned, giving her full attention to her glass.

Satisfied, I rushed to the restroom. I still had *some* decorum, no matter how small.

I bent over the sink and wiped the smudged mascara under my gold-speckled, blue eyes, grumbling in defeat. I looked exactly as I did when I broke up with Jared a few days ago. A hot mess. My brunette hair splintered out like I went through a windstorm, and I tried like hell to smooth it down to no avail. My cheeks flushed with color, and my lips were parched, aching for water.

I did the best I could and took out my red lipstick from my jacket pocket and applied it over my full lips. I managed to tame my hair down a bit, making myself appear half decent.

Content with my appearance, I glided out of the doorway and sat on a mahogany barstool. I ran my fingers through my hair and waited for the bartender to notice me.

My necklace came to mind, and I pulled it from under my shirt and squeezed it in my palm; my other hand tapped the bar top rigorously as I traced the key before shoving it back underneath my shirt.

Why would anyone want this piece of junk? With a silver key in the shape of a hexagon and an engraved crescent moon on it, it looked like some cheap knockoff. And it was only a simple keepsake from my mother with some weird written language on it I couldn't comprehend. Not that I desired to find out what it meant or what Raagini was talking about. It only soured my mood when I thought about her.

The bartender appeared in front of me, and I jerked backward. "What can I get you?"

I rubbed the nape of my neck and eyed the shelves of liquor. "Whiskey and ginger ale." I desperately craved something strong but also something that wouldn't upset my stomach, and this was the perfect concoction.

The bartender plopped the drink down with a bored expression—not holding back any of their hostility.

I guess they didn't like my DILFs shirt either. Go figure.

"Fifteen dollars," the bartender said in a pinched tone and with glazed-over eyes.

Forcing my jaw not to drop, I handed my debit card over. Small tears welled in the corners of my eyes, but I quickly blinked them away. The thought of my bank account plunging any further crushed my soul.

I'm fine. This is fine. It's not like I had an eviction notice on my apartment door or got fired for punching some creep who grabbed my ass last night.

Oh, wait . . .

I chuckled humorlessly and rested my forehead on the cool bar top.

Sulking wouldn't save me or give me my job back. Figuring out my plans going forward was my best bet.

I launched upright, grabbed my drink, and took a sip. Relaxation enveloped me like an inviting blanket as the icy liquid warmed my stomach. My worries seamlessly melted away.

BELLE BRIAR

"Found you," a sultry voice sang behind my ear.

2
IN THE DARK

"**G**et lost." I slammed my drink down.

Jared poked his head over my shoulder as his black curls brushed against my cheek. He stepped back and his mesmerizing green eyes locked on mine.

I groaned and twisted my body to evade his touch. "Did you not hear me?" I asked, the venom seeping from my voice.

Could he not take a hint? I wanted some peace and quiet, and his presence did neither for me.

"Ouch. I'm devastated." Jared placed a hand on his heart like I physically wounded him. And man I wish I had.

A frown expanded across my face as he flashed a smile—one I used to love, but now it only pissed me off. His flirty antics were just plain annoying.

Jared leaned against the bar and looked me over. He didn't

bother sitting down on the barstool. Which told me: he didn't plan on sticking around, or he didn't want to wrinkle his tailor-made suit that molded to his muscular physique perfectly.

God, I hated him.

"Clearly." I glanced past Jared and at his two friends loitering behind. "Hello, Chad One. Chad Two. It's been too long. I missed you guys." I gave them an insincere salute, but it looked more like a flick of the wrist.

Chad One scoffed as he turned and muttered *psycho* to Chad Two.

I didn't remember their names, and frankly, they didn't deserve my effort. They were rude to me while Jared and I dated, so why bother playing nice now? Wait . . . did they call me psycho?

That's two for two tonight. Hot damn, I was on fire.

"We need to talk." Jared shooed the Chads away and proceeded to act like we didn't break up a couple days ago. "Addy, I miss you. Why haven't you returned any of my calls?"

"You know why." I continued to not give Jared my full attention and swirled my glass. The ice swished around, and for a split second it muted everything around me.

"So?"

My eyes widened and I scanned Jared's face, his dark eyebrows furrowed. "So, what?"

"Can I buy you a drink?"

If I said yes, would he think he's forgiven? What a dumb question. Of course, he would.

"Fine."

Jared's face lit up and he waved the bartender down and ordered my favorite drink.

The bartender plopped the whiskey sours in front of us, gave Jared a wink, and went back to helping new customers.

Unbelievable. I chugged the last of my drink and grabbed the next. I tapped my fingers aggressively on the bar top again—holding my tongue.

Don't be petty, Addy. Don't be petty.

"Seduced the bartender already, I see." Damn it.

Jared's deep chuckle reverberated in my ears as he brushed his curls back and leaned into me. His gaze didn't falter. "I seem to remember you liked it when I seduced you."

Jared pulled the barstool out and sat down.

My face scrunched in disgust. Did I really date a man this full of himself?

A hollow laugh escaped my throat. "So did the other woman you brought into your bed," I muttered, gripping my glass tighter and stirring the ice.

This was a sign I needed to raise my standards.

Jared ruffled his hair and ignored my dig as he brazenly took a sip of his drink. He remained poised but stayed silent. He glanced at my drink and then back at me. He held a deadpan expression, but it eased back into his normal, flirtatious smirk.

Jared had some nerve to act so nonchalant. My hand itched to dump my whole drink over him. If I stained his suit would that ruin his night like he shattered my confidence?

No, no. I evolved. I didn't need to seek revenge. I was above that. *Kinda.*

I banished all my intrusive thoughts and stretched out my free hand, stopping my aggressive taps. "Yeah, past tense. I did. Not anymore."

I chugged my second drink in a matter of seconds, contemplating if I wanted Jared to keep me company or if I should take my chances with Raagini or the crows. They all sounded atrocious, but I leaned more toward my other two options than him. I needed to choose the lesser of the three evils, or whatever.

The shelves of liquor shifted out of place and my whole body went numb as my thoughts muddled together.

I turned to face Jared, but the room spun around me. "What the f—" I didn't even hear my head hit the bar top before it all went black.

☾

An endless sea of darkness encompassed me. My body stiffened from the metal pressed against my wrists and ankles. Someone had gagged my mouth and bound my eyes in cloth.

I thrashed and thrashed again, attempting to rock the chair, but the more I tried, the more hopeless it felt.

A rush of cool air caressed my exposed arms, and my heart slammed against my chest like a frantic lion trapped in a cage with every intention of breaking out.

Sleep paralysis. Yeah, that explained everything. I passed out at the bar and now I couldn't see or move.

A vivid nightmare. That's it.

Light footfalls echoed around me, and it pushed me over the edge. No, nope. *Jared wouldn't do this to me.*

My hyperventilating escalated as the smell of rust and bleach assaulted my nose. It all felt way too real. *Too familiar.*

The echoes rang louder and quelled my thundering heartbeat.

Yeah, I was going to die. Crazy ex mutilated and dumped ex-lover in the forest because he couldn't handle seeing her in public, hot and semi-happy-ish.

An icy hand touched my face. It took me out of my thoughts, and I flinched so hard I shook the whole chair. If I could see myself now, I bet I looked like one of those shaky chihuahuas that needed to keel over and die.

They removed their hand from my cheek, and chills edged down my neck. I couldn't stop trembling as the sudden presence of others surrounded me.

"Where's the old hag?" a gruff voice demanded, cutting through the stillness of the air.

The erratic beats of my heart started again, pounding harder against my chest. *Thump, thump, thump, thump*—like white noise—blocking out everything so I could slip into oblivion, or so I really fucking hoped. Anything was better than this.

If the man expected me to answer . . . he had me gagged and blindfolded—I couldn't speak or defend myself even if I wanted to.

The room fell silent again, but I knew people still hovered around me.

The cold draft surged stronger through the room. The autumn breeze nipped at my fingertips and sent goose bumps all over my bare skin.

They tore the cloth from my face; light blinded me until my vision refocused.

I gawked in horror at the man looming over me. His alabaster hair shone like the moon descending to earth, lighting the grungy warehouse in his wake. The men and women surrounding him paled in comparison. Overshadowed by his otherworldly brilliance—it was disturbing. He resembled the God of Death ready to reap the carnage he had instigated.

Only one thought occupied my mind.

What does a man like this want from a broke, slightly delusional girl like me?

A gnawing pain cemented itself within my stomach the moment when our eyes met.

I knew instantly if I didn't find a way to escape those amethyst-colored eyes fixated on me, I would probably die in the most gruesome way possible. And I really wanted to live and not end up as an episode of *Dateline*.

"Anyone care to explain this?" the man asked again without raising a single decibel, but it carried throughout the room regardless and resounded off the steel walls.

One of the bulky men with slicked-back brown hair and yellow, slitted eyes carried himself with an immovable stance like a gargoyle; his massive build and crinkled face looked just as menacing. The blonde woman beside him had a similar, formidable pose but she also remained stiff as a board.

My gaze went back to the man with alabaster hair as he crossed his arms; his black tuxedo shifted as he lifted his sculpted jaw. His face pinched into a grimace.

No one dared to respond to the man who made the earth tremble with two simple questions.

The eternal silence ate away at me until Jared's grating voice scraped against my ears. "Ryas said she was the one who had it." He paused, fidgeting before he worked up the courage to speak again. "You promised you would let her go when you got what you wanted."

Of course Jared camouflaged himself in the corner. I swear if I died because of that cheating bastard I would rise from the depths of hell and haunt his pathetic ass until he croaked.

I gave Jared the nastiest glare I could conjure despite my circumstances, but he avoided me like a spineless prick. *Typical.*

I didn't dare glance back at the man standing before me and kept my focus on Jared, but Jared's continued silence made me increasingly more nervous.

What did Jared even mean when he said I had it? The stupid key?

From the corner of my eye, the alabaster-haired man turned to Jared. His face twisted in disdain as his domineering posture became more apparent. He looked down on Jared like an insignificant bug he could squash whenever he desired.

"It's a pity I have to repeat myself. I said I would consider it. Now my generosity is wavering." The man didn't give Jared any more attention as he looked back at me.

I wished to disappear or melt into the chair so I wouldn't have to face the man any longer. I mean, couldn't he continue to take out his animosity on Jared? That would be a win for the both of us. Fuck up his night, dude, not mine.

The man untied the cloth and ripped it away from my mouth.

In a low voice, he said, "Where is it?"

My mouth hung open. I wanted to say something, anything, to get out of this situation, but I got the feeling if I did, he wouldn't appreciate the killer jokes that would spill out of my mouth like vomit.

I gulped. My mouth turned bone dry despite the words aching to pour out.

A flicker of light resembling a purple flame appeared in the man's eyes, and he snatched the necklace off my neck.

I gasped from shock or flinched or maybe both before I realized what he had taken from me.

The man glowered as he turned to a lady in a midnight blue dress and black heels. "Valeria, get rid of her."

"Of course." The woman, Valeria, smirked, appearing from the dark; her blonde hair almost reached the cement as she bowed.

Jared took one step closer. "Wait you said—"

The man clicked his tongue and stalked toward Jared, glaring.

"What happens to someone who refuses to follow one of *my orders*?" Malice dripped from the man's voice as he gripped Jared's shoulder. All the color drained from Jared's face as he stammered to speak, but ultimately stayed tight-lipped. The man laughed and bent down, inches from Jared's face and whispered, "Good boy." The man let go of Jared and snapped his fingers, and the others faithfully followed behind him as they walked out of the room.

Where in the mafia hell was I?

Jared mouthed the words *I'm sorry* and followed reluctantly behind them.

The reality of my situation sunk in, and betrayal and anger hit me all at once like a festering wound, worsening the farther Jared walked away from me.

"You coward!" I screamed.

I cursed and cursed at Jared again until his black curls disappeared from my view, and my voice went hoarse. Until I no longer heard his footfalls echo throughout the warehouse.

Until my anger turned into desperation.

3
VANQUISHED FOES

"**O**h god." I sniffled. "What did I ever do to deserve this?" I cried out between sobs. The woman pulled me behind her with such brute force my feet could barely keep up. So I carried on with my worthless plea. "I may have stolen a few things in my youth and hijacked a car, but who hasn't impersonated a valet and taken a Lamborghini on a joyride? It was stupid teenager stuff. I swear, I'll repent," I cried out again.

I rambled on and on like it would somehow bring on *deus ex machina* and save me from this nightmare. But real life didn't work that way, so I worked with what I had—which didn't feel like much.

The woman dragged me to a black SUV with no license plate. My heart rate dropped, and my teeth clattered.

No one had a car without a license plate unless they planned on doing some shady shit like burglary, trafficking, or going *on a stabbing spree.*

I thrashed and wiggled against her, and I somehow escaped her grip and took off toward an open field. The forest beyond it appeared so far away, and I knew I wouldn't make it in time before she snatched me. I frantically searched for a paved road, but only dead grass filled my vision for miles and miles.

My best chance of surviving: running and not looking back. If she managed to stuff me in the back, I was as good as dead.

I continued my pursuit to the open field despite my odds. Dealing with mice, snakes, and ticks seemed more pleasant than begging for my life again.

My breaths came out in short, jagged bursts as the night sky loomed over me with millions of scattered stars illuminating the field like a stage light.

My hands tied behind my back, I stumbled as I ran for my life.

I didn't even make it ten yards before her body slammed me into the ground.

The wind knocked out of me, I rolled onto my side and gasped for air. My hands and knees covered in dirt, she picked me up and flung me over her shoulder like a sack of potatoes.

I couldn't catch my breath before she chucked me into the back of the SUV.

The woman put her slender pointer finger to her ruby lips and whispered, "Don't make a sound." And she slammed it closed.

The engine turned on, and she peeled out of the empty parking lot.

Every bump and turn sent me flying. I tried to kick my way out, but the constant whiplash made it impossible.

My head smacked against something and a loud *Ooof* escaped me.

My vision blurred, along with my concentration, as a strong queasiness settled in my stomach. I honestly thought my drinks from earlier might flee my throat and paint the whole back.

The SUV screeched to a halt.

The silence suppressed my breathing altogether. Or had I forgotten how to when the door shut and the crunching of dead leaves rang in my ears?

The closer the sound came, the more a deep-rooted turmoil churned inside me.

The back clicked and popped open.

Rust, pine, and salt hit me all at once.

I squeezed my eyes shut and clenched my hands into tight fists. My nails dug into my palms and a sharp twinge of pain shot through me. Blood oozed and trickled down my wrists.

I heard the click of her tongue as she dragged me out by my shoulder.

My knees smacked onto the gravel and another *Ooof* escaped me.

I cautiously opened them, and a rusted sign saying Hades Cliff in an off-white color towered over me.

The crashing of waves hitting sharp rocks launched me into another panic. I rambled on despite her previous threat. "From one girl to another, your boss seems like a dick—"

"He's not my boss and you talk too much."

The woman pushed me in front of her and all I could think

about was why this place was so infamous and had the second name of Widow's Peak.

Rumors swirled around after so many deaths. The townspeople swore the River Styx resided right below the cliffside, and that Hades himself would cry out to all the damned and condemn them to jump, leaving countless grieving widows behind. Oh fuck. Was I like the damned in the story?

"Don't move," the woman barked as she shoved me onto a bench facing the ocean.

A small squeak slipped out as the view stole my breath in a holy fuck kind of way—my focus remained on the spiked rocks at the bottom, harsh tides thrashing up against them.

All my blood drained from my body, and I gulped. "You honestly don't have to do this. I mean, you guys probably have the wrong girl," I whispered more to myself than to her, shaking like a newborn calf.

I was content with staying on this bench for the rest of my life. If I had claws, I would have dug them into the sides, so she would have a hell of a time prying my cold, dead body off it.

The woman scoffed. "We're out of his territory." Her chilling stare froze me in place. "Now . . . the coven wants you and the keys, but I have another agenda, first. Tell me where Larisa's grimoire is?"

"Larisa? Wait . . . My mother?"

"You have ten seconds before I throw you. Don't test me," the woman hissed, baring her canines, her face full of contempt.

"I haven't seen her in over a decade, and the only thing she left me was the stupid key necklace that man stole from me!"

I almost keeled over and died again for the second time tonight when her glare turned into a thin smile.

"Wrong answer. Have fun in the other realm. I'm sure you'll come crawling back in no time like a cockroach that just won't die. You are your mother's daughter, after all." The woman unbound my hands, pulled me to my feet, and pushed me off the cliff, waving as I plummeted. "Next time, come up with a better answer."

The wind ripped and lashed at my clothes as my hair plastered to my face, blinding me from my impending doom.

I clenched my eyes and butt, anticipating the end.

A clear, dense substance invaded every crevice of my body. I wheezed for air, but nothing came in until I slammed ass-first onto the cold, hard bottom of the ocean waiting for myself to slip away—but it never came.

Groaning from the impact, I blinked and blinked again. But trees and shrubs surrounded me instead of harsh tides and an unforgiving current.

Stuck, dumbfounded, I didn't leave the spot where I landed, and it seemed like hours passed before I laughed maniacally to myself.

I was so out of my element.

I pushed myself off the ground and brushed the dirt off my jeans. If I fractured something from the fall, I wouldn't be surprised as my adrenaline wore off, and I felt strangely high-strung.

I pinched myself, anticipating again for my world to morph into frigid waters and sharp rocks, but my brain kept deceiving me.

Was this how the body copes with dying of hypothermia or drowning? Easing the body into a slow and painless end full of colorful hallucinations?

The sky, painted like a canvas with strokes of cerulean and plum, had two moons parallel to each other. Miniature beings in all hues of green and translucent wings quavered across the soil.

"Thank the Fellow! The prophecy has come true! Our mighty savior has blessed us with her arrival!"

Intense sobbing and cheers came from below as hundreds of winged creatures resembling dolls with wide eyes and wispy limbs flooded around me. My sight lowered to their exoskeleton legs bending outward.

I could have gone my whole life without seeing it.

"We beg you! Vanquish our foe and we shall grant you our most prized possession!" a high-pitched voice cried.

"Hurry!"

I narrowed my eyes, stupefied. Was I tripping balls, or was I in some weird level of hell?

No, hell wouldn't have cutesy, bug-like creatures.

Tiny screams erupted again, and they pointed toward a creature lurching at them.

The more I looked, the more my vision focused, and it mutated into an eight-legged creature like some twisted species of a spider, crimson dripping down its white-striped back and a huge stinger. About the size of a house cat, the creature jabbed at a pixie the color of the forest with an orange dress covered in frills and pink flowers. They looked like a scoop of orange sherbet.

"Will you not help us?!"

I wrinkled my face, repulsed by the pool of saliva dripping from the creature's mouth.

"You guys need me to kill"—I pointed to the terrifyingly sized spider-creature—"that?"

Tiny screams erupted again, and they scattered all over the place.

Oh my god. This was too much, but I guess I was well past not indulging in crazy, so *fuck it.* I needed some good karma after all this supernatural BS.

I took my boot off and crept up to the spider cornering a group of them and slammed my boot down again and again. I winced and gagged all at once as it popped and ruptured into a yellow goo. The smell of rotting flesh flooded all my senses.

Squeaky cheers came from behind me, and the fluttering of their wings started.

"Our magic!"

I scraped the remnant of its body off my boot and shook the putrid-smelling goo off it. I squirmed at the realization I had smacked a massive spider to death.

So, two witch ladies, talking crows, some Legolas-looking motherfucker, and now pixie creatures?

I was well past insanity. I couldn't tell what or who was real even if it bit me on the ass.

A male pixie hovered at my side. A white cap in the form of a rose rested on his head as he wore junipers and a frilled, gold-laced, black tunic. Bunched-up bodies hugging and crying tears of joy stood behind him. I assumed they were pixies. Tiny bodies and little wings—what else could they be?

The forest-green pixie bowed before me. His big, pitch-black eyes blinked at me. "My people and I are forever in your debt." He rose and clapped his hands and my whole attire changed in an instant. "You are an honored guest. We feast tonight for our victory!"

I was stunned as the weight of my clothes left my body and soft and airy fabric replaced them. My black jeans and T-shirt morphed into a light pink, baby doll dress with puffy sleeves and ruffles. My world went dark as something obstructed my view.

A flower crown materialized on top of my head, and it matched the cap of the male pixie in front of me.

All right, this was about as far as I could manage without losing all my marbles. I looked like a pink princess who had an unhealthy obsession with balloon sleeves.

I stepped backward again. "Thank you for your generosity but I need to get back home."

"Let us discuss the details over the feast. We must *honor* you," the tiny pixie grinned, and he was oddly cute except for his dagger-like teeth. Those were a little frightening.

"No, no I can't."

Retracing my steps as they swarmed me, I slipped and fell; the density of the air thickened as a weird sensation vibrated throughout my body. I couldn't breathe as my world went dark.

I crashed stomach first onto the ground, rolled onto my back, and coughed.

I laid in the middle of the road not really grasping my reality until I looked down and saw the pink, frilled dress still clung to my body.

This was not how I wanted to spend my birthday.

4
UNINVITED GUEST

Highway S50 went on and on, but no headlights from either direction. *Cool.* Why would I hitch a ride from a stranger, especially past midnight in a pink fluffy dress? The fact I couldn't call for help was what sucked; my phone died when I ran from my apartment.

The sign glaring above me read the nearest gas station was five miles away, but it didn't help me one bit. I was mentally kicking myself for not memorizing someone else's number besides Jared's when I had the time.

Clicking came from behind me, and I whipped my head around and assessed my surroundings.

Sequoias towered over me like skyscrapers as overgrown ferns littered the forest floor; I couldn't see anything at all.

"It will be back," a croaky voice called out.

Another one chimed in, "She will be back."

"Yes, yes."

I snapped my head up and the murder of crows with black beady eyes stood in the middle of the highway, rubbernecking like I had grown a third arm.

For once in my life, I was happy to see them.

I sighed. "Oh, thank god."

They all craned their heads and uttered the same words as if functioning like a hive mind. "God has nothing to do with us, Adeline."

A chill ran down my back. My relief vanished and my anxiety intensified.

If I had imagined this whole shit show of a night then I really belonged in a madhouse. But seeing as I still wore the dress, I couldn't deny the truth any longer.

"Why are you following me again?" I asked, rubbing my temples, so done with this whole ordeal. Wait. They did say something about a key last time. Were they really after it too?

They all gasped and croaked amongst each other.

"It's been ages!"

"She finally speaks!" they cried out, jumping up and down.

All their claws scraped against the road as their overzealous chatter filled the air and reverberated off the trees.

I stood there, annoyed. Could they not answer a question in their goddamn life? "Yes, it's all very lovely."

It had been years since I last witnessed them, yet I couldn't place the exact memory. But why would they resurface now? *Why stalk me?*

They responded with no hesitation like they heard my

thoughts. "For protection. The barrier is weakening."

"Your presence has been revealed," one-eyed said, clarifying.

The crow hopped forward lifting its beak at me; the apparent scar revealed it as the same bird from earlier, Gren.

I peeked at the rest of them and back at Gren, perplexed and a little aggravated. I could have used their protection earlier. If they couldn't protect me then, how could they possibly protect me later?

Ah, maybe they could claw someone's face. That might come in handy. "Why didn't you help when I needed it, and what are you protecting me from, if it's not from being literally kidnapped and pushed off a cliff?"

They only perched there silently and shook their beaks.

"You weren't in immediate danger," Gren finally responded.

I tossed my head back and laughed. I'd hate to find out what they considered immediate danger. "Fine, but the stalking needs to stop. Only one of you can follow me. I can't have all of you guys squabbling twenty-four seven. So, only one." I pointed my finger at Gren. He seemed like the most level-headed, and I would rather deal with one than thirty. "You."

Gren froze, peeked at the others, and nodded, signaling them to leave.

"We won't be far."

"Just in case."

"We will be waiting."

They gave each other looks of disapproval but ultimately listened and disappeared into the forest, leaving Gren by my side.

"Care to explain anything?"

Gren's silence ate away at me as his beak pointed to the

ground. He stole a glance in my direction while fidgeting—if crows could do that. Either way, it looked more like twitching his feathers than anything else.

"Your mother's coven is after you. I'm sorry, I wish I could say more," he said with a hint of sorrow in his voice.

I scoffed and kicked a few pebbles off the road and continued walking. I really hated how it wasn't my first time hearing those words.

So my mother really was a witch. *Great.* Super normal stuff.

I rubbed my temples again out of frustration. I yearned to question Gren further, but he didn't look like much of a talker and had apparently taken an oath of silence. How convenient.

My legs grew weak and restless. I lost track of how many miles I hiked once we passed the gas station.

The moon mocked me under its lambency. The cruel taunt lit the path to Lucien's place—making it painstakingly obvious I should have stayed inside for the night with Raagini. Then maybe I wouldn't be in this never-ending hell-loop.

I tossed aside what little pride I had left and knocked on his door. I waited, fiddling nervously with my hands. Several clicks later and the door swung open.

Lucien stood there, shirtless and in black boxer briefs. His exposed chest reacted to the chill in the air as his muscles flexed from his tight grip on the side of the doorframe. His eyes slit before he fully took me in. They widened and his jaw dropped. Maybe he saw Gren, too, but I doubted it.

"What happened? Wait, what the hell are you wearing? Oh, shit. I forgot. I'm so—"

I held my hand up and waved for him not to finish. "Bad date."

Lucien didn't seem to buy a word of it as he looked at the dirt covering my hands and knees, and my palms stained and bloody with deep purple bruises forming around my wrists.

Lucien crinkled his nose, and he removed a spiderweb out of my hair, shaking it off his fingers. I was surprised he didn't say anything about the flower crown.

Lucien wiped his hand on his boxers. "Water or hot chocolate?"

"Hot chocolate," I whispered.

"Go sit down and relax. I'll be right back." Lucien walked into the kitchen and started the water on the stovetop.

I followed behind him and plopped down at his kitchen table, nervously tapping my nails. The tears welled at the corners as he turned his back to me and disappeared into the living room. All my pent-up emotions surged through about to break the gates wide open, but I wiped the few ones that escaped. I took one deep breath and pushed my feelings down.

Gren perched on the top of the chair beside me and stared at me for a long second. "You have nothing to fear," he stated as if it were a fact and something he had control over.

His voice carried so much conviction I almost chuckled.

I gave Gren a silent nod for his effort. He was an odd contradiction. His menacing exterior was deceptive because he was strangely cordial.

The whistling of the tea kettle startled me, and my whole

body tensed under the sound.

Lucien strolled back in, and I relaxed back into the chair. His muscular build was now hidden by a baggy gray hoodie and black joggers, and his light blond hair was shoved into a trucker's hat with only a few stray strands peeking out.

Lucien fixed up the hot chocolate, even dropping in a few marshmallows like I was five and he was nine again. When I went through hell and back at the Kelleys' house for having a smart mouth—he was always there, comforting me.

Lucien set the hot chocolate on the table and sat beside me. I smiled weakly and mouthed a small *thank you*.

Lucien nodded as I clenched the cup in my hand, unable to lift my eyes from the tile. My hands turned clammy, and my pulse spiked.

The pressure returned, enveloping my body tenfold. How could I get out of this crazy cycle? If they kept coming after me, what then?

Lucien grabbed my shoulders, and I flinched; his firm grip startled me, and I flung myself backward. I almost knocked myself over, but he caught the chair before I hit the ground.

Lost in thought, I didn't realize Lucien moved and now hovered inches from my face. So close his cool minty breath touched my cheek.

Lucien's eyebrows furrowed. The worry was tangible in his expression.

I averted his gaze like a coward and stared out the bay view window.

Lucien broke the silence first. "You should live with me. You can save money so you can get back on your feet. I'm not saying it's forever," Lucien said, attempting to sound persuasive, but it only interrupted my previous thoughts.

The offer seemed tempting, but what if he got caught up in my mess?

I didn't want to go back to my apartment. It didn't feel safe, but I also didn't want to make it dangerous for him here either. *Ah, maybe I shouldn't have come over but . . . he was all I had.*

I peeked over at Lucien, his face consumed with worry. The tension between us ate away at me and I couldn't stand it.

Our eyes met, and I grinned like a fool. "Are you going to kiss me or what? I have to warn you, I haven't brushed my teeth yet," I teased as I annoyingly poked his cheek.

Lucien took his hat off and slammed it on my head. He tilted the bill down, blocking my vision so I couldn't see his expression. "You're so weird. You know that?"

I raised the hat and Lucien seemed more peeved than before.

He turned and fell back onto the chair next to me.

The mood went from serious to playful back to serious in a matter of seconds.

It made me uncomfortable.

I didn't look away from the cup again. "I'll think about it, okay?" I lied.

"Good, at least you still have some brains left in there. And you know you can stay as long as you want. The guest room has a change of clothes, and you can get cleaned up after this." Lucien patted my shoulder.

"Babe, come back to bed," a sleepy voice called out from his bedroom door.

5
FEIGNING IGNORANCE

A petite woman with long, dirty blonde hair in burnt-orange shorts and a baggy gray shirt stepped out of the doorway. She was tiny compared to me, like I could fit her into my back pocket or the palm of my hand. Lucien had a type, and she fit it to a T.

She yawned and rubbed her eyes as she glided toward us, unaware I sat right next to Lucien.

"Oh." The woman peered at me, tipping her head. "Hi, I'm Lynne. You must be . . . Addy?"

She grinned, but it faded quickly the closer she got.

She probably noticed my strange appearance. It didn't take a genius to figure out I went through some shit tonight, but no way would I let some stranger take pity on me.

So I summoned my best customer service voice and softened

my expression like nothing happened, like I hadn't walked twenty miles to get here. "Yes. It's lovely to meet you. Although, I wish it was under better circumstances," I laughed, smiling until my cheeks stung.

I gave Lucien a quick what-the-hell look. He never said anything about dating a new girl, and now I felt like an ass for showing up. I thought we told each other everything.

Ah, I was being petty.

Lucien finally opened his mouth and closed it again like he couldn't muster up the right words.

I gripped my cup tighter and ignored the fact he lied to me. A minuscule lie compared to everything else. So I let the hot chocolate warm me from my fingertips to my stomach with each sip. I almost felt normal—almost. I still carried a gnawing emptiness, but at least the liquid calmed my nerves.

Lucien spoke in a hushed tone like I wouldn't hear him. "Yeah, my little sister might be living here. I told you during dinner, I believe." He turned his body to face her and avoided me.

I almost sprayed his kitchen table with hot chocolate as the words "little sister" left his lips.

Confused, I whipped my head to the side and attempted to get his attention, but he had an unwavering focus on her.

Lucien gave Lynne a side smirk revealing his dimpled cheek and she blushed.

Sly bastard. I knew that look. I had witnessed it countless times before. He was feigning ignorance like he could charm his way out of it. And Lynne ate up his lies like they were a four-course meal.

I cringed and wrinkled my nose at his gross display.

"Of course." Lynne beamed and spun back to me. She twirled the side of her baggy shirt in her hand and grabbed my shoulder with her other, pressing her nails down before she resumed. "I would love it if we could get to know each other, but it seems like you have some things to discuss, and I have work in the morning. So I'll leave you guys alone. It was nice meeting you, Addy."

She glided over to Lucien's side, cupped his cheeks in her hands, and kissed him, deeply. They smiled at each other through locked lips, and she mumbled a sweet *good night* under her breath.

Lynne leaned back and waved goodbye with a cheerful face. I felt like I had to return it.

She came in and out like a ray of sunshine, and if I were to compare myself again, I was more like a violent storm striking thunder at random.

I didn't utter a word as I watched her disappear into Lucien's room.

After the door clicked shut, I turned to Lucien and whisper-screamed, "Little sister? Little sister? I know you didn't just refer to me as a nun." I shook my head in disapproval.

How long had they been dating? Why didn't he tell me? Why lie? A similar tinge of pain burrowed its way into my chest, and I didn't know what to make of it.

"There's the Addy I know." Lucien smiled his dumb, smug smile, and his stupid dimple sprung out. "And you can't say shit. Unless you can tell me word for word what happened to you tonight?" He lowered his eyebrow, waiting for a response.

Now, I couldn't find the right words. I gaped at him about to speak but all my words eluded me.

I couldn't tell him the truth.

I turned my head, unable to hold his intense eye contact.

Lucien laughed and shook his head. His light waves swayed with each turn. "I knew it. Secretive as always."

Yeah, I was a hypocrite, but I couldn't tell him that. I was already jobless. A broken disaster of a human being who could only take and never give anything in return. A whirlwind of red flags. I knew it all too well. I didn't need to pile on more—like how my ex kidnapped me, and the only way I escaped was by mere chance as a freaky lady pushed me off a cliff. How I might have saved a swarm of pixies from a massive spider, and now a talking crow perched five feet from his face, and it wasn't the first time, nor would it be the last. I would sound insane to anyone if I uttered those words out loud.

"She seems nice," I spoke, dismissing what he said and expelling the thoughts spiraling in my mind.

Lucien rolled his eyes but still allowed me to change the subject. "She is. I like this one a lot, Addy."

I scoffed under my breath. Lucien's nice way of saying don't fuck it up for him, but I'd say he already messed it up by lying to her about us being siblings.

I squeezed the cup until my knuckles turned white. "Got it." I had no right to be angry, and he didn't need to help me. So I stopped myself before I could act any more childish. "I hope this one sticks." I gave Lucien a clumsy grin.

Lucien nodded, and we didn't spend any more time on the subject. "I was going to drive you home, but I think it's best if you stayed the night. I'll take you tomorrow."

I relaxed my grip and tapped my fingers on the cup. "Uh, yeah. Sounds good."

"Good night," Lucien said, mid-yawn.

"Wait." I cleared my throat and attempted to sound as calm as possible. "I mean . . . good night."

Lucien frowned without saying another word and nodded.

After a couple hours of no sleep and straight binge-watching romantic comedies, I found myself yelling at the female lead to run, not walk, away from the dark, tall, and mysterious guy attempting to ensnare her with his witty comebacks and devilishly good-looking face. It was a fucking trap, girl. Run.

That's when I knew I needed to stop watching TV. I was sounding more jaded by the second.

I got up, brushed the crumbs of chips off me I raided from Lucien's cabinet, and took a shower. And it cleansed all the dreadful emotions away.

I stepped out and dried myself off. I leaned halfway over the sink and splashed my face with cold water. I glanced up at the vanity mirror and took it all in.

It was crazy what a hot shower could do for a person.

My reflection looked more like an echo of my past self. My blue eyes speckled with gold had a glimmer of hope ignited within them like wildfire to an arid forest. I thought they had lost their sheen—their spark—but they were now glowing under the light filtering through the window.

When was the last time I had felt this safe? Where I didn't have to peek over my shoulder or worry someone or something might be following me. I was constantly on edge, and I didn't realize it until now.

I pulled my phone out of the charger and walked out of the bathroom and into the guest room. Hesitating, I picked up the outfit Lucien gave me off the bed.

The orange and pink stripes with a white collar shone against the black and red plaid comforter; I couldn't tell which was uglier.

I felt like a person dressed for a kid's show as I slid on the atrocious brown khakis. I honestly think he chose this as a cruel joke because I knew his taste wasn't that bad.

I didn't have to look in the mirror to know my outfit was absolutely ridiculous. I grabbed the crown and outfit the weird little creatures put me in, still in shock my life turned into this, and shoved it in the bathroom trash can.

I swung back to the guest room when a light reflected off the dresser and blinded me.

My jaw dropped.

6
MURDEROUS INTENT

I mulled over the chances of how the necklace made its way back to me. Did someone drop it off? Did Gren get it back for me?

My hand shoved in my pocket as the edges of the key poked my fingertips.

I had a horrible feeling about this.

I sighed, pulled my hand out, and clicked the seat buckle in, twirling my thumbs—suddenly self-conscious of how I looked in this god-forsaken outfit.

Lucien jumped in on the driver's side and turned the ignition a couple of times before it eventually started. He desperately needed a new vehicle because this 1991 Jeep Cherokee had seen better days, but I couldn't tell him that again. It would be like insulting his pride and joy—his baby.

And I really couldn't judge; I didn't have the money to even buy myself a vehicle.

Lucien cupped his mouth and shifted away, one hand holding the steering wheel as we drove off.

A glimpse of a smirk stretched across his face as some weird, muffled gasping noises escaped his mouth. I leaned toward him and inspected his odd behavior.

Lucien's tight gray shirt betrayed him; I saw *everything*. His whole body trembled from his bulging pecs to his fingertips.

The nerve of this man. "Are you seriously laughing at me?"

Lucien erupted into a fit of laughter. Between wheezes, he gasped out, "Your outfit"—he sucked in another breath—"is gold. Hold still." He rummaged through his joggers and pulled out his phone. "Let me take a picture to commemorate this beautiful moment." He leaned sideways; his back pressed against the car door as his eyes remained on the road.

Lucien's deep chuckle tickled my ears as I threw my hands up to shield myself from getting an unwanted photo. "Hey! No. This outfit will be burned at the stake, and there will be no evidence left behind," I threatened him.

"Such malice inflicted on such a lovely outfit for no reason." Lucien sighed, his voice exuding extreme amounts of sarcasm.

I reached out to bat his phone away, but he quickly snapped the photo and shoved it into his back pocket with a shit-eating grin.

How cruel. Yet, I couldn't help but return his smile. Lucien's laughter was infectious.

"See, you're already feeling better." He shot me an eyebrow wiggle. "And come on, it's kinda cute."

How long did this man plan to ridicule me?

He laughed again—so hard he had to physically dig his hand into his left side to stop and wiped literal tears running down his cheeks.

I groaned. "Yeah, yeah. Soak it in now because this will never happen again." I stuck my tongue out and scrunched my face into a frown.

I glanced outside the car window, curious if Gren trailed behind, but nothing besides the dim red taillights reflected off the paved road.

"Never say never." Lucien winked and gave me another cocky grin. Without fail, his dimple sprung out, shining like a beacon in the dark. "And if you're worried about your outfit, here." He took off his black trucker's hat and placed it backward on my head. "There. Much better."

Somehow, I highly doubted it.

I glared at him with an obvious pout, noticing his messy light blond hair had a dent, but surprisingly, he didn't look bad if I was into that boy-next-door face.

"Oh, by the way. I hope you don't mind. We're going out tonight and Lynne begged me to invite you."

"Way to make a girl feel special." I paused. "Uh, sure. Sounds fun." I forced myself to sound pleasant, but it came out more high-pitched than I intended.

My stomach churned from my words. Was it because I didn't know Lynne yet?

☾

We pulled up to my lousy apartment complex littered with sketchy people who waited for their next fix beside their cars. Numerous times, some creep had sneaked up behind me and asked if I had a lighter. It scared the living daylights out of me each time, but I held back my obvious discomfort and always told them about Cee's gas station right down the road.

Luckily, Lucien walked me to my door so I didn't have to deal with another one of those situations.

He stopped right under my door frame, his jaw hanging open.

"Who . . . who did this?" Lucien's face twisted from his sweet expression into pure rage. "Was it that asshole, Jacob? I swear to god I'll kill—"

"Hold on, it wasn't him." I rubbed my forehead, attempting to come up with a good lie while trying not to laugh at how he purposely got Jared's name wrong. "I, um. Kicked down the door because I locked my keys inside, and the manager was off."

Lucien creased his eyebrows, not believing a word of it. "You know you could have called me or at least a locksmith."

I dangled my phone in front of his face. "Battery died and I couldn't remember your number. Just my luck, huh?"

Lucien's phone vibrated and he glanced down.

Without tearing his face from the screen, he said, "I think I should wait until you get your door fixed. Lynne says she's taking care of a pest problem so I can stay here—"

"No." An awkward laugh bubbled out of my throat. "I mean, it's fine. The manager is in the office. I'll handle it." I grinned, hoping he wouldn't pressure me further.

"All right. I guess I'll see you tonight then?"

I had an urge to tell him no. I really didn't want him to leave, but I wasn't his girlfriend. I didn't have the right to ask. And I also didn't have in me to keep lying to him.

So I nodded in agreement and let him walk away from me.

I switched on every light and rushed to my dining room table. My eyes remained focused, not daring to look at the open bedroom door, nor any dark corners. Instead, they remained on the view outside the window—right on Lucien as he jumped into his Jeep and drove out of the parking lot.

My guts wrenched as he disappeared from my sight.

Nervously tapping my fingers on the side arms of the chair, I tried to ground myself. Sweat beaded near my brows, but the room held no warmth. On the contrary, a stark chill saturated the air and nipped at my neck.

A huge black blob smashed against the window, and a blood-curdling shriek shot out of my mouth.

I almost died from heart palpitations but quickly recovered and steadied myself.

Gren pressed against the window, tilting his beak as his black eye blinked slowly at me.

Annoyed that things kept jumping out of nowhere, I still pressed my hand on the glass and let him hop in.

I dropped my chin and pointed my index finger at him. "Never again."

My heart or sanity wouldn't survive another jump scare. It seemed my life had turned into a horror flick, and no matter how many times someone or something popped out, I couldn't stop screaming.

"Something's wrong. You have to leave now." Gren urged me forward, flailing his wings. Quakes of trepidation encased his body as he scanned the apartment.

Gren spoke again, but he talked so fast I couldn't comprehend a word. "Hold on. Hold on. Breathe." I reached out my hand and smoothed his feathers down.

"The others." Gren hesitated and his vocal cords caved and his voice came out clipped. "They're gone." He shook his beak, not saying another word.

I opened my mouth but shut it. How could I comfort him when I couldn't even comfort myself?

I got up and paced around and ended up settling by the stove beside the old, crusted pan of mac and cheese sitting there for god knows how long. Two, three days? A week?

My hands gripped the side of the oven, and I threw my head back and grumbled.

The possibilities were endless.

Valeria could have killed them to scare me, or someone else could be taking out the obstacles to get to me.

Should I skip town? Ah, even if I wanted to, I couldn't afford it.

Gren's feathers trembled, and it amplified my stress.

"It seems we're both in a bit of a bind," a deep voice growled from behind me.

7
GLAMOUR AND DEATH

I made a split-second decision. The fuck if I was getting kidnapped again.

I grabbed the nearest object and swung the week-old mac and cheese pan at the intruder.

I squeezed my eyes shut and bashed with all my strength, screaming at the top of my lungs. I didn't stop, too afraid I might hear the sound of flesh and bones getting pulverized by my kitchenware.

My clammy hands restricted my grip on the pan. I feared the worst—that it would slip through my fingers, and I would drop the only thing I had to defend myself with.

I worked up the courage to peek through my eyelashes once I stopped shrieking, gradually lowering the pan to my side. I was gobsmacked as I blinked at the floor with not a single drop of blood on it.

Did I imagine myself swinging? No, I distinctly remember trying to beat the living hell out of the intruder.

My chin lifted, and the pan slipped through my grasp. The cacophony of clangs as it hit against the tile made my pulse go haywire.

If it was humanly possible to drop dead from a heart attack as a somewhat healthy twenty-three-year-old who survived on premade sandwiches and mac and cheese, then I would have died right where I stood.

I gaped at the man—arms crossed, without a scratch on him. His alabaster-white hair tied back in a loose ponytail. A heavy contrast to the black suit molding to his tall and muscular frame.

The man still resembled Death and it freaked me the hell out. The only thing he needed to complete the look? A scythe and a black robe—if Death had an otherworldly complexion with glowing purple eyes and pointed ears.

Yep. I needed to find a way to escape. *Fast.*

This raging lunatic already had my psycho ex drug and kidnap me. End result? Some creepy lady pushed me off Hades Cliff!

I didn't want to associate myself with this man ever again. He caused me more trouble than I could manage.

He pinched his face into a scowl and wiped the mac and cheese off his shoulder, grease seemingly staining his expensive suit.

Murder. The only word I could use to describe his sharp, lowered gaze.

Oh my god, I fucked up.

I turned my head back to Gren and signaled him with wild

eyes, attempting to tell him now was a perfectly good time to protect me and claw the bastard's face so I could make a run for it. But Gren didn't flinch, as if someone cast him under a spell.

"Gren?" I whispered, but he remained silent, perched on the dining room table.

Fear engulfed my body as I twisted back to face the man, who seemed a little too entertained by my distress. The corner of his mouth coiled up with amusement like my reaction fed his sadistic appetite.

"No one can see or hear us. Humans are fairly easy to manipulate, familiars even—" Shadows shot across the room and pulsated in waves around us as Gren snapped his beak in my direction, horrified.

The shadows vanished, and Gren went back to silently perching there.

My attention fell back onto the man, confused. "No need to demonstrate your power. I've had a hellish twenty-four hours, so get to the point. Why are you here?" I asked, attempting to sound strong, but the quiver in my voice revealed the truth.

The man ruffled his hair as if my words made him uncomfortable when he was the one who snuck into my apartment! What was this? A free-for-all? Did someone put a sign on my door that said *Come scare the living shit out of Addy; it turns her on*?

Oh, wait. I didn't have a door anymore.

A chuckle fled my throat and the man's eyebrows shot up; his face littered with confusion.

I waved my trembling hand, urging him to continue.

He grunted in response but carried on with his weird spiel. "Your place reeks of magic. You might be more useful than I first anticipated since you weeded out a rat in my ranks."

"Way to state the obvious," I said, remembering the crazy witch lady smashing my coffee mug against the wall.

So magic left an invisible residue, or did he have an abnormally strong sniffer?

I went back to the oven and gripped the sides, trying to stop my legs from giving out on me.

If the witch lady wanted to pop out of my fridge, too, I would consider it normal now.

"I can sever your ties with the key if you help me find the other one. You'll be free to live your mundane life without these persistent disturbances."

I spun around and grabbed ahold of his collar, squaring him up. "Don't fucking lie to me." I scanned his face, but not even a hint of a lie, only disgust when my thumbs brushed up against his skin.

The man swiped my hands away and adjusted himself. His jaw clenched at my words.

"I cannot lie."

A snort escaped my lips, and I covered my mouth. From my recent experience, *what man couldn't lie?* "Whatever helps you sleep at night, bud." Oh my god. Did I want to get myself killed?

In the blink of an eye, the man cornered me. My back pressed against the oven. My butt probably turned on a burner with how much I jerked backward.

The man leaned close and whispered in my ear. "By all means, take your chances by yourself. See how much it takes before they break you. I'll be waiting at Death's Paradise for an answer."

I blinked and the man disappeared, evaporating into thin air, or maybe he messed with my mind and strolled out the front door.

I stood there, stunned, and rubbed my temples, not entirely sure what my best options were.

8
REAP WHAT YOU SOW

I propped my elbow on the side of the car door and rested my chin on my palm. I fixated on how the moonlight peeked through the pine trees and reflected off the ground. I wished for it to clear my head, but a million scenarios crossed my mind, and none of them ended well.

I ignored the conversation between Lynne and Lucien once they chatted about trivial things like going on a hike this Sunday to Crescent Falls because the weather app said it would be seventy degrees with not a cloud in sight. Lynne turned around from the passenger side all giddy with sparkles floating in her irises asking me if I was interested.

When I would rather be pushed off Hades Cliff . . . again.

That's what I wanted to say but I held my tongue and told her a polite *no, thank you*. I already had my fill of hikes, and the thought of third-wheeling with them didn't excite me.

And if I had to see Lucien act all cutesy with her any longer I might vomit.

I also had more pressing matters to worry about than stupid hikes. I needed to make sure my sanity survived the night and my life went back to normal.

I lifted Lucien's hat off my head, brushed a few flyaways behind my ear, and put it back in place.

Given the time to reflect on my decision, the outfit Lucien gifted me didn't seem all bad anymore compared to the shirt I snatched and put on in a hurry. I hadn't done laundry yet—for obvious reasons—so the only clean clothes in my dresser were the absurd graphic tees I started collecting when I turned thirteen. I remember wearing them thinking I was so edgy.

What a joke.

Now I only wore them as pajamas, and without fail, they became a little ritual for me every time I went to bed. However, I regretted my decision to collect them. I looked like a freshman frat boy with a shirt that read "A dirty hoe is a happy hoe" with a picture of a woman gardening.

Honestly, how did I think this was my best option even if I was in a rush? I should have contemplated it more.

Maybe it did beat the shirt Lucien picked out, *I guess.* Now I didn't have to walk through the front doors of the hottest night-club in Hollow resembling Steve from *Blue's Clues.* That was a plus, I think.

My whole body screamed in agony as I lifted my chin. A tad pathetic how sore my body felt from swinging a small pan around, but in my defense, I had swung like my life depended on it.

"Hey, we're here," Lucien said, bunching his forehead as he glanced back at me.

"Sweet." I unbuckled my seatbelt and stepped out of the Jeep, avoiding his concerned expression.

Lynne walked incredibly fast and stood right by Lucien, locking hands with him, and shot me a glare as we crossed the street.

Did Lynne expect me to grab Lucien's other arm? Why did she feel the need to act jealous if Lucien said we were siblings? Did she think some *Game of Thrones* shit went down here?

I smiled gently, avoiding Lynne's dagger eyes and lifted my head at the building in front of us. Death's Paradise's massive black sign with purple stripes and white letters loomed over us and illuminated the entire block.

I cracked my knuckles, but it did nothing for my escalating anxieties.

The electrifying music vibrated the ground the closer we got to the entrance.

We only stood a couple of feet from the front doors when I wished Gren had come with me. Then maybe I wouldn't feel so utterly alone. I didn't mind if I looked like a cross between a frat boy and a pirate if it meant he could offer me his odd comforts.

But Gren required some time to grieve and process what he witnessed. Of course he was on edge after finding drops of blood and feathers a few miles out from my apartment. Thankfully, no crow bodies—which meant they could be somewhere. *Alive.* I tried to tell him, but he remained unconvinced and said he needed to investigate more and would find me later.

So I had to meet this man alone. Great. Nothing weird ever happens when a woman meets a sketchy guy alone. Totally safe.

I accidentally made direct eye contact with the intimidating bouncer who stood like a statue and gave him a graceless wave as I hurried past him.

Shoved awkwardly in the corner as Lynne and Lucien danced sensually, I watched from a distance as all the drunken idiots on the dance floor pushed me more into the wall. They synchronized their bodies to the thundering beats, and I wished I was one of them, forgetting all my worries. But I had an opportunity, and I wouldn't let it slip me by. I also couldn't rely on Raagini to resurface, and avoiding Valeria was the most logical plan.

"Oh my god! Addy!" a woman shouted over the music. She held a martini glass as she swayed to the song thumping over the speakers.

I pinched my whole face like it would magically make my vision better, but I still couldn't recognize the voice.

The slender figure walked closer until I made out more of her features. Her black waves bounced with purpose as her floral romper exaggerated her long legs and complemented her stiletto heels.

"How have you been?" she asked, blinking innocently as her brown eyes glimmered back at mine.

Her smile exposed two gapped teeth, and it somehow made her seem more sincere.

I couldn't help but grimace a little. Who was she? I felt like an ass, and it didn't help remembering faces wasn't a strength of mine.

I looked her over again, but nothing came to mind. "I've been good," I lied through a masked expression. "How have you been?"

A coworker from a previous job I worked? School? Foster

care? God, this might drive me nuts.

"That's good at least. I heard what happened, and what the customer did to you. Outrageous. Tyler was wrong for firing you," she said, shaking her head. She leaned down and brushed my collarbone. I jerked backward. "Oh, you had some dirt on you. Sorry, force of habit." She grinned.

I moved my hand and impulsively wiped where she touched.

Oh, Tara. The girl who went on vacation for weeks when I first started working at Cosmo's.

I rubbed the nape of my neck, uncomfortable with the topic. "Yeah, I didn't think I'd get immediately fired for punching a customer after he grabbed my ass, but what can you do?" Actually, I didn't have to resort to violence but goddamn it, I had a short fuse because of Jared. And the customer calling me angel face didn't calm my nerves one bit.

"Shitty manager. The nasty pervert deserved it." Tara nodded as if agreeing with her own statement. "Let's catch up! Want a drink?"

My voice came out strained. "Sure." The song ended, and Lucien wrapped his arm around Lynne's waist as they swayed back over to my side. "Oh, by the way, this is my friend, Lucien, and his girlfriend, Lynne." I gestured at the two of them.

My concentration went to the bottles of liquor on the wall as they all introduced themselves and I stood silent like always. Lynne and Tara clicked and talked about some name brand I never heard of. It was fine though; it would make it easier for me to disappear without them noticing.

I turned away, hoping to drown myself in some drinks before I met the man handing out deals like he was the devil.

A firm hand gripped my shoulder, and my breathing hitched. I spun around.

Fuck, Tara scared the shit out of me.

"Yes?" I asked, a little confused. Why did she have to give me a heart attack? She could have said something first.

"This round is on me." She smirked as she twirled the maraschino cherry in her empty glass.

"Oh, cool." Only two leather barstools were left, and one practically screamed my name.

"Yay." She perked up and clapped her hands together as her nails clinked around her glass. Then she grabbed my shoulder with a surprisingly strong grip as she said, "It was nice meeting you guys, but I'll be stealing this little cutey for the night."

Lucien and Lynne both nodded in agreement as he gave me a thumbs-up like I needed it.

Unable to protest, Tara dragged me to the bar, plopped me down on the empty barstool, and ordered us two Reapers. I never heard of the drink, but I hoped it had a strong whiskey flavor. But I doubted it and bet it tasted as unpleasant as it sounded.

I was still going to drink it.

I drummed my fingertips on the bar and took it all in. The stench of booze and smoke swarmed my nostrils as the dance floor overflowed with more people. The flashing neon lights chaotically darted across the place.

My eyes landed on a VIP Room sign written in silver letters.

"You will lose it all."

I snapped my head back at Tara. "Excuse me?" I asked, unsure I heard her correctly.

"I like your shirt." Tara pointed at me; her voice was barely audible over the pulsating music.

It was only paranoia.

No way she said that.

I glanced at the sign and back at her, smiling. "You're teasing me, huh."

"Never. It's edgy. I like it." Tara gave me an innocent wave.

The bartender placed the two drinks down in front of us, both with a deep crimson color and a cherry on top.

I chugged the whole drink and asked for another. After the second one, I would slip away.

"Oh!" Tara cleared her throat and set her drink down. "My aunt has an apothecary shop in Samsville about an hour away, and she recently lost her full-time employee. It's not much but if you're interested, I can put in a few good words for you. I know Tyler probably slandered your reputation here." Tara trailed off, hitting her manicured nails on the rim of her glass.

I hadn't thought about getting a new job but if my life was going to go back to normal soon, I needed to take all the help I could get.

My face softened. "Sounds great." Money was money, and I was in desperate need of it.

"Okay cool! I'll text you all the details when I visit her."

I gave her a smile and watched the bartender drop our second round in front of us.

If only I could sit here and enjoy some girl talk, but that was a luxury I couldn't afford.

So I chugged my drink again as it slid through my throat like lead, and I shifted toward her. "I'll be right back; I have to talk to someone in the VIP room." I pointed at the door behind her.

"Oh, sounds fun! I'll come with you," Tara insisted.

"No!" I launched up from the barstool. A couple glared in my direction, but I ignored them and wriggled out the tension in my hands. "It's private. I'll come find you when I'm done. I swear."

Tara pouted but nodded and went back to eye-fucking the bartender.

Tara didn't seem bothered by my abrupt response, but I should still make it up to her later.

I weaved through the crowd, bumping into a few sweaty shoulders before I stared at the door in front of me.

If I assessed the man's vibe right in the short amount of time we talked, then he was the pretentious prick who owned this club and lounged behind this door without a care in the world.

9
THE DEAL

I gripped the door handle, and my life flashed before me. Memories came in tiny bursts and fluttered around in my mind like a butterfly evolving through time.

Some held importance, like my first impression of Lucien—a scrawny and tall prepubescent boy with rich gold eyes dripping like honey every time he had a mischievous idea. Even then, he was incredibly easy to read. That's probably when I knew I found someone I could trust.

Some were much darker than I remembered. Where I was trapped in a basement for days on end, clawing at a door until my nails grew brittle and blistered with blood. Until my voice went hoarse, and my eyes dried out from my frantic cries for help that had always gone unanswered.

The Kelleys never liked how I *saw* things. My sheer existence became the embodiment of evil to them, and no matter how hard they tried, my soul couldn't be saved. It seemed almost laughable now because, in the end, I was seeing more things than ever before.

But I hated mulling over the past. It did nothing for me except bring out the scared little girl I desperately wanted to hide.

Now, I had to walk through that door with these memories seared into my brain—relentlessly corrupting my consciousness and spreading their seeds of doubt like a flame to a drought-ridden forest bound to eradicate the inhabitants.

It made me wonder, how many times would I have to suck up my emotions and push them down until a gaping hole replaced my heart?

My hands trembled as I twisted the door handle, and I let out a shaky breath—one I didn't know I held in until now.

I pressed my fear down and propelled myself forward with each treacherous step. My options were slim, and if I could end it all by striking a deal then I wouldn't hesitate any longer.

The cold and damp hallway lights flickered on and off. The heavy vibrations of the music faded gradually until my shallow breathing grew louder, and my betraying heartbeat thumped aggressively against my chest. An eternity had come and gone before a white wooden door emerged with the symbol of a gold and silver crescent moon resting right above eye level.

Muffled voices came from behind the door. An eruption of laughter shot through the stillness, and I flinched and stepped back.

I shook out the tension enveloping my whole body and pressed the fear down again; so far down I was blinded by rage instead.

If I died here, I would at least die with some dignity, or at least try to. Damn my cursed, fickle heart.

The door clicked, and I stepped inside.

The laughter died as I took in my surroundings. The room stunk of cedar, booze, and cigars. And all the walls were painted black except for one mirrored side making the place appear larger. The only furniture occupying the place was a ruby-red leather sofa and a glass coffee table with an ashtray in the center.

A small cloud of smoke from a recently finished cigar began to smother the place.

Two women with long azure-blue hair and matching silver cocktail dresses with clear spiked heels lounged lazily as they sipped on what seemed to be a thick purple wine. My vision landed on a bulky man with raven-black hair, tinting blue each time the revolving lowlights touched him. He sported a white tuxedo and had squished himself between the two ladies, his arms wrapped around their tiny waists.

His bright-red eyes lit up and swirled like a flame as he noticed me. A spine-chilling smirk stretched across his face and gooseflesh rose behind my ears as it kissed my neck.

I escaped his prowling gaze and eyed the group of men occupying a round table with another wooden door behind it. They all lifted their heads and leered at me, unamused I had interrupted their game of poker.

Their soft whispers sent my pulse into overdrive.

The raven-haired man spoke, and it was just as slimy as his appearance. "Ah, Kaschel said someone new might show themselves tonight." The man stood up, and he was taller than I expected. He smoothed out his tux and flicked his wrist at one of the other

71

guys sitting at the table. One launched from their chair, scurried to the other door, and softly knocked. He must have heard something because he turned back to the raven-haired man and nodded, and the man's face twisted into something truly wicked. "By all means, walk right through that door and don't mind us."

The amount of doors I had to keep walking through to get to the man named *Kaschel* was a tad excessive.

I didn't say a word to the raven-haired man, too afraid he'd take it as an invitation to approach me, and my sanity could only handle one psychopath tonight.

I hurried past them and avoided all nosy looks and swung the other door open and shut it behind me.

"Sit." The crackling of the fireplace made Kaschel's alabaster hair stand out and caused his words to sound more ominous as a coppery glow cast throughout the room.

He compelled me to listen, or maybe I felt too jumpy to disobey as my legs dragged me to an empty chestnut-colored wingback chair while he lounged on the other.

My eyes focused on the top curve of Kaschel's chair and avoided his detached expression, too afraid I would beg like a coward. God, my courage flickered as much as the flame before me.

Where did my conviction go?

I scanned the walls. Nothing but shelves of leather books weathered by years of neglect.

Kaschel tapped the arms of the chair, and my attention darted back to him. I only heard the hissing fireplace and my poor, palpitating heart.

His long alabaster hair fell loose, freed from his ponytail as he leaned back; his chin pointed up, scrutinizing me, and the tie he wore earlier now unwound and exposed his brawny chest.

He appeared more relaxed than I had ever been in my entire life, and for some reason, it ticked me off.

I salvaged what little confidence I had and broke the silence. "I'm here. What's the deal?" I crossed my arms and attempted to sound irritated, but I probably just looked constipated and in pain. I would have to work on my intimidation tactics.

Kaschel's face twitched into a half-smirk but quickly went back to a sour expression of disinterest. He leaned forward, only a couple feet away from me. I physically dug my nails into my upper arms, so I didn't flinch back from the threatening aura naturally oozing off him.

He clicked his tongue in disdain and lowered his chin, ignoring my question. "Where is it?"

In my pocket, but since it was the only leverage I held over him, no way would I tell him that. "Why does it matter? It's not like you can hold on to it for long."

My words pinched a nerve in Kaschel, and he launched forward and clutched both sides of my chair.

I retreated inward, but he had me pinned, and physics made it impossible for me to dissolve into the chair and disappear, no matter how much I wished to.

My breathing turned shallow, and I couldn't tear myself away from his bright purple eyes. The edges stirred with darker specks as if they were floating amethysts—both terrifying and mesmerizing.

Kaschel bent his head to the side, so close his cool breath caressed my cheek. "Like I said before, you help me find the other key and I help you sever your connection to it, freeing you from all this unwanted attention. *Deal?*" He leaned back, but his arms still gripped the sides of the chair.

I wanted my life to go back to normal more than anything, and as crummy as it sounded, I think he was my best bet. I didn't give two shits about the necklace if it kept thrusting me into crap like this.

I shooed him away. "Fine, but why do you even want my mother's antique necklace so badly? It's just a piece of trash."

"*That piece of trash is mine,* and I will have them both back. There's nothing else you need to know," Kaschel growled as the flames crackled and hissed, making the light dance across his face.

Someone was a little too possessive. Note taken. "Ookay then. Make sure you keep your word." I glared and pointed my finger at him.

Kaschel smiled and it was strikingly handsome. One that would sweep any woman off their feet, but not me. No—all it did was make my stomach wrench into a massive knot like I made the biggest mistake of my life.

"I always do." Kaschel bent down and kissed the back of my hand. His lips zapped through me like an electrical current, searing into my flesh. I yanked my hand away and bit back the scream bubbling in my throat. I watched in shock as a silver crescent moon etched onto my skin like a tattoo. "A little insurance." He gave me a slimy businesslike grin, let go of my hand, and walked toward the opposite corner of the room. "We leave at sunrise. Ryas will show you to your room."

10
MOONLIGHT
AND STARDUST

Kaschel chanted in a language I never heard before. The fire raged and expanded as if his words agitated it. The shadows bent in chaotic but sylphlike motions across the room—until one broke away from the corner.

The shadow morphed into something else entirely. The deafening cracks of bones pulling and snapping together pierced my eardrums.

A woman emerged from the darkness. Her heels clicked against the floorboards as she glided to my side. Her effortlessly loose white curls bounced with each stride. Her long legs glowed against the fierce flames bursting out of the fireplace and settled back down.

My mouth hung open as a woman literally materialized before my eyes.

"Ryas, take her to the guest suite," Kaschel said in a low but commanding tone.

My attention snapped to Kaschel. He walked back to his chair, sat down, and crossed his arms without breaking eye contact with me.

If Kaschel's posture could kill . . . I would be dead from the displeasure radiating from him.

My presence alone seemed to irritate him.

I shouldn't feel intimidated though, but my head could think one thing, and my body would still react differently. God, could I go back to my old life where I only dealt with shitty customers, not power-hungry, supernatural weirdos?

"Of course." Ryas bowed her head.

All my suppressed emotions erupted out of me as I glowered at Ryas. "What in the actual hell was that?"

I had many, many questions, but the more I wanted to know, the more they kept stacking on top of each other, one after another. I couldn't keep up.

Ryas grinned, captivating but deadly. I wanted to run away and never look back, but I also wanted to throat-punch every fucker in this room who wouldn't give me a straight answer.

I knew it wasn't an option, but a girl could dream. My attempt would be futile—but I really didn't want to recall my previous stab at it.

So . . . Jared meant this woman found me. The one who told Kaschel my whereabouts.

About my necklace.

A thought stirred in my mind and loitered a little longer than I would have liked.

They probably spied on me from the beginning. So Jared only approached me for the key?

Actually, I had no desire to know the last part. That sorry excuse for a man would rue the day he met me if I ever saw him again.

Anger cascaded through me. I felt manipulated and *insane*. Would Kaschel even keep his promise? How would I escape if he didn't?

Think, Addy. Damn it, *think.*

Why couldn't my brain ever function when I needed it to?

I stole a glance in Kaschel's direction, and he held my gaze as he spoke. "Enlighten her on proper etiquette. I'm growing rather aggravated by her uncivilized demeanor, and I can't have her acting out of sorts while accompanying me." He waved his wrist, gesturing for us to leave, and apparently that's all it took.

Ryas herded me out of the room, but my rage returned before we stepped out of the doorway, and I couldn't hold my tongue.

"I can see why Valeria stabbed you in the back. Your shit personality could use some improvement." I had a mouth, and I knew it. It had gotten me into many dangerous situations before, and this time was no exception.

I needed to learn how to whisper or shut up—like, did I have a death wish or what?

Kaschel stood up and stalked toward me. "On second thought . . ." He pointed his chin down and smirked—one that screamed he planned to torture me. I hoped he would have a change of heart as my line of vision stumbled upon his open shirt. His pecs practically burst out of it. "I will escort her, and you can gather some of her things, but be quick. I don't have all night."

I would much rather bet my life on Ryas's temperament than his. I also wanted to live as much as my mouth said otherwise, and she seemed like a safer option.

"I'm good," I said abruptly, nervously hitting the side of the leather armrest.

Damn it. I *really* needed to shut the hell up. Why of all times was I having word vomit?

"Don't worry. I don't bite." Kaschel snatched my wrist, and his whole hand devoured mine.

I slanted my eyes in distrust and tried to wiggle out of his grip.

What an ominous thing to say to someone you barely knew. Did I have to worry about him being an absolute creep too?

I crinkled my nose at the thought as another chant left Kaschel's lips. The shadows balled together and formed a massive gaping black hole in the wall. He dragged me behind him, and I stumbled over my feet. My focus was fixed on the endless void before us. "First time might be uncomfortable. I'd hold my breath if I were you," he said and pulled me through.

The darkness clung to my clothes like phantom hands grabbing me and pulling me under, but the substance rubbing against my skin felt thicker than water and smelled of stardust and moonlight. I could hardly comprehend anything as we shot through and landed in a massive hallway decorated with gaudy antiques and dreary oil paintings. The decor resembled some thousand-year-old vampire mansion; if this was his taste, I really didn't want to see the inside of his chamber.

I staggered for a split second as bile threatened to rise, but Kaschel caught my waist. He instantly yanked me and my body squished up against his firm chest, but he quickly shoved me away once I regained my balance.

I patted my clothes down and shot him a murderous glare. How violating, whatever the hell it was, some portal shadow-shit.

Kaschel hauled me behind him again, and my legs struggled to keep up with his pace.

We entered what appeared to be a loft with the same gloomy and unwelcoming aura as the hallway.

My eyes darted to a familiar black curly mess sprawled out on a chair as he sipped a full glass of wine.

Speak of the devil. Did Jared believe he deserved to enjoy a drink after all the bullshit he put me through? Oh, hell no.

Jared spit his drink out and launched up. "Why is she here?"

Kaschel raised one hand and it silenced Jared. "If I snapped her neck right now, she would resurrect. As irritating as it is, she's bound. I wish I had sensed it sooner. Right now, I need you to gather the others and find the witch."

Jared nodded. But all I could think about were the words, *snap neck* and *resurrect*. Would Kaschel have tried it out if I didn't agree to the deal? What kept him from testing the theory out?

The conversation ended, and Kaschel tugged me behind him again.

Jared's dumbstruck face fueled my wrath. If it wasn't for him, maybe I'd be on my loveseat watching rom-coms and eating ice cream out of the container like a normal girl mourning a bad break up. Not being dragged by some lunatic.

My pettiness won and I flipped him off.

Extremely juvenile, but what the hell? It seemed like a reoccurring theme for me tonight, and Jared deserved it. I also would be lying if I said the look of horror on his face didn't satisfy me.

Relishing in the idiocy of my actions, my mouth twitched up in delight as Jared disappeared from my view.

I needed that win, no matter how trifling.

I twisted back to face Kaschel and smashed into his back.

His gaze fixed on me screamed that he was baffled, wondering how I could act so pleased at a time like this.

My smile faded as a weathered door caught my attention.

Kaschel turned the knob, opened it, and dropped my hand. "You have a couple of hours before we leave. I suggest you sleep in the meantime."

He pushed me inside and shut it without giving me a chance to process what he said.

I sighed and brushed my fingers through my hair and inspected the room.

It had a Victorian gothic aesthetic with its midnight blue walls and black spiral bed frame with intricate designs carved onto the pillars. The closer I got, the more it looked like skulls with flowers protruding out of the eye sockets. A mirror on every wall except for the one with the vanity dresser beside the bed.

I sat on the mattress, and the fabric was softer than I imagined. I launched myself backward, and the cool comforter subdued my cluttered mind.

The silver tint of Kaschel's mark on the back of my hand glowed in the candlelight and I wondered, *If this meant our deal was set in stone, what would happen to me if I broke it?*

One tear escaped, and I almost let the floodgates open when a knock on the door jolted me upright.

Didn't Kaschel just tell me to get some sleep? Then again, he didn't seem like the type to respect someone else's privacy by knocking.

I groaned and left the comfort of the soft fabric and walked to the door. "What?"

11
THE TRUTH

No one spoke, and I half thought I imagined the knocking.

"Hey," Jared whispered, and his rough voice ground against my ears.

I brushed away the tear staining my cheek and pressed my hand against the door. I stayed so strong at Hera's Palace. I held it together so well when he caught me by surprise.

But Jared said one word and my fickle heart drained me of all my sensibility.

One word and all my walls came crashing down.

I physically fought back the tears as a surge of our memories tainted my mind.

We dated for a year. One fucking year.

Until a few days ago, when I stopped by his place to surprise him after my shift with his favorite pasta in one hand and a bottle of red in the other.

Nothing prepared me for what I saw next. When I caught him with someone else in the same bed I told him I loved him in. The same bed I woke up in. Where I kissed him passionately.

In that same bed, someone else wrapped around his body—entangled in the sheets as they devoured each other like wild animals.

How did I hold it together then but not now?

I didn't even threaten to stab one of them; I only dropped the bottle of wine.

It shattered on the wooden floor and stained the walls and my work clothes.

I was soaked, and just as shattered as the wine bottle.

He tore my heart out, and I didn't think it could get worse.

Oh, how the world had a funny way of proving me wrong.

I bit my tongue and whispered back, "*Fuck off.*"

Jared groaned, and I imagined his defeated expression through the door.

Silence fell and I thought maybe I said enough and spun back toward the bed when a hand phased through the door, then a leg, then a torso, until Jared stood behind me.

Jared's tall, athletic frame prowled toward me as his piercing green eyes stunned me. In a similar suit to the one he wore at Hera's Palace, but this one matched his curly hair and fit better than the last.

God, why was I still attracted to him?

I took a step back and landed safely on the bed. I should have put two and two together that Jared could also be something else—whatever monster with the ability to phase through walls.

"No." I pointed my finger at him. "You can't do this to me right now." I turned away, inhaled. "You drugged me, kidnapped me. Get the hell away from me!"

My anger and sadness mixed together, and rage and despair blinded me.

Jared put his hands up and crept closer. "I'm not going to do anything. Addy, please hear me out."

I laughed and it left my chest hollow.

Not like he was offering me a choice in the matter. "Okay but stay where you are and don't test me." I skimmed the room and snatched the deep purple candelabra resting on the vanity dresser. "I will hit you if you get any closer." I waved it at him.

It was a threat I fully planned on keeping, no matter how ridiculous I looked, or whether I could even hurt him. I still had no clue what he was.

Jared stood still as if contemplating what to say next.

He spoke as soft as freshly spun silk. "I didn't know when we started . . ." He rubbed his fingers through his hair and broke eye contact. Heavy circles marred his complexion like he hadn't slept in days. He was a wreck, a heavy contrast to his normal put-together appearance. "I didn't think Valeria would harm you. I thought she had a weakness for humans ever since her coven murdered her lover, but I didn't know she'd be a spy. And once Ryas found out you had the key and told him, I couldn't . . . I couldn't disobey."

Jared fidgeted with his hands, displaying extremely high-strung behavior even for him.

And no matter how on edge Jared appeared, his explanation

served no purpose.

It was worthless and a little too late.

"Whatever your excuses are, they won't change my mind. Now if that's all, *leave*."

Jared took another deep breath and continued to fidget with his hands. "The night when you saw me—"

"Don't even go there. I'm not in the mood."

"It didn't mean anything."

Wow. He was insane, and what kind of excuse was he trying to fabricate? Did he not hear the absurdity of his words?

I saw everything now.

A narcissistic man who justified his awful behavior. "Get out. I have more important things to worry about, in case you haven't noticed."

"Listen to this last part, please."

"Get out," I said again. I didn't care to hear more. I was done. He stepped closer and I screamed louder, "GET OUT." My hands trembled as I waved the candelabra at him like a mad woman.

Hell, I was a mad woman.

Jared flung his hands up in defense, stepped back and whispered, "I'm sorry. I guess it was too soon, but I wanted to tell you before we had to travel together." He pouted like he was some lost puppy, shifted back, and phased through the door.

I crumpled to the ground. The weight of his words pierced through my armor and affected me more than I cared to admit.

12
WINDOW OF OPPORTUNITY

I couldn't sleep after my encounter with Jared, but I needed to cry. To scream and throw a fit—to feel every bubbling emotion burst out of me, no matter how painful or ugly. I needed it so I could let go of whatever part of our relationship I still clung to.

I embraced the sorrow and bitterness and went through every possible scenario leading me here—but the outcome never changed. My mind circled to the necklace and the last memory I had of my mother before she disappeared.

Her big doe eyes had held so much concern that day as she desperately searched for something and went through the house like a tornado until she found it.

I recalled her snatching my hand and shoving the necklace in my pocket and rushing us out of the kitchen.

I rode shotgun in her cobalt blue Cadillac, looking up at her—hypnotized as she drove us down the freeway. The windows were down, and her long, black, wavy hair whipped behind her as the hot air caressed our faces. Her tanned skin and dark eyes illuminated as the sun fell. The car wobbled each time it glided over a crack and bump in the road as she chanted along to the radio blaring through the speakers. Her signature cigarette in hand was perched slightly out the window.

Her attention never left the road as we both hummed along to our favorite song until we reached a worn-out cabin in the middle of nowhere. She may have acted free, but I still saw the irreversible damage someone had left on her, and the spark of anxiety revealed through her quivering hands as she opened the car door.

My only memory of her was a cloud of confusion. I didn't remember walking into a cabin. I didn't remember a goodbye. A hug. *Nothing.*

I only recalled waking up in the Kelleys' house, unaware my mother left me.

I had no idea what made the necklace she gave me so special, or why it chose now of all times to put me in constant danger— or why it even came back to me.

I wrestled with the memory over and over again, as if something new would come to mind, but the more I dug, the more it left me empty and confused.

I craved answers, but first, I had to deal with my connection with the necklace. I rolled to my back and stared at the black ceiling.

"You look like shit."

I launched up and nabbed the candelabra still at my side and waved it around.

Ryas strolled out of the darkest corner of the room with a menacing smile on her face.

I couldn't believe my heart still worked from all the jump scares these psychos put me through.

I never wanted to witness her crawl out of the darkness like the girl from *The Grudge* ever again. "What do you want? I'm sure I still have some time before sunrise," I said, my tone loaded with irritation.

Ryas tossed a bunch of clothes on the bed and crossed her arms. "Get ready. It won't stay in one place for long."

I raised my eyebrow. "Stay in one place?"

Ryas shook her head and chuckled. "You really are so naïve, even with a familiar."

All I could think of was witches with brooms and black cats, and them making potions in a huge cauldron or some shit like that. Was my mother really part of a coven?

Gren popped into my mind. Wait, was he frantically looking for me after what happened?

I scrambled to my feet and stood in front of her. "Could you possibly get a crow for me? He would be waiting at my place. Possibly by my window. Probably brooding." I rambled on, ignoring her detached expression.

Why couldn't I leave Gren? I didn't owe him anything. But with what happened to his brothers, maybe we could offer each other moral support since we were both alone.

Ryan grinned and I scooted back; her frightening eyes contained nothing but chaos. "Yeah, I grabbed him." She reached her hand through the thick darkness and tossed him to my side.

"Now hurry and get ready."

She disappeared and left me shell-shocked. I eyed Gren who shook his wings out like he was drenched in something slimy, his feathers all sticking together.

"Hi." I couldn't think of anything else.

Gren lifted his beak, angling his one good eye at me. "You are a walking, talking danger magnet. I can't leave your side for a second."

"Hey, I didn't have a choice," I lied.

Gren sighed. "They're coming for you, Adeline. Did your mother teach you nothing about magic? I couldn't fix the barrier without my brothers. I'm-I'm sorry."

Gren had said similar words before. *What barrier?*

I settled Gren's feathers down with a pat hoping to calm his nerves. "Everyone keeps saying the same cryptic words to me. Who's coming for me? What barrier? I need answers."

Gren hesitated. "I'm under a sworn oath. It would destroy me . . ." He gave me a defeated sigh as he lowered his beak to the bed.

How frustrating. "Okay, I won't pry any further."

Who was I kidding? Everyone avoided giving me direct answers like I was the plague. And Gren conveniently couldn't tell me because of an oath?

I had no idea who I could trust and it scared the hell out of me.

"Thank you."

My smile waned as I pushed the uncertainty down. "Do you know anything about the person I made a deal with?"

"I'm not sure about the fae. I don't have much information on the Unseelie. I'm only versed in the dark arts of ours. Not theirs."

Gren raised his wings into a shrug like I should know the last bit of information.

I erupted into a fit of laughter.

This was all so absurd. I wondered if it was more plausible I was locked up in a psych ward right now than knowing I made a deal with an actual faery.

I patted Gren again. "All right, thanks for trying to explain."

The clothes bundled together beside me were, of course, my graphic T-shirts. At least she brought a pair of black jeans and boots. I wouldn't look *that* ridiculous.

I slid the dark green shirt over my head and grumbled, frowning at the bold letters like it would somehow alter them, but they remained the same and read "Life's too short, so let's fuck."

I had to remind myself my wardrobe didn't matter. I didn't need to impress anyone. Who cared if my outfit seemed like a teenager dressed me?

The mirror suspended in front of me revealed my worn-out reflection.

I detangled my hair and wiped the smudged mascara from under my eyes. The hell if I was wearing this outfit and looking like an unhinged raccoon—I had to maintain some form of dignity for myself.

If the sun had risen, I couldn't tell. The place resembled a dungeon without any source of natural light, but since Ryas showed, it meant Kaschel might come for me soon.

"Try not to disappear from my side so much," I told Gren as I veered from the mirror and watched how he pecked the bed, circling around the same spot, attempting to get in a comfy position before he plopped himself down.

"Of course." He blinked and somehow, I doubted he would hold true to his words.

I let out a controlled breath and wiggled my hands. The anticipation sent shivers down my arms.

The door swung open, and Kaschel stood there in odd attire.

Where were we going that required a sword in its sheath strapped to his hip? If I had to choose words to describe his outfit *medieval-times chic with juniper trousers* seemed to fit.

Yeah, he had questionable taste.

"Ah, so the little flea isn't going to make me drag her this time." The side of Kaschel's mouth tugged into a smirk, but it vanished as he fully took me in. He turned his back to me; his tight black tunic had a deep V, leaving nothing to the imagination as his broad shoulders practically devoured the doorframe. "Let's go, and make sure you bring the necklace with you. We don't have time for mistakes," he said and disappeared into the hallway.

A nagging thought told me I was in for one hell of a ride, and obviously, not the hot kind.

13
BLÀTH FALLS

I jogged to the hallway. I peeked both ways and saw Kaschel already ten meters away, and I hurried to his side. I was annoyed he couldn't wait—like did he need me here or not? He sure didn't act like it.

It's hard to expect anything from Kaschel, but some common courtesy wouldn't kill him. I highly doubted he could manage something so simple since he kidnapped me once already. He was on a losing streak in my book, and playing nice was poison to a man as pretentious as him.

Also, why did he keep referring to me as a parasite?

I took long strides to keep up with his pace and craned my neck up to glare at him. "Thanks for the endearing nickname, but I already have one," I said, sarcastically. "It's Addy. Short for Adeline. Got it?" I enunciated by hitting my pointer finger on my collarbone.

Kaschel chuckled with no hint of amusement. "Oh? I didn't think I asked for your name."

Kaschel didn't glance in my direction again. He just kept walking, and it was pretty goddamn infuriating. He was a total dick.

"Listen, here, faery man. My life has been turned upside down because of your shady-ass shit. Tell me what I'm supposed to do for you so I can fulfill our deal. I would love to hike my happy ass home sooner rather than later where we never have to cross paths again."

Did I have a death wish? Probably. Did I care? Absolutely not. I had no more fucks to give.

Kaschel's silence felt endless as we walked down the hallway. His long hair was pulled back neatly and flowed gently behind him. I craved yanking his stupid ponytail to the ground and seeing what kind of face he would make, but then he might justify using the sword at his hip to impale me. Yet, the small amount of patience I had left dwindled to nothing, and I felt more reckless by the second.

Had I always been this self-destructive?

Kaschel halted and my face smashed into his upper back, nearly knocking me over. He didn't lose his balance while I practically had to clench every muscle from my butt to my toes to stop from falling. I might have also snatched a fistful of his shirt to assist myself. Though I *really* wished I had caught his hair instead.

I released Kaschel's shirt and patted my hands on my jeans. I disregarded his maddened disposition and glanced at the two women with azure-blue hair in matching all-black outfits. They both had two short, silver, pointed objects around their belts.

Most likely daggers of some sort. The red-eyed man, the same creep from the nightclub, loomed over them. He sported similar attire as he stood brooding in the corner, leaning against the wall.

Kaschel creased his eyebrows and hardened his face into a scowl and resumed ignoring my existence. "Are the others there yet?"

"Yes. They're waiting for your command, and if we leave now, we'll make it there before nightfall," the red-eyed man said calmly as he fiddled with a switchblade.

Apparently, everyone had a thing for sharp objects here. I bet they had nicknames for them too. Maeve, Striker or Blade. Or something truly laughable like *Stabby*.

Jared walked through the opposite door—his hair messy, a loosened tie around his neck, and a wild look in his eyes. "Therion knows we have one of the keys."

Kaschel rubbed his temples and grunted. "Who did he send after us?"

Jared hesitated. "Everyone."

Kaschel side-eyed Jared. "You're with me. Zyair and the twins go see what Oberon's up to. Ryas go to my study, find the relic, and then help the other two." Kaschel growled the last part and snatched my hand and chanted the same words as before. The shadows materialized as he turned to face me. "This might be more uncomfortable than the last time."

I couldn't protest as Kaschel pulled me behind him and the darkness engulfed us and clung to me like tar. I inhaled but couldn't breathe. My time there felt stagnant until a hint of light appeared. We fell through and I smacked ass-first on the floor. I flipped to my side, on my hands and knees as I puked my guts

94

out. I wiped my mouth, rolled onto my back, and groaned. Gren shot through after me and patted my back with his wing.

I lifted my chin and gave him a weak smile.

Jared walked through, unaffected, and approached me. Concern furrowed in his brows, but Kaschel placed a hand up and prevented Jared from getting any closer. "Worry about yourself. Now go assess our surroundings. It's been a minute since I've been on this side."

Jared nodded and phased through the wall, leaving me alone with Kaschel in some spooky cabin. Dust clung to a crimson and gold tapestry like someone had neglected the place for years. A brick fireplace, one cherry-colored wooden table, and only two chairs occupied this room. It reeked of mold and decay. I could hardly keep it together. It didn't help I puked all over the floor and curtains. Now, it stunk of both death and vomit.

"Do you mind never doing that again?" I coughed out as I lifted myself off the ground, legs wobbling as I compelled the bile back down.

"Not gonna happen," Kaschel snipped as he stalked over to the table, crouched down, and thumped the wall with his knuckles.

"Please then, enlighten this little flea on what's going on so I'm not an aimless parasite."

Kaschel shifted and glared at me, but it seemed to have worked and he bit back. "The necklace you have is a key someone stole from me, and I need to find the other one . . ." He stopped tapping the wall and skimmed me over. "You're rather annoying. Has anyone ever told you?" He raised a brow.

Kaschel didn't want an answer, I knew that; he was just being a rhetorical asshole. Well, two could be rhetorical assholes.

"And you're rather arrogant. Has anyone ever mentioned that to you?"

Kaschel scoffed and didn't spare me another word as he concentrated on the wall again. I kept my eyes fixated on his alabaster hair as his ponytail rested in between his muscular shoulder blades.

It's like Gren read my mind and shook his beak.

I didn't really plan on pulling his ponytail. It was only a passing thought. I liked to believe I had more maturity than that.

"What are you looking for?" I probed, and Kaschel exhaled in response. "All right." *Not in the talking mood.*

I swung around and left him there to tap the wall like a lunatic and went to explore the rest of the place.

Nothing appeared out of the ordinary—just an old cabin requiring some serious TLC. I peeked down the dark hallway and proceeded to walk in the opposite direction of Kaschel. Spending the time scouring was a better pastime than forcing myself to stay in the same room as him, suffocating under his overwhelmingly dreadful company.

Decay wafted through the hallway; the pungent smell brewed a new type of disgusting with each step as my senses screamed at me to turn around and not open the silver door handle.

Convincing myself I developed an immunity to the dark and creepy was easy when the existence of a six-foot-four monster stood on the opposite side of the cabin. I mean, how could anything else intimidate me now when Kaschel was so close?

The door clicked open, and I flung my hand up to cover my mouth.

14
DARK SPELLS

One hand clenched my side as I placed the other one tightly over my mouth and nose to stifle the rancid fumes. A body with its lower half burned to a crisp laid in front of me, tied up against an iron bed frame. Bile rose in my throat, and I gripped my stomach harder.

The laceration on their open chest appeared deliberate and had a ritualistic pattern. The more I studied, the more gruesome it became. A carved crest of twisted horns on their forehead, and their ears were ripped clean off. The creature seemed alive when it happened; a face frozen in fear as a huge area of dry blood stained the white bedsheet.

A low hissing buzzed in my ears, but I couldn't find the source of the noise.

It petrified me.

I took a step backward, refusing to look at this torture chamber of a room any longer when my boot connected with something crunchy on the ground. It flattened under my shifting weight; reluctantly, I raised my boot off the floor.

A shriveled, pointed ear stared back at me.

Bile rose higher in my throat, and I emptied what little contents I had left. My eyes turned bloodshot and watery, blurring my vision as my body retched until my insides settled and I couldn't take it anymore.

Only a true monster could do this.

The erratic flutters of my pulse writhed within my chest, hindering me from calming down and breathing.

I guess I hadn't become numb to everything yet.

I wiped my mouth and swerved back to the door, my face colliding with Kaschel's firm chest.

And before I summoned a squeak or sound, Kaschel spoke. "Barbaric, isn't it?" he asked, not tearing his gaze from the mutilated body resting on the bed.

His expression remained unreadable: mad, frustrated, humored, or indifferent—they all meshed together. Honestly, not knowing what went through his mind was another thing that truly terrified me.

One of my hands betrayed me and shook profusely as it pressed against his abdomen, exposing my unease. My other hand clung to his shirt.

I sidestepped away, letting go of Kaschel. I didn't need comfort from him, even if the situation was unsettling.

"What kind of person would do this?" I didn't expect an answer, nor did I really want one.

I just didn't want to stand in silence any longer than necessary.

Kaschel recited the words in a daze, and I couldn't help but get lost in his deep voice as it rang melodically in my ears. "Greed is truly ugly." He stopped, broke out of his stupor, and bent down to face me. His light, cosmic eyes bore into my soul. "Weaker beings let their animalistic urges consume them and covet what they can never have."

The words *greed* and *urges* danced alongside each other, spinning wicked thoughts as I tried to grasp the meaning behind what he said.

I scanned for Gren, but he had disappeared, *again*. Where did that little fucker hop off to? A "Hey, I'll be right back" wouldn't kill him.

My eyes narrowed as Kaschel's words registered in my mind. "Why would you take me to a place like this? I'm sure you could have portaled us somewhere with less serial killer vibes and more, I don't know . . . welcoming vibes." I winced from my abrupt words and faced the wall.

The sadistic man laughed.

Kaschel actually laughed, and it was low and throaty.

I spun around and gave him a you're-fucking-crazy look.

I was judging. Harshly. He was demented.

"A fae spirit resides here," Kaschel announced.

My brows furrowed and I waited for him to elaborate, but he didn't even grunt. Apparently, he thought those words equaled a full-blown explanation.

Would I get an aneurysm or go bald first from frustration if another person said one more coded phrase to me? With my luck, I'd get both simultaneously.

Kaschel so rudely blocked the doorway with his shredded physique, and I squeezed behind him to get out. I swore if I stayed any longer, I might end up puking my guts out again.

For some stupid, unknown reason, I peeked over my shoulder, and Kaschel's shadow thingy devoured the body like it was a midnight snack.

I shuddered, picking up my pace as I hurried down the hallway. Did he have some collection of dead bodies I didn't know about?

The last thought loitered in my mind as I rushed back to the front, pulling out a chair.

My nails clicked against the table.

I didn't know how much more I could handle. The more I found out, the more it thoroughly made me want to rip my hair out.

Why did my mom leave me with the key? Why hide me from her coven?

Dropping my forehead to the table, I lifted my head and slammed against it again, and again.

Hopeless, everything felt utterly hopeless. If I died right now, I would die a clueless idiot.

Something brushed against my shoulder, and I squeaked, shot up with my eyes closed, and swung my hands in defense.

My hands collided with a solid surface, and I blinked.

I groaned and smacked his chest again for good measure. "Can you guys stop being so fucking creepy and warn a person?"

15
A COVENANT OF LIES

"**Y**ou were . . . acting odd." Jared frowned.

I rolled my eyes at his dishonest behavior. "And this place doesn't feel more odd? Your concern is misplaced."

Jared leaned closer, brushed a few loose strands of hair out of my face, and tucked them behind my ear. "I will always be concerned about you."

His scalding touch lingered against my skin and burned a crater through me, forming a void where my heart should have been.

I swatted Jared's hand away. "Don't ever touch me again," I seethed. Repulsed by his touch, I shook the lasting feeling of his skin against mine and changed the subject. "Did you find who, or whatever, we need? I don't think I can stand another second by your side," I said, ignoring the flicker of dejection in his face.

I bet Jared only pitied me, and his false sympathy—or whatever else swirled through him besides rejection—had my skin crawling.

Jared walked a few steps away with his back to me, wavering. "Of course, and yeah . . . something along those lines."

Jared's hushed tone held no hint of sadness, nor did he sound angry. He seemed more empty than anything else.

Not that I cared.

I didn't say a word to him and instead, I silently watched him disappear into the hallway.

I faintly heard them talking, and it sparked my interest. I tiptoed toward the room and hoped to god the old floorboards didn't squeak under my weight as their deep voices crescendoed off the walls.

I peered through the cracked door as Jared made hand gestures, and Kaschel stood there with his arms crossed, his face pinched in annoyance.

"He said there isn't enough for all of us to cross over since the balance is off and it could collapse any moment. The potential of getting stuck in between is extremely high."

Kaschel rubbed his temples like nothing was going according to his plan—if he even had a plan. I had no idea what he was thinking, and getting stuck somewhere else didn't sound great either.

Why did none of our options seem reasonable? The place Jared spoke of couldn't be worse than this murder cabin.

Kaschel finally spoke, and he laced it with so much venom the walls quivered. "I will go with her while you go to the others and make sure they stay off our tracks. I don't need to deal with more witches or bounty hunters when I'm at half-power."

"Sir, I think it would be best if I came with—"

"Did you not hear what I said?" Kaschel snarled, looming over Jared with a spine-chilling expression.

Kaschel's head leaned to the side, and Jared's stance made him appear frail in comparison.

"I know I could be of assistance." Jared trailed off, shoving his hands in his pockets.

Kaschel chuckled. "Have you forgotten what I've done for you? What you've sworn to? You also led them right to us. So, tell me, why should I allow you to disregard my orders? Why are you so hung up on some *human*?"

Jared stood there, hushed. "Forgive me . . . I wasn't aware she was the one with the key. I thought you were hunting down a witch who stole them centuries ago. I don't understand why she's—"

Kaschel clicked his tongue. "Yet, she has it, and until I find the other one—" Kaschel bent his head toward the cracked door. "If you intend on spying, try to be a little less aggressive with your breathing. You sound like a rabid goblin, and it's rather distracting."

I flung up my hand to cover my mouth and gathered the courage to defend myself, but I quickly realized I didn't need to. Not to a prick like him.

My eyes wandered to Jared, but he always avoided my line of sight. What a coward; how was I ever hung up on him in the first place?

I huffed. "I wasn't spying if I could hear your grating voices from the kitchen." I so badly wanted to flip Kaschel off or stick my tongue out, but with what little pride I had left, I held on to it like my thread of fate, and I walked away without sparing them another word.

I closed the front door behind me, sat down on the steps, and ran my fingers through my hair, still half-tempted to rip it all out in frustration.

But that would make me insane.

I placed my chin on my palm, propping my elbow on my knee, and looked out into the forest.

When I escaped this hell loop, I needed a vacation. A long one, but a vacation also required money—money I didn't have. So I needed a job first, and to work for a while before I could even think about taking time off. A delusional girl could dream though. Hawaii or Cancun didn't sound terrible. Some tropical scenery with fruity mixed drinks right on the beach where I could bury my toes in the sand and sip without care. Maybe meet a hot foreign guy.

The kinks could be handled later.

I tipped my head back and shut my eyes, inhaling to relieve the tension.

Sleep sounded incredible right now, but no way would I nap where a murder took place with two shifty-ass men. *No, thank you.*

My head dangled farther back as I laughed, and it was dry and vacant of any joy.

The wind picked up and stroked my skin. The chill in the air soothed my chaotic mind, and I was almost thankful for it.

"Are you ready to tell me where the grimoire is?"

I whipped my head up and studied the forest. Nothing.

"I wonder: Will you forfeit his life, or will you save him?" a hypnotic voice purred in my ear.

My senses were clouded with fond memories of Lucien. His bright cheerful face invaded my mind, and I couldn't think of anyone but *him*.

A tsunami of pain surged through me. My temples throbbed with desperation as an ache settled into my chest before lashing out at my arms and legs—like pins and needles—as the memories spun into gruesome nightmares of Lucien's skin melting off his bones as he crawled toward me.

The voice taunted me further. "Do we need to try the hard way . . . again?"

The abrasive voice echoed around me.

I demanded it to stop.

It had to stop.

A rapid fire of vicious oscillating voices plagued my ears, and if I didn't obey them I somehow knew my body would combust and burn the forest to cinders.

I stood up and began walking.

Then jogging.

Running.

My legs pushed me forward, blending the forest into a blur of deep green and umber as my feet left a wake of dust behind me.

I captured glimpses of Gren flapping his wings furiously as he kept up with my speed.

He held his beak open, but I only caught every other word.

"It's . . . trap . . . come . . . your!"

A deep sense of dread cemented itself in my chest, and anguish hit me harder. The pain relentlessly corrupted my concentration.

I pursued the loudest voice with everything I had.

Two blurred bodies manifested in the distance and grew more vivid with each step.

Lucien, on his knees, mouth gagged with a shadow-like substance—entirely different from Kaschel's—wrapped around his body like a rope. His glistening face reflected dread and suffering. Valeria stood above him, grinning.

A rush of fury hit me. Raw emotions clawed their way to the surface, fighting for their spot alongside my rage.

Terrified and *helpless.*

Valeria's jaw broke apart into a hideous smile as it stretched to an unnatural length.

"Is this convincing enough?" Valeria mused as she pointed to Lucien. "Or should I demonstrate it for you?" Valeria's eyes flickered a pitch-black as she belted out a cackle.

I stumbled back.

My heart thundered against my chest; my hands clenched into tight fists. "What do you need? I don't have the grimoire," I gritted through my teeth.

My eyes focused on Lucien like if I turned away he would disappear forever. But I couldn't open my mouth to console him. I couldn't think of a single fucking word to say to him.

Lucien didn't deserve silence, but my voice and mind were failing me.

"Oh, sweetie. I won't stop hassling you, but my boss is growing quite impatient, so here I am for the keys."

16
FOOLS BE DAMNED

All the pain from earlier vanished, but now tremors of panic penetrated my mind, spinning a thousand disturbing scenarios. Not a single one offered a way out for both Lucien and me.

"Well, your boss will be disappointed because I only have one." I squeezed my fists, my nails pinching into my palms.

The sharp pain kept me grounded so I didn't fall apart and beg for our lives.

Somehow, I knew it wouldn't do me any good.

"Tsk-tsk. You're no fun at all." Valeria grabbed a fistful of Lucien's golden locks and pulled him up to his knees. A muffled groan escaped his lips as he staggered to his feet. She grabbed his cheeks, squeezed them tight, and turned his face to hers. "I can see why you're so enamored with him. He's such a cutie, isn't he?"

Valeria compelled Lucien to nod his head at her remark, and his look of terror made me sick as her elongated jaw moved. It twisted and curled with bone spurs protruding out of her tight skin. She was a nightmare coming to life before my eyes.

"Valeria, your problem is with me, so why don't you let him go, and we'll come to an agreement on our own?" I bit out each word again, not wanting to see her manhandle Lucien any longer.

Lucien didn't deserve this, yet here he was because of me. I could have avoided his house, his help, but I didn't.

Valeria twisted Lucien's face, and our eyes met as Valeria's sharp words pierced me like a double-edged sword. "Please, we're friends now. Call me Val." Her face curved into an ungodly smirk and put her sharp canines on display. She paused like she waited for me to respond, but I didn't say a word and she carried on. "I'm so happy you rid me of that imbecile. Fumbling around with half his power desperate to restore it." She laughed. "You see, men." She shoved Lucien back onto his knees with her boot pressed to his back. "They always go headfirst without thinking, but look where that got him? Stuck playing tag with a bunch of bounty hunters. No, you need to play the long game if you want to win."

Her black eyes sparkled with malice as she stared behind me.

I rotated my body and witnessed Gren slamming himself against an invisible force. The ripples of his power shattered against the barrier as a black mist enveloped him.

The ground moved beneath me, or maybe my body trembled.

Could she not get to the fucking point?

I clapped my hands, aiming to control my ruse, and not show my obvious fear. "How clever. Now please, save us both the trouble and tell me what the hell you want me to do?" I pulled the necklace from my pocket and dangled it in front of her. "You can have it for all I care; just leave Lucien out of this."

"You really are a fool." Valeria shook her head. "It doesn't work that way, or I would have taken it from Kaschel the first time around. So here's the deal. Retrieve the other key, bring them back to me, and open the door for *her*. Simple. Okay?" She popped her fingers against each other and an unnatural snapping noise reverberated around us.

I shuddered.

How could I steal from Kaschel? I made a deal with him. And open what door? To where?

Valeria yawned. "I'm growing bored." She wrenched Lucien up again, snatched his arm, and shattered it like a glass.

Lucien's muffled cries pierced me to the core as his arm, broken in half, slumped to his side.

I rushed to Lucien, kneeled, and cupped my hand under his jaw. Tears stained his blushed cheeks, and I gently wiped them away.

And I lost it.

"Okay! Okay, I'll do it!" I pleaded with her and my eyes narrowed, overflowing with fury.

Valeria lifted her hand to cover up her laughter. Her mocking gesture was meant to enrage me further. She wanted to continue toying with us.

"Good." She pulled out a pocket mirror laced with silver thorns and a skull with three golden vipers spilling out of its mouth and eye sockets. "The next red moon will be the only time you can use this to get to my location."

"What about Lucien? His arm?"

Valeria chuckled, shook her head, and pulled him up from the roots of his hair again. "This thing?" She snapped her fingers, and he disintegrated into a black gooey substance between my fingers. "It's what you could be casting, yet you chose to stay ignorant."

The goo spattered onto the dirt, and I grasped at it like it would somehow offer me stability and bring him back. "What have you done?" I choked out.

"Oh, lighten up. He wasn't real." She tossed the mirror; it hit my chest and fell to the ground. I hesitated, but ultimately picked it up. "Now, hurry up or Lynne will have a splendid time experimenting on your friend. And knowing her . . . you don't have long."

"Wait!" I had mere seconds to ask my bubbling questions.

"Oh?" She turned slightly toward me.

"Is he safe? And at least tell me about the keys and why I'm the centerpiece for some war I didn't even start."

Desperation didn't look good on me, but at this point, I would take answers from just about anyone.

Valeria perked an eyebrow as if debating whether to humor me or leave me ignorant.

"Have you heard of the story where the saying, 'ye without sin shall cast thy stone first,' came from?" Valeria asked. I squinted at her, confused, so I just nodded. "Well, it's a similar story. A witch accused of adultery, but for her, she had to prove her innocence by stealing something of greater value for our lord. However, by the time she had them in her possession, she was as plump as could be with you. I'm sure you can put two and two together." Valeria blew me a kiss, twisted into a raven, and vanished into the shade of the trees.

The echoes of her words jumbled together, and I couldn't make sense of them. *Stealing. Adultery. Lord?* What screwed up shit did my mother put me in?

17
OTHERWORLDLY

The ground rumbled beneath me as the barrier dissipated. Gren's vociferous voice thundered through the pine trees like a vengeful apparition wreaking havoc. "You need to listen!" He flapped his wings and glided to my side. "You can't trust her!"

I stared at the dirt soiling my hands and knees. "It's not like I had a choice," I mumbled, lifting my gaze to Gren. "I needed the pain to stop."

My words had caught him off guard, and he stood still for a moment.

Then he patted my back with his wing at an awkward angle.

If I had told myself a month ago a bird would be consoling me, I would have laughed my ass off at the sheer absurdity. Yet, he perched there, comforting me.

"Thank you, Gren, but you can stop now." I forced a smile, stood up, and dusted off my hands and knees, but the dirt still clung to my clothes.

So Lucien and I were both played for fools. He had no idea the woman he adored was toying with him.

My heart clenched and I tried like hell to stabilize myself as I clutched my hand to my chest.

Gren spoke, cutting me off before I spiraled further. "You need to learn magic. It's the only way to deal with them. And I'm sorry. I should have known sooner. She was a part of your mom's coven, and she did everything in her—" A violet light shot down from the sky and struck Gren's chest like a lightning bolt.

Gren whimpered as the magical current pulsated in waves until it evaporated.

"GREN." I scrambled to pick him up. "Are you okay?" I smoothed his feathers out, and a couple fell from where the bolt struck him.

"Yes," Gren croaked. He shook his wings as they expanded to a couple of feet. "The oath is more potent than I anticipated."

"I'm starting to see that nothing comes without a price."

Gren didn't respond, but he knew what I meant.

My options kept getting more limited, but it didn't matter. I wouldn't let anyone harm Lucien. There were some lines I would never cross, and letting a friend die in my place was one of them.

I would figure out the rest of the details later. Right now, my focus stayed on retrieving the other key.

"The fae is coming. Don't speak a word of it. No one can be trusted until we know our plan of action. I know you won't leave your boyfriend to rot," Gren whispered.

I almost corrected him, but it held no importance if he thought Lucien was my boyfriend, so I nodded my head.

In a millisecond, Kaschel towered above me and scanned the area. His lips pressed in a fine line, his hair now loose and tousled. He looked chaotically untamed.

Gren stuck his beak out and glared at Kaschel, oddly cute for a crow.

"Your presence disappeared and now the air is thick with magic. *What happened*?" Kaschel growled, scrunching his face in aversion.

I wondered, if he thought I might betray him, would he cut me down where I stood?

I raised my chin and crossed my arms. "Can a girl not sit in the forest and be one with nature? It's called meditating, you should try it sometime. It might fix your egotistical personality." I pointed at him and headed back to the cabin.

Kaschel appeared stunned and he fell short of words—for once—or he didn't want to indulge in my craziness. Well then, the feeling was mutual.

I trusted him as far as I could throw him. So telling him about his ex-lackey coming to visit and threaten me? Didn't seem like the best idea until I understood the whole picture, which got more skewed by the second.

Gren and I wandered more than ten meters before the sinister cabin came into view.

"You're going the wrong way."

I shuddered from his voice—a delicate whisper in my ear. He hadn't budged a muscle and stayed in the exact spot I left him.

Was he using magic? Uncalled for.

I took a deep breath and turned around. He definitely planned that. What a petty man.

With my head held high, I trudged to Kaschel's side. "Then where to?" I asked and let all the annoyance roll off my tongue.

The side of Kaschel's mouth curved into a smirk, and I yearned to wipe the conceited look right off his face.

God, he irked me in more ways than one.

Kaschel bent down, his face inches from my ear. I could snatch his ponytail if I wanted. And fuck, did I want to. My hands had an itch, and I longed to scratch it. What was the worst that could happen?

The beckoning impulse was an intense temptation, but I didn't need to test the theory out.

I've been in more life-threatening situations than I could count and adding another to the list didn't seem like my brightest idea to date. So physically antagonizing a fae? Nah, I was good. I wanted to live.

"Blàth isn't far from here, so we'll walk," Kaschel said, but that meant absolutely nothing to me.

"And once we get to Blàth?" I probed, but Kaschel grunted in response like all my questions annoyed him. But if he answered them instead of acting like an enigmatic asshole, then, maybe, I would give him some grace and shut up. "Great. Really straight-forward."

I stole a quick peek in his direction, but he proceeded to ignore me.

My legs grew weaker by the second. I had no idea how long we walked. Maybe two or three hours? His idea of close was incredibly off.

My stomach growled in protest, and my cheeks reddened as it cut through the silence of the forest.

My insides rumbled again, about to cave in and gnaw away at themselves. But no way would I ask Kaschel for food. We would stop eventually. He needed sustenance too . . . right?

My body screamed at me, trembling and on the verge of exhaustion, dehydration, and probably starvation when Kaschel stopped, and I crashed into his backside.

The sun descended as the sky illuminated in red and purple hues, highlighting the blue undertones in my skin. The crescent moon glowered down on us, and a chill edged down my spine.

The wind came alive, swirling around us and the soft hums of the water pillowing over faded in the background.

The beauty of the falls was unmistakable.

A low ticking resounded off the water like an imaginary grandfather clock counting down the seconds.

Kaschel's purple eyes reflected brilliant specks of light, and I wondered if he heard the ticking as well.

The world slowed down except for Kaschel and me as the sky exhibited otherworldly signs and ripped in half. I stood there speechless, disorientated, and most of all, captivated.

Kaschel snatched my hand, and it expelled me out of whatever force attempting to pull me in.

"You're not accustomed to the magic in my world. So don't touch, eat, or talk to anything. Got it?" Kaschel's eyebrows bunched together, and he pursed his lips.

"Uh, yeah. Sure," I mumbled, not even sounding convincing to myself, but he didn't seem to care.

Kaschel nodded his head, and we walked through the rift cutting through the soil to the sky as it swallowed us whole.

18
GRIGS, SPARKS, AND TRICKERY

The portal shoved and spit us out in a forest overrun by ferns taller than me and ivy wrapped around the trees as the branches coiled in bizarre angles. They were all covered in needle-like thorns about three inches long as a thick fog hung right below my waist. I would be lying if I said it didn't look like we walked right into a horror movie. This place gave off some serious, serial-killer vibes just like the cabin, and I wouldn't be surprised if a psycho popped out of a bush.

God, I was so sick of dark and creepy.

Why couldn't the portal drop us off at an inn or pub? I was famished and in dire need of a drink and sleep.

Kaschel, in his element, as his muscular build complemented his formfitting all-black attire and boots. All he needed? A machete instead of a sword to cut through the overgrowth.

I, on the other hand, was ready for bed, not ready to rummage through a goddamn forest with spiked trees splintering in all directions. With my luck, I was going to get myself impaled.

Kaschel shook my hand off.

Out of habit, I wiped my palm on my shirt—slightly upset at myself for holding on to his for so long.

"Stick close. These woods will warp your sanity if you let them. It's no place for someone like you."

I rolled my eyes. "No shit. You're incredibly good at stating the obvious."

Kaschel chuckled under his breath and roamed deeper into the eerie forest, leaving me behind. I scurried close enough to his side that if something jumped out to murder us all, I could easily shove him in the way and save Gren and myself. Or at least, stall whatever creature was determined to attack us long enough for me to escape. I was shameless, so what?

I trudged behind Kaschel through the thicket of ferns, and with each step he pulled a branch forward and let go, whacking me with an ungodly amount. My rage bubbled to the surface and almost burst when the forest thinned out, and a dirt path came into view.

Kaschel hurled something in my direction, and darkness shrouded me.

I ripped the thing off, glanced down at it, and back at him.

"It has an enchantment and will disguise your human scent, but you must keep your face covered. We're in *Dearmad a Dhéanamh*; the border between the courts. There are no laws, so don't wander off or do anything stupid."

I didn't hesitate and draped myself with the black cloak. I

struggled with the button in the front for a few seconds, and Kaschel's heated glare bore a hole into my skull.

Didn't he know the more he stared, the harder it was for me to attach it?

I fiddled with it for a couple more seconds as sweat rolled above my eyebrows and it popped into place.

I cleared my throat and avoided Kaschel's agitated expression. Only a hint of his emotions flickered across his face, and they screamed, *You're a dumbass.*

"How long do we have to be in . . . this place?" I asked, choosing to ignore his patronizing look.

A chill crept down my neck, and from the corner of my peripheral, a million eyes blinked and vanished into the ferns.

I gasped and shook the nerves away.

Kaschel didn't appear worried, or he didn't notice them. I couldn't tell which, so I tried not to overreact.

It's fine. Totally normal stuff when you walk through a portal to another world.

"I need to meet with an old friend. He'll know how to find the second key and break the spell that has you bound to this one."

Wow, how detailed. Sounded easy if he said it like that. The sooner we got the second key, the sooner I could save Lucien. So I stayed silent and followed Kaschel down the dirt path.

We reached a stone building with a wooden sign reading Eros's Saloon.

Creatures filled the streets; it had the same appeal of a farmer's market, but a grittier one with carts full of oddities. The place stirred with boisterous chatter and clanking noises as the ground rattled from all the heavy foot traffic.

Kaschel shoved us past a group of, well one thing had to be a fae like him, but with jet black hair, pure obsidian eyes, and bat-like wings, but he was one of many creatures we walked by. I caught a glimpse of a centaur. She had the look of the forest with sprouting horns covered in moss and withered flowers. A hundred tiny gray creatures shot past us. Their black beady eyes and translucent wings buzzed like a swarm of horseflies.

Their unified shrieks pierced my ears, and I launched my hands up to cup my ears, but Kaschel snatched my wrist.

No one else even flinched at the god-awful sound but me.

I yanked my wrist away, and Kaschel grunted and proceeded to the doors.

He opened the front entrance, and a hauntingly soft tune captivated me. My attention fell on a willowy creature with ghostly white skin playing a lyre harp.

A smell wafted the room and had the variation of pine needles, wheat, and coriander all muddled together; it reminded me of a shot of gin. It packed a punch but ultimately settled down and enveloped my whole body with its warm embrace. The tempting aroma drifted through the room, stronger than the smell of the sweaty creatures dancing.

My whole body tensed as we barreled through the sea of creatures, making it to the bar top; I tapped my fingers rhythmically as they squished us against it.

An ogre-like creature leaned over the bar, drooling from its tusks. I averted my gaze, and it landed on a fae. Tall and handsome, but unlike the other one I saw earlier. His hair was golden, but not the normal type of gold. A color of gold more rich and dazzling, and his eyes, a deep coral burning with so much intensity for the woman next to him. Although, in comparison to the woman he flirted with, he appeared rather dull. Her beauty overwhelmed the room; her long silver hair and icy blue stare could pierce any heart.

I snapped out of my weird stupor as I forcibly squeezed harder against Kaschel. Gren perched on the edge of the counter tilting his head at me. We were all packed together like sardines, and if I said I was uncomfortable, that would be an understatement.

Yet, I didn't protest or make a sound as a goblin-like creature walked up to us. His skin was lumpy with a swampy, greenish tone, and he had an exaggerated crooked nose. I tried not to stare and decided to look straight at Gren with wide eyes.

Gren saw right through me and mouthed, *You have nothing to fear.*

I almost scoffed and spit all over the bar. It had to be his favorite line.

When in fact, I had so much to fear.

But Gren's words held some weight to them. I felt relatively calm, but I still couldn't stop drumming my fingers. A bad habit of mine I couldn't quit.

"An ale and a water," Kaschel said as he tossed a few silver coins on the counter, and the goblin nodded its head and snatched them.

The goblin grabbed a mug from under the bar, pulled the tap handle, and slid the amber ale toward us. I licked my parched lips as my mouth instantly watered. He slid a wooden cup full of water in my direction, and I hesitated.

A musty smell flooded my senses, and I gagged and pinched my nose.

Could I have gotten something without a suspiciously spoiled smell to it?

I doubted it. Was this why people in the wilderness drink their own piss on the brink of dehydration? Because they were so dehydrated they didn't care?

Did I say I'd rather drink my own piss?

I pinched my nose harder and chugged it as fast as I could. I inhaled and squirmed as the water oozed down my throat. Kaschel's chest pressed against my back as he chuckled at my obvious discomfort.

I quivered as it hit my stomach. "Did you poison me?"

"How could I have poisoned you? It's just water. You should be fine," Kaschel said in a smug voice, and it sent vibrations against my back. "You should use that brain of yours, even if it is the size of a pea."

I mumbled some unrefined words as I compelled the water to stay down.

I moved my squeezed elbow and accidentally smacked the creature next to us. I peeked over, and the man glowed yellow and had an impish aura to him. Then the bastard winked at me.

I shuddered and turned back to Gren.

Kaschel's attention was focused on something in the distance. "Stay right here. I need to handle something."

"Wait, what do you mean?" I asked, but he didn't hear me over the music or crowd, or maybe he chose to ignore me, again. Highly possible.

I faced the bar as Kaschel shoved past people and disappeared from my view.

A sharp pang hit me at the nape of my neck, and I tried to rub the intense spasms away.

A blazing inferno stirred inside me as the color of the room turned to a pinkish hue.

If I ever experienced walking on air, this was pretty damn close to what I imagined it would feel like. A myriad of iridescent hues swirling around me shimmering like fireflies. My body was weightless as the light danced around my skin and warmth consumed me.

My pragmatic world turned to brushstrokes of pastels. The crowded bar suffocated me until I wobbled outside, slid down the wall, and tipped my head back.

I smiled with closed eyes as a numbing sensation overtook my arms and legs, but it didn't feel like pins and needles. It felt warm and fuzzy like someone stood there tormenting me with a silky feather.

Light footballs echoed around me.

I dropped my head down, squinting. "Gren, when did you get so . . . small?"

I tilted my chin up wondering if Gren could carry me. I laughed as the sound left my lips. *Of course, he could.*

I patted what I assumed to be Gren's head. "You can carry me, but just don't drop me." I hummed along to the faint music and tossed my head back and closed my eyes again.

Euphoria swirled through me, but a faint burning sensation itched all over my skin. My feet dangled off the ground, and I whistled at Gren's strength.

Gren carried me like I said he could. "See, I told you. You just had to believeeee." I tipped myself farther back and I blinked.

But a million sets of tiny eyes appeared, not Gren.

An audible gasp escaped my lips.

I lifted my hand and pinched the cheek of the closest one in proximity, a crowned forest-green pixie dressed in trousers, flowers, and jewels.

"You're the little pixie from before," I murmured, and the vibration of my words tickled my lips and crept up to my ears.

"Grigs," he said sternly.

"Greg?" I scrunched my face, not sure what the little creature was saying.

"We're grigs." He aggressively tapped his chest.

I grinned. "Bless you."

The little pixie rubbed his temple and shot a glare at the ones loitering behind him, then focused back on me. "You left suddenly. Your prize still awaits you." He grinned and his needle-like teeth peeked through his light green lips.

My eyes widened at the sparkling wings on the back of the pixie and my impulsiveness won. I traced my hands along the set of iridescent wings, and the only way I could describe the feeling was rice paper. I shook out the tingling feeling and giggled.

They all gasped and whispered, shooting hectic looks at one another.

The crowned pixie, shocked, held on to his wings like I was about to steal them away from him. "Oh, no." He turned away from me and my world went in and out. "How much did you give her? I said bring her here, not drug and drag her!" The pixie let out a dramatic sigh. "No matter. Lay her here. She can rest while we prepare the ceremonial feast."

My mouth instantly watered from the word *feast*, and I almost asked them what they were having and if I could join them when

Kaschel caught the corner of my eye, glowing before me.

His existence was otherworldly, more so than usual, and not in the grim reaper type of way where he'd reap my soul if he had the chance and drag me down to the fiery pits of hell. No. He was *enchanting*.

My fingertips to my toes tickled, and a wave of giddiness washed over me as all the little pixies gasped again and shot a look right to the crowned pixie.

A weird buzzing hit my stomach as Kaschel scooped me up and spoke, his voice in a low growl. "I leave for a second and I find you not only disappeared but have been dragged to this filthy place by a horde of grigs. What am I even looking at?"

So Kaschel was saying the little creature was a grig, not a Greg.

I let out a loud cackle and squinted my eyes at them. His name being Greg made more sense. Grig? What utter nonsense.

"She's ours!" the crowned grig yelled, blocking Kaschel's path with me.

"I'm afraid you will have to wait. She's a little preoccupied with some affairs at the moment," Kaschel said, clicking his tongue.

"You don't speak for her." The tiny grig crossed his arms, and I had the urge to pinch his adorable cheeks again.

Kaschel crouched down low and flicked the grig into a dirt wall. "I forgot how bothersome you little vermin are." Kaschel snatched my wrist and tilted it downward so they could see the crescent moon. "This means she's *mine*. So don't cross me."

The tiny grig stood up and pointed at Kaschel. "You will regret this!"

Kaschel chuckled and walked away from them. All I could see now was Kaschel's face and the tips of the trees passing me by and how the moonlight reflected off his pointed ears. Now more than ever, I could tell he was a faery.

I wondered if I called him that would it piss him off?

Kaschel noticed I was staring, and I erupted into a fit of laughter. His face pinched into a scowl. His choppy alabaster hair framed his square jaw perfectly. A faint pink scar starting at his plump bottom lip went all the way down his neck to under his loose shirt. I hadn't noticed it before.

And I was dying to know, *did he have more like me?*

He tilted his head. I mimicked him and watched as his lips moved up and down again. "Trouble seems to find you no matter where you go, doesn't it?"

I reached out my hand and pressed my finger to his lips. "Shh-hhhhh, faery man. Shhhhhhh." I stopped, brought my hands to his back and moved them downward, feeling every muscle along the way. "Do you have wings too? Where are you hiding them?" I patted his back when I couldn't find them and squeezed his firm cheeks. "No surprise you've got such a great backside."

Kaschel snatched my hand and pulled it away from him. I followed the sparkles around his face and an uncontrollable urge hit me.

"Booooop." I squished Kaschel's nose with my pointer finger, and his dark eyebrow shot up. "I caught the sparkles for you," I said, crinkling my nose, suddenly annoyed he didn't appreciate my generosity. "Not like you would care, you Geralt-looking motherfucker."

Kaschel's lips moved again, but a dense fog occupied my mind and thickened until it all went blank—except for a soft melody pulling me to sleep. I let it carry me as my whole world spun to darkness.

19
PASSION OR HATE

I was lulled back awake by the rhythmic sound of water droplets. The cold sensation splashed against my feverish cheeks and cascaded down my neck.

I tipped my head back and stared at the vast sunset as the rain doused me. The sky was slowly consumed by opaque rain clouds as the sun dipped down and the two moons ascended. The bleak night couldn't overshadow the countless stars' splendor as a deep desire churned inside me.

I reached my hand out and tried to pluck each and every star from the ever-changing kaleidoscopic sky.

I closed my fist, brought it to my face, and opened it.

Frustration steamed within me and flushed out the last remnants of desire as I studied my empty palm.

I huffed and threw my head back, and the fuzzy feeling overtook me once again.

I studied Kaschel and traced his face lightly with my finger-tips. His skin, smooth, yet still rugged and firm—maybe from his clenched jaw.

Kaschel's face seemed to only know one facial expression: the same grimace he sported earlier as his dark brows squeezed together in vexation. A heavy contrast to his slicked-back hair drenched from the rain as it gave off a silverish tint in the moon-light.

He radiated like a beacon in the darkness ensnaring you with his celestial glow. Only to drag you down to hell and let you burn for all eternity. He was a trap, an enchanting but oh-so-cruel trap. A god of war and calamity ready to destroy everything in his wake. Even with the wave of giddiness flowing through my veins, I knew he was a lethal venom slowly poisoning me the more I stared.

My breathing hitched and I skimmed ahead as Kaschel carried me princess-style through an eerily lit street that had long been abandoned.

The intense pounding of Kaschel's heartbeat sent tremors through me, yet it moved, slow and steady.

A grogginess consumed me, and a thundering pain hit me right above my temple.

My concentration muddled as my vision blurred—going in and out as the world danced in throngs of prismatic lights around me.

My vision cleared, and once again we appeared at a location teeming with laughter cutting through the dense air.

I rubbed my eyes and widened them, suddenly aware of

everything.

"L-let me go," I squeaked, glancing up at the dark stone build-ing with the sign that read Galleget's and shoved myself away from his burly chest.

Kaschel didn't give me the time of day and answered in a clipped tone. "You were being facetious."

I wiggled my legs and tried to get out of Kaschel's hold, but I couldn't rival his strength with my fatigued arms.

I sighed in defeat. "Please let me go."

Kaschel lowered a brow in suspicion. "And let you act as a fool and do as you please? Look where that got you."

"It's not my fault you laced my water with something," I grumbled as I crossed my arms.

Like hell if I would act like that of my own volition. I was stubborn, not stupid.

The corner of Kaschel's mouth curved upward. Somehow my words amused him, and it pissed me off.

Kaschel tilted his head to the side, and his striking jawline tensed as he responded. "What a bold accusation, but I'd take no pleasure in drugging you, nor anyone."

"But you get off on kidnapping and threatening? Oh, wait. I seem to remember being drugged by one of your dumbass lack-eys." I chuckled under my breath.

"You weren't the person I ordered to be kidnapped."

"Yet here I am."

Kaschel scoffed and went back to ignoring me. He came to a halt and dropped my legs without warning. I almost fell ass-first onto the ground but managed to catch myself. I shot him a death glare, hoping it illustrated how much I detested him, but I knew my resting bitch face was weak.

He shook out his hands, nonchalantly stretched out his shoulders, and focused his attention back on to me with such authority I staggered back.

"If you touch or look anyone else directly in the eyes, I can't say I have it in me to save you from another horde." Kaschel gave me a once-over.

"How chivalrous of you." I rubbed my throbbing temple as the pounding in my skull intensified.

Kaschel grunted and walked through the front doors.

20
SMOKE AND SPICE

The building resembled a labyrinth with hundreds of multicolored doors. Some painted a deep, passionate red while others a luminous violet. Each one had a different symbol at the top, but I had no desire to find out what they meant.

My gaze focused on the marble floors as a heavy lavender perfume and smoke permeated the place. My nose crinkled, retaliating against the putrid fumes.

I tugged on Kaschel's shirt, but he acted like I didn't exist. I muttered under my breath in frustration. I felt like a nuisance when someone ignored me, and it aggravated me to no end. It reminded me of my childhood when no one listened—who only wanted me to keep my mouth sewed shut. I knew all too well how I resembled the boy who cried wolf—but with talking crows. Back then, the Kelleys grew sick of my cries for help and wanted me silent and obedient like a lapdog.

It was an insecurity of mine. I could handle someone pushing once or twice, but Kaschel kept lodging a knife into my wound and twisting it.

I had to get a response. I couldn't stand it. I wouldn't let someone treat me like some docile pet. Not anymore.

I whisper-screamed, "Why are we here? Please tell me you have a valid explanation that's not as perverse as it seems."

Kaschel didn't stop walking nor did he entertain me with a reply.

I quickened my pace to match his long strides and lifted my hand to yank Kaschel's ponytail. Maybe then he would listen, but he unexpectedly stopped. My hand grazed his hair, and I barely pivoted in time so I didn't collide with his back.

A tall creature stood behind a front desk with grayish skin and webbed fingers and a long and wispy body with black hair, red eyes, and a thin dress.

She purred. "Room for one or . . . would you like some company?"

She literally purred like a cat as she leaned over the desk with her cleavage spilling out. I struggled not to make direct eye contact with them as they pointed outward.

I shivered and blinked and willed myself to ignore everything around me. I probably looked stiff and uncomfortable like I didn't belong here—which I didn't nor did I want to.

I think I was going to barf. Valeria's company sounded better than trying to understand what the hell went through Kaschel's mind.

He still wore an unimpressed frown, but to be honest, I didn't think anything would excite a pretentious man like him.

Kaschel leaned forward, hovering over the desk, and towered over the lady with an evil glint in his cosmic eyes.

In a deep voice, he said, "No we won't be staying long but . . . if a fae named Levisus happens to pass through asking for me, please escort him to our room." Kaschel winked.

The woman ate his fake kindness like it was her last supper and metaphorically melted into a puddle before us.

I held back the bile threatening to come up for the third time today and shuddered at the gross display.

The lady only barely noticed me, and her nostrils flared in excitement. "Oh!" She widened them more as she scanned me over. Goose bumps trickled down my arms and legs as I cautiously stepped backward. "You could make a lot of coins here, darling. A lot of our customers loved to be served by your kind. You'd live lavishly," she said, emphasizing the last syllable with a deadly smile.

I stared at the lady's frightening set of teeth. If anything, she reminded me of an anglerfish, and it only made her more terrifying.

Slack-jawed, staring at the lady like an idiot, I couldn't put any words together. The only thing crossing my mind—did she just offer me a job?

I forced out a high-pitched, "Nah, I'm Gucci, girl."

I had to physically stop myself from facepalming and burying myself into a hole. Honestly, where did that come from? Was I some forty-year-old ex-frat guy rejecting a woman? Why was I always thinking of frat guys?

I massaged my forehead and groaned. To be fair, quick responses in tough, creepy, or awkward situations weren't my forte. I always ended up saying dumb shit.

The lady tilted her head in confusion and blinked slowly like she wanted me to elaborate, but no meant no. Or in my case, Gucci did.

"How kind. I'm sure she'll think about it a little more," Kaschel answered for me with a straight face, and the lady's response was a little too overjoyed for my taste.

"Wonderful." The lady clapped her hands together. "Follow me. I'll show you guys to your room." She beamed at the both of us and walked out from the back of the desk and toward a hallway I swore wasn't there two seconds ago.

A scream erupted from a room, and goose bumps rose all over my body again. What the hell did people rent these rooms out for?

A pit formed in my stomach once the lady stopped by a gold and silver door with an intricate pattern on it. All I could think about was Lucien and if he was okay. And how much time did I have left until a blood moon?

And I haven't seen Gren for a while, where did he go?

Snatching Kaschel's shirt, I pulled him to eye level. "Where is Gren?"

Kaschel placed his hand over mine and pried my fingers off him.

With an annoyed expression, he asked, "Why would I keep track of your *pet*?"

I frowned, shook his hand off mine, and faced the hallway again.

The lady opened the door. Its loud creak ricocheted down the hall as she gently waved us in.

I gulped and took one step forward.

21
A CONTRADICTION

My sight drifted to the massive canopy bed with a silky white comforter and black curtains draped around it. The marble floors swirled with white and silver. A place designed for royalty, yet it felt like it was meant for cheap entertainment.

A couple of creatures dressed in short, crimson, satin garments filtered into the room as they set multiple dishes and drinks on a table in the corner. The fragrance of freshly cut fruit filled the air and delectable meats and cheeses placed on golden trays glowed in the candlelight—or maybe, the food itself glowed from the many pearly-white candelabras scattered across the room. Some magically dangled from the painted pitch-black ceiling with specks of silver.

Deep in my gut, unease screamed for me to get the hell out of this place as all creatures bowed before they left the room, leaving the front desk lady behind.

She tilted her head to the side and blinked, her slanted eyes comparable to a reptilian. "May I offer you guys anything else?"

Kaschel didn't budge, and fear swarmed me as sweat beaded above my brows.

Why did her question feel so sinister?

My heart rate escalated as Kaschel mulled over her question like he would actually consider it.

I unclenched my hand from the cloak and walked away from him and to the couch. I plopped myself onto it and let the cool leather soothe me.

Kaschel's face turned from composed to infuriated as he glowered at the lady. "No. Again, we won't be staying long," Kaschel stated coldly as he grabbed the door and shooed her out.

The front desk lady didn't say another word and bowed and scurried out of the room as Kaschel slammed the door behind her.

He threw something in my direction and stalked over toward the table in the back. The object bounced off the side of the couch and onto the cushion.

A chocolate protein bar in a blue and yellow wrapper.

Kaschel kept his gaze fixed on the table as he talked. "Eat. It seems you can't even handle water from my world. But he should be here soon enough." He grabbed a plate and plucked samples from all the delicious food and snatched a chalice, pouring a deep purple liquid into it.

I looked back down at my dry protein bar and flung myself back against the couch. I sighed heavily. It was entirely unfair he could have a four-course meal while I had to savor this dried-up protein bar with nothing to drink.

Kaschel now lounged on the bed, legs crossed, enjoying his meal. My face gave away my animosity as my lips curved down in irritation. Hanger got the best of me and an intrusive thought forced its way into my mind. *I hope he chokes on those grapes he seems to be enjoying so much.*

"If you keep staring, I'll start to think I captivated you with my ethereal beauty." Kaschel wiggled his brows, and I snorted at the stupidity of it. Embarrassed, I shot my hand to my mouth and turned away from him. "Or are you staring at the food with such lust? I won't stop you from eating, but if you do . . . don't blame me for what happens next." He tossed another grape in his mouth.

I could have sworn his face lit up in a smug expression.

My eye twitched at Kaschel's accusation. "Is that a threat?"

"You tell me, little flea, since I get off on kidnapping and threatening." Kaschel taunted me as he twirled his chalice in his hand, leaning against the headboard of the bed.

His black shirt and pants molded to his body perfectly. His pecs practically burst out of it as the indents of every muscle couldn't be hidden by mere fabric. The flickering candlelight illuminated his light features as his hair radiated like starlight.

His face was too relaxed for someone who had no control over his precious keys.

God, I craved wiping the condescending look right off his face and throwing the nearest object at him—which happened to be the protein bar. "Could you not offer me any better alternatives? You are magical, are you not?"

Kaschel chuckled. "Glamour and magic are one in the same but also entirely different."

"All right, Gandalf, can your glamour change this crusty protein bar?"

Kaschel cocked an eyebrow, debating on whether to entertain my question. He flicked his wrist, and a black shadow cast from him shot across the room and devoured the protein bar, transforming it into a beef dip; my mouth watered instantly.

I bit down and it dried my whole mouth—its rough texture assaulting my tongue like I took a nibble out of sandpaper. My face pinched into a sour expression. I glanced down and it was the same protein bar Kaschel had thrown at me.

I shot a glare at him and Kaschel winked. The bastard actually had the audacity to wink!

Kaschel tipped his head slightly, wearing that stupid face full of vanity. "I warned you, did I not?" he asked and took a bite of bread.

I swore, I might jump over this couch and give him a piece of my mind. And if I died from this dry-ass protein bar getting stuck in my throat I'd haunt the living shit out of him to the point it broke his soul—if he even had one.

"Ah, so you're nothing but a glorified magician. Noted," I grumbled between bites.

A deep chuckle reverberated through the walls, and I snapped my head back to Kaschel, dying in a fit of laughter.

My face scrunched into scowl, peeved he found my anguish amusing. "How mature of you, faery man. Are you laughing at my sad excuse for a meal while you eat like a plump, arrogant king sitting on his high horse?"

"You forgot guilefully sitting on his high horse. I have schemes you are unaware of." Kaschel perked up one eyebrow.

I crossed my arms. So Kaschel had jokes? "What a contradiction. I think you're more ignorant than anything else." I enunciated the word *ignorant*.

Kaschel shrugged. "What's wrong with being a contradiction?" he asked as he proceeded to take a long sip from the chalice.

"You're either one or the other. How can you be cunning and so haughty? I'm sure that awful personality of yours would get in the way of your critical thinking. I mean, people like you tend to overestimate themselves and underestimate others."

Kaschel chuckled again in defiance. "Everyone has strengths and weaknesses. Doesn't imply I can't be cunning. Maybe mine is my ego. I am a fae after all. I quite enjoy playing games if the mood is right." Kaschel's eyes carried a mischievous glimmer as they danced in the low light.

Did I want to ask what type of games he was referring to? Hell no. So I averted my gaze and choked down the dry protein bar.

A thunderous knock on the door startled me upright. My soul left and came back as my heartbeat settled back down.

"Come in." Kaschel, unfazed by the abrupt knock, took another swig of his drink.

22
THE SCÀTHS

A muscular man stepped through the door wearing loose gray slacks and a cream tunic with black boots. His sharp features set me back; his dark complexion was a striking contrast to his short, silver hair. His sharp features were similar to Kaschel's but his eyes held a darker hue.

The devilish smirk suited the man as he glanced at me and back at Kaschel. "I see you've changed your kink preferences since the last time I saw you. Were the sirens too clingy? I figured you'd be more worried about your throne than tossing around some half-breed, but then again, you always were a wild card." The man shrugged his shoulders and each muscle in his chest flexed with him.

Kaschel's lip jerked upward. The amusement in his expression—brief but indelible. He set his tray to the side with all his attention on his drink as he swirled it between his fingers.

Kaschel didn't take his sight off the chalice as his words grew thicker than the wine he drank. "I don't relish digging up past mistakes. Those were dark times, Levisus. It seems everyone is trying to test my patience."

Levisus places his hands on his chest, a spark of enmity in his face. "To the previous Unseelie King? I would never be so bold, my lord."

Kaschel chuckled with so much insincerity my body tensed up. "Drop the formalities and bullshit." Kaschel uncrossed his legs, leaned farther back against the headboard, and took another sip. "You know what I need."

Levisus stalked around the room like a predator and circled closer toward me than Kaschel. He appeared more intimidated by Kaschel, which was understandable. My aura didn't actually scream, *I could kick your six-foot-four fae ass*—no matter how much I glowered at him.

Didn't Kaschel say they were friends? Why was the tension so palpable?

Without turning his back to Kaschel, Levisus sat on the couch beside me. He tilted his head and skimmed me up and down.

Levisus's face stirred with sinfulness and chaos. My body went stiff, but for some reason, I couldn't turn away from his enthusiastic stare.

Levisus grinned, lifted a finger, and poked my shirt right below my collarbone. "Sounds fun. *I'm in.*"

Gooseflesh raised on the back of my neck. Not wanting to indulge him, I kept my mouth shut.

I looked down and squinted at the words *Life's too short, so let's fuck* and sighed. I mean, what was I thinking when I put it on? This godforsaken shirt might be the death of me.

It was settled. I was burning my whole collection of T-shirts once I returned home.

Levisus studied my face, and his thunderous laughter echoed throughout the room.

He wiped a tear from his cheek and took a deep breath and patted my back so hard, he almost launched me off the couch. "No need to worry. I don't take what isn't mine." He laughed again, leaned farther into the cushion, and lifted his head back to look at Kaschel. "You must have found one. Oh, my . . . and it only took a couple of decades."

Kaschel didn't respond for hours, or it felt like hours, as I sat there trying to breathe as shallowly as possible so the only noise in the room wouldn't be my heavy breathing that resembled a rabid goblin.

Yeah, him calling me that still ticked me off.

Kaschel got up, strolled over to the table, and poured himself another glass. "I'm surprised your silver tongue hasn't been cut out yet."

Levisus eyed me as he purred, "The ladies seem to love it."

I shuddered and Levisus's smirk widened as his gaze wandered back to Kaschel.

Kaschel gradually stepped further away from us as he spoke with an authoritative voice that shook the floor. "You're here . . . so, I assume, you still want your brother saved from the Scáths?"

Resentment radiated in Levisus's eyes as he shot up and stalked over to Kaschel, who now leaned against the bedside, not bothering to budge a muscle as he brazenly sipped on his wine.

"What makes you think I'll help the one who put him there?" Levisus growled as he slammed his hands against the side of the bed.

Kaschel raised his sight from the chalice. "You're here, are you not? Or are you here for something as foolish as revenge?" The side of Kaschel's mouth moved into a thin smile like the mere thought amused him; Kaschel openly mocked Levisus now. "I thought you were more clever than this. We both know the council made that decision."

Levisus scoffed as he picked up his arms and crossed them against his chest. "And you stood there and did *nothing*. I'd rather ask Samuel than your pathetic ass." His glare intensified with such hostility I swore a fight would soon break out.

Kaschel's face darkened as Levisus loomed over him. "I'm afraid it's impossible. Were you banished alongside me?" Kaschel waved his hand dismissively. "It's such old news. At least yours is still alive . . . Well, somewhat."

Levisus turned away, his expression unreadable as he lowered his chin, contemplating the possibilities before he peered back at Kaschel. "Swear it."

Kaschel leaned forward with a vicious glint draping over his face. "You're going to have to be a little more specific and come now . . . Where's your sincerity?"

The fury emanated off Levisus in waves—the ground rumbling beneath us as he clenched his hands into fists. "Will you free Daene, safely. *Please*," he bit down the last part, his neck muscles straining as he kept his jaw clenched.

Kaschel launched his head back and chuckled. It was deep and every bit as antagonizing as he meant for it to be. It made me realize again how cruel his nature was and how easily he could change in the snap of a finger. He was the embodiment of depravity and mischief; a wicked, immoral fae.

Kaschel took great pleasure in watching Levisus beg, unmistakably so.

If this was how the fae behaved to each other . . . then the sooner I got the second key, the better.

I stole a glimpse at Kaschel and saw him wave his hand again. "Fine. Daene was my favorite twin anyway."

Kaschel turned this whole conversation to work in his favor, and it sent more shivers down my body as Levisus fiercely held his tongue.

The room stood silent as both men didn't take their eyes off each other. I had the urge to speak up. I needed to see where Gren disappeared to, and I needed a plan, fast. I didn't have time for their petty catfight to continue.

I rested my hand on my cheek and clicked my tongue, which forced both of their attention onto me. "If you guys are going to strip each other's clothes off, please allow me to leave the room first. No matter how hot it may be, I'm a little traumatized from the last time two people did that."

Both men stood there gaping at me, too shocked at my words to respond, but I didn't care. Their prolonged pissing contest needed to end.

Levisus grunted in defeat, but his face revealed a flicker of elation. "My cabin isn't far from here."

Kaschel watched me as he sat there speechless with a clear look of disgust and shook his head in disapproval.

"Seems like you guys want to make up." I shrugged. "And if

it's too embarrassing because of my presence . . ." I trailed off as I stood up and stretched my legs, letting a small squeak out. "I'll let you guys sweat it out, or whatever you want to do with all this intense eye contact."

"Ooh, I like this one." Levisus grinned as he closed the distance between us. He bent down, inches from my face. "My offer still stands, all jokes aside. I'd be much more fun than the old prude over there."

One loud laugh slipped out as I awkwardly stepped away from the couch. "I'd rather not." God, it was almost unreal how quickly Levisus switched between temperaments.

Levisus sighed dramatically. "It's your loss."

Kaschel cleared his throat, and our attention snapped back to him. He lowered a brow, skeptically. "Can I trust you're not ignorantly working for my uncle? He will promise you many things only to double-cross you when the opportunity presents itself. His tongue is sharper than the sword you wield."

Levisus laughed and thankfully walked in the opposite direction of me. "I may want my brother back, but I would never work for a weasel of a man who slaughtered thousands of his own just to put himself on the throne. Even if it means I have to work with his impetuous nephew."

Kaschel ignored Levisus's snide comment and nodded his head in agreement.

Levisus clapped his hands together. "Great, we should leave before the banshees arrive. We wouldn't want to become one of their targets."

"I thought they were only spirits who warned a family of an impending death?" I blurted out.

My foster mom always mumbled about the fae and how they're worse than the devils. It made me wonder how she thought I was the crazy one and not herself.

Levisus's lip curled into a crooked half-smirk. "And you believe everything you hear?" I didn't respond, and that apparently signaled him to continue. "Their preferences are children, but when the pickings are slim, they don't mind adding a few various souls to their collection."

23
UNSIGHTLY BEINGS

"**S**top trying to scare her," Kaschel grumbled as he straightened out his black shirt.

His intense physique was ridiculous. I wanted to claw my eyes out just looking at him as I watched every muscle in his arms flex. It's like everyone around me spent all hours of the day at the gym. I would love to think it was glamour and they were disguising their true selves; I, on the other hand, could not hide my lack of muscle mass and weak stamina.

Wow, what a jealous thought, but how could they expect me to run away from danger when I got winded in five seconds?

It was asinine. I wasn't built for this. I wasn't some fae warrior who's lived through countless battles with a thirst for blood and riddles.

I was some broke bitch orphan who could barely hold down a

dead-end job. My idea of a good time wasn't going off on an otherworldly adventure and being hunted by the occasional demon or monster. No. I wanted to watch my favorite TV shows on repeat. I needed fluff. Some romance, happily-ever-after bullshit that makes me feel warm and fuzzy despite my hellish life beating me down. That kind of fluff.

Yet here I was—where a banshee, or whatever else crawled around in this god-forsaken world, could easily drag me by my hair and throw me into some creepy glass display. Getting kidnapped again? No thanks.

I knew I was the easy target in the group, and it frustrated me to no end.

I had never relied on anyone except for Lucien my entire life. Now I had to hope Kaschel would help me out of the goodness of his heart for some silly keys? What a joke.

No one here was on my side. I had to make sure I reminded myself, so my focus remained on saving the only person who mattered. God, I missed Lucien, and I hoped, somehow . . . he was doing okay despite it all.

I clenched the key tightly in my pocket. My attention was on the door as Kaschel stalked over to my side, shoulder-checking Levisus along the way.

They acted like two college bros who needed to let go of their pride and hug it out.

And I thought I was a petty one, but they proved me otherwise.

Kaschel lowered his head, and his gaze darkened with a flash of dismay swirling in his amethyst eyes. "Are you able to walk farther?" He dropped a brow like he was concerned for my well-being.

The concern was not for me but for what I could or couldn't accomplish on our dumb quest to find the other key.

I desperately wanted to scream at the top of my lungs and tell Kaschel off. That, fuck no I'm not okay. I was dehydrated and the crusty, dried-up protein bar only made it worse. I wanted to eat, cry, and sleep.

My lips pulled into a thin line and I forced a jaded smile. "Yep, all good. Could even run a marathon. I feel so incredible." A hint of sarcasm oozed from my voice, but Kaschel didn't notice or care. Probably the latter.

"Good." Kaschel turned away.

Levisus interjected. "Love, I wouldn't mind carrying you if it becomes too much." He winked at me, and I couldn't tell if he was joking or not.

My frown worsened, and I couldn't hide the aggravation in my voice. "Worry about each other, and if Kaschel gets tired, you can princess-carry him. I'll manage."

Levisus's smirk turned into a pout as he sided-eyed Kaschel. "I would offer, but I think he'd slit my throat if I did. Royals." Levisus tsked. "So quick to resort to violence."

Kaschel's eye twitched as he stiffened up.

Now they teased each other like childhood friends. It piqued my interest, but not enough to ask them directly.

I poked Kaschel's chest, nearly breaking my finger in half. "If you're so concerned with me slowing you down, why don't you do that shadow thing and transport us? It would save us the trouble and save us from your complaining."

Kaschel rubbed his temple and leaned closer to me. A few

strands of his alabaster hair tickled my cheek.

His cool breath caressed my ear as he asked, "My shadow thing?"

The hairs on my arms raised, and I wished to retreat inward, but I was so sick of being intimidated. So sick of people pushing me around.

I hated not having control.

I stood my ground and faced Kaschel, lifting my chin to lock eyes with him, my finger still pressed to his chest. "You heard me. Unless it's too much for you to handle?"

I had always been ballsy, but I hoped my luck hadn't run out before Kaschel's patience for me grew too thin.

Kaschel sneered and turned slightly away as he brushed his loose strands behind his pointed ear.

The veins in his neck tensed up as he bit down and looked back at me. "That's not how it works."

I raised an eyebrow, waiting for him to elaborate. "He can only go where a fae's soul is haunting and hasn't crossed over to our lands yet," Levisus said, plainly.

"Don't make me laugh." I imitated a fake laugh. "What are you, the Grim Reaper? No wait. The Lord of Death?" Wow, it sounded even more laughable out loud.

Any hint of anger or amusement from earlier had drained from Kaschel's face as he said, "No, and it's not important. We need to leave."

Kaschel stalked over to the door as Levisus stood next to me and leaned down.

Levisus brought his hand to his mouth and whispered, "He gets testy when people call him that. Try king of the unsightly or shadow daddy. He absolutely loathes the last one. I use it all the time if I want to push his buttons."

"Pfft." I choked on my own spit and threw my hand to cover my mouth, stifling the laughter back down.

I inclined my head to meet Levisus's mischievous grin as he held his pointer finger to his lips, hushing me when Kaschel snapped his sharp eyes in our direction.

I didn't know how to respond. Levisus was a loose cannon. I mean, did he really say *shadow daddy*? No. I slapped my cheeks to snap out of it.

It had nothing to do with me. I didn't need to be curious, and I definitely didn't need to call him *that*; I needed to bury it. I cleared my throat and stayed silent as I trailed behind the two guys walking a little too fast through the endless corridor. The noisy chatter penetrated through the walls and muffled everything around me.

I tried to focus on how I would find Gren and talk to him alone without the pointy-eared bastards overhearing us. Kaschel had to have super-hearing, which only made it hard to sneak around.

We stepped outside of the building, and I took a deep breath. The suffocating smell of lavender-infused perfume affected me more than I thought.

The streets thinned out. Not a soul in sight as the rain had ceased. The two moons were spellbinding as their glow lit a path to the impenetrable forest.

I skimmed the area, but I couldn't see Gren anywhere.

My jaw was taut as my heart palpitated roughly against my chest. An intrusive thought forced its way into my mind. *If Gren left me, I truly would be alone.*

The flapping of wings came from behind me, and all the built-up tension left my body as I twisted around to the building's entrance, seeing Gren perched at the top.

He glided off the ledge and plopped to my side. My shaky breath steadied, and I exhaled, patting his feathers down. "You scared me," I murmured.

Gren tilted his beak and glanced at the forest. "You know I would never leave you. I just felt something, but it vanished. I'm not sure if I imagined it or not."

I stood silent. I didn't want to deal with any more supernatural BS. I barely survived Valeria's torment. If she desired, she could have killed me.

God, it seemed like my life was only spared by those who wanted something from me.

"I sensed a faint, dark aura from our world but it's gone. There's a ritual that will—"

A bloodcurdling screech resounded off the forest trees. Then, only a deafening stillness as Kaschel scooped me up and pressed me firmly against his chest.

His gaze fell on Gren. "Can you scope out the area and see how much time we have?"

Gren reluctantly nodded and disappeared into the night sky, right toward the horrifying sound. But all I could think about was . . . would Gren be okay?

Kaschel glanced back at Levisus. "Is your place warded?"

Levisus scrunched his face. "What do you take me for? A half-wit? Of course it is."

"Was that a banshee?" I asked, but I regretted my words. I

sounded like an idiot. I guess in these types of situations, I was one.

I wished sometimes I kept my mouth shut.

I pushed myself away from Kaschel's chest, but his grip only tightened. "I didn't think they would find me so soon. I thought we had more time. How careless," Kaschel snarled under his breath.

Gren reappeared, and he looked frightened by what he witnessed.

He croaked out, "Thirty meters away, but it's gaining on us faster. Maybe five minutes max."

Kaschel nodded, but kept his focus on Levisus as he said, "Lead the way."

24
CROSSING BOUNDARIES

I longed for Kaschel to set me down, but I already knew his answer, and if I was honest with myself, no way would I outrun the creature. Admitting one's flaws and shortcomings made it okay to stay in his arms, *right*?

So I pretended to wiggle my way out. But thank fuck he had a death grip on me. If he had dropped me right now, I'd probably throw away all my pride and latch onto him.

"Don't let go," Kaschel said, firmly.

Don't worry, I didn't plan to, was what I wanted to tell Kaschel but instead, I mumbled a short, shaky, *whatever*.

I whipped my head up and inspected his face, pinched into a scowl as his dark brows bunched together, his square jaw clenched tightly.

Was he going to run or not? I thought the creature was gaining on us. Did we really have time for him to stand here looking constipated?

I waited for Kaschel to explain further, but eerie silence enveloped us, and my heart thumped so aggressively I bet Kaschel heard each individual beat.

My eyes were parallel to Kaschel's full lips, anticipating an explanation. When he didn't utter another word, I studied the faint scar running down his bottom lip. It was scarcely raised with a light pink hue as it trailed down his neck and disappeared underneath his shirt.

I wondered if Kaschel got it from a battle or from the creature currently chasing after us.

"Wait. Why exact—" Levisus looked at the sky and launched himself upward, cutting my words short.

White wings expanded and contracted behind him, and I gaped in awe.

The silky feathers retained an iridescent glow. Levisus looked like a celestial being ascending back to heaven, but the deadly talons at the top revealed their true nature.

He vanished from my line of sight, flying effortlessly into the night.

I eyed Kaschel, half expecting him to elaborate on what the fuck just happened, but as a man who valued keeping his secrets, he ignored my wild stare.

Kaschel looked above us, disregarding my what-the-hell expression. "I wouldn't open your mouth for a while," he said, propelling us off the ground, making sure I had no time to refuse.

His dark wings expanded and carried us with so much momentum. I squeezed myself harder against his chest and tossed my arms around his neck.

Kaschel's wings were the polar opposite of Levisus's—covered in obsidian black feathers with a plum tint to them—and if the moonlight hit them just right, they radiated like a violet flame soaring through the darkened sky. They made Kaschel's presence more menacing than it already was.

I clutched my hands tightly together as the wind whipped around us.

We moved so fast I could barely peek my head up and look over Kaschel's shoulder. The sky passed by in a blur of midnight blue and gray like watching a movie stuck in fast-forward mode. I couldn't decipher a single thing—only streaks of twilight.

Now was not a good time for me to realize I had acrophobia.

I pressed my face against Kaschel's rugged chest again, and his steady heartbeat slowly throbbed against my ear. It calmed me as my heartbeat settled back down with his. Then, he turned us upside down and nosedived.

A high-pitched scream escaped my lips, and I clenched my eyes shut. I swore my soul left my body when the wind violently thrashed against us.

Everything stood motionless now, like death took away all the pain and panic cementing itself in my bones.

My eyes fluttered open.

Both Kaschel and Levisus's wings contracted and disappeared into their backs.

Confusion devoured my mind but now was not the time to question it.

Kaschel dropped us in the middle of a forest with dense weeds the color of a pale green. The trees surrounding us had white bark and black protruding lines running down them with yellow-tinted moss covering the bottom and thinning out at the top.

A low fog cast around us as the air grew thick with condensation.

The crooked branches contorted in different directions when either of us flinched or moved a muscle.

So the forest was alive. *Disgusting.*

Gren managed to keep up with them as he landed by our side.

"You can let go of me now," Kaschel said in a flat tone; his face riddled with aggravation.

I peered down, horrified to realize how I entangled my body with his. I looked like some leech or a snake suffocating its victim.

I dropped to my feet and smoothed my hair out, but I knew it probably resembled a rat's nest the more I tried.

I coughed. "I think I prefer your shadows."

Kaschel's eyes flashed an animated glint, but it vanished so quickly I thought I imagined it.

Kaschel fixed his sights on Levisus as his tone shifted, now low and gravelly. "You better hope we didn't make my presence known to the others."

Levisus walked right past us as he spoke. "Would you have preferred we strolled our happy asses over here? You know as well as I do that if we ran on foot . . . it would have dragged us both back to our court."

Kaschel tipped his head back, and grumbled, "Fuck."

No one else spoke as we came upon a burned tree split in two.

Perplexed, I squinted at Levisus, but I had been here long enough to know there was some trick or enchantment to it. So I watched him crouch down in front of the charred tree as he chanted under his breath. He stood up, stepped forward, and vanished.

"Your turn." Kaschel ushered me forward, and my body collided with the portal.

My movements slowed down like I was thrust underwater, but my breathing stayed short and controlled as the world surged around me in tidal waves until everything reverted back to normal and the shifting stopped.

A gray-colored cottage with an enormous tree in the center of it materialized in front of us. It stretched out for miles in the sky, like a skyscraper with a reddish-brown bark weathered by the elements, chipped and discolored. It matched the oddly shaped door curling outward with a ram's horn as a door handle.

Gren shook out his feathers and glanced around the area. "I'll keep watch."

I looked back at Gren with some urgency in my voice. "I'd rather you stay inside with us."

I waited for him to say okay, but that answer never came.

"I'm not comfortable when someone I know isn't keeping a look out."

Levisus laughed as if half-entertained by Gren's remark. "I will sense if something or someone tries to break in, so don't worry a cute little feather on your head."

Without hesitation, Gren said, "I don't trust your intuition."

Levisus shrugged and walked inside.

I crouched down to Gren. "Just come inside."

Gren shook his beak. "I will be fine."

He patted my back with his wing, and it was the most ridiculously wholesome thing that's ever happened to me since—ever.

Damn, when did my life get so sad?

I sighed and ran my hands through my hair but nodded my head.

My sight fell back on Kaschel, who looked bored to tears by our conversation but stayed close behind me.

So it appeared Kaschel wasn't going to let me leave his side. *Great.*

I stood up and stepped through the doorway.

The decor was as sleazy as Levisus's personality. It had two matching white leather couches with a fox's fur draped on the top of one and a coffee table with a marbled, topless mermaid as the centerpiece shimmering from the black-bricked fireplace.

A wooden bar was positioned in the corner of the room and a golden light illuminated it, only making the rest of the place dark in comparison.

Levisus yawned and strolled over to the bar and poured himself a stiff drink. "Want one?" He looked at me with a lopsided grin.

Kaschel didn't pay any mind to Levisus as he stalked over to the couch and sat down. He leaned back and draped his arms over the top and rested one leg over the other.

Kaschel tilted his chin up; his eyes sharper than daggers as his voice lowered. "How long do we have until your barriers fail?"

Levisus took a sip of his drink. "Maybe ten or twelve hours."

Kaschel glowered at Levisus as if contemplating his next move before he spoke. "Is that enough time for you to make a tracking spell for the second key?"

"And a separation spell," I added.

Levisus raised an eyebrow, seemingly insulted by Kaschel's

question. "Your faith in me has dwindled to nothing. I assure you, my lord. I can manage both."

"It has been a couple of centuries. Who knows if you have lost your touch or not?" Kaschel asked with indifference.

"Testy. Then I will be in my lab." Levisus bowed sarcastically with his drink in his hand. His gaze wandered over to me. "I know what you're thinking. You're surprised I'm more than just a pretty face." He bent over the bar and swirled his drink. "We could have some fun before I have to work tirelessly for that big, brooding oaf."

I attempted to keep my mouth shut, but the words flowed effortlessly off my tongue. "Dude, read the room."

Levisus mused, "I have, and you look like you need to relieve some stress, and I'll happily oblige."

Kaschel uncrossed his legs and leaned forward with a murderous air to him. "Do I have to remind you of your brother? My patience with you is growing thinner by the second."

Levisus didn't seem to care, and he clicked his tongue in defiance.

Did Levisus not care that we were in danger? We only had a certain amount of time before that thing broke through whatever barriers surrounded us. Now was not the time to act casual.

Levisus exaggerated his pout. "Such a mood killer. Next time then." He blew me a kiss and disappeared into the hallway.

Kaschel didn't budge a muscle as he carelessly said, "Sit."

My legs had a mind of their own and moved toward the opposite couch and awkwardly sat me down.

The crackling fireplace gave me a strange sense of déjà vu. The familiar light flickered against Kaschel's face and cast a coppery glow through the room.

His alabaster hair was in disarray, freed, and rested right below the deep V of his black shirt.

His head tilted back against the couch with his eyes shut.

25
A MISCHIEVOUS FAE
AND THE GULLIBLE

Kaschel didn't move a muscle, refusing to acknowledge the two of us occupied this room. I couldn't comprehend how he could sleep at a time like this. Or how either of them could act so unconcerned with everything going on.

"You seem to have a bad habit of staring at others and it's quite distracting," Kaschel muttered under his breath.

He lounged with no cares in the world. It always irritated me how apathetic he behaved.

I rested my cheek on my hand and compelled myself to stay strong like I had so many times before. I might be stuck in an undesirable situation, but the feelings of helplessness I knew all too well. I could handle this.

I was so done with my Addy-only, pity party.

And damn all these cryptic assholes keeping me in the dark.

I demanded answers, and I wouldn't stop until I was satisfied.

"So, a royal, huh? Why are you out here playing the part of a petty crime lord when you should be up in your ivory tower? Why aren't your servants the ones scrambling for the keys?" I asked, half-mockingly.

I was poking the bear, but I got this far with my unfiltered mouth, and nothing had happened yet, so let's see how far I could push him until he gave in.

A soft chuckle left Kaschel's lips, deep and seductive, and it tickled my skin in all the wrong places. He slowly opened his eyes and moved his arms from the top of the couch, positioning them on his knees.

He leaned forward and took me in.

His stare felt hot against my skin. My nervousness rose as his wild look burned right through me.

He broke eye contact, and I emptied my breath.

Kaschel focused on the fireplace behind me. The faint flames danced across his face as the crackling of the fire cut through the silence.

Kaschel spoke in a soft, velvety tone and it sent gooseflesh down my legs. "Why should I indulge your curiosity and tell you my life's story? If I feed a beggar scraps once . . . they always come back demanding seconds, and I'm not as charitable the second time around."

I bit my lip, avoided facing him and traced my fingertips along the seams on the side arm of the couch. "Comparing your life's story to food scraps . . . you must feel quite pathetic to be reduced to nothing."

Kaschel stood up and prowled in my direction until he towered above me.

He held a bloodthirsty spark in his eyes along with something else I couldn't determine.

He bent down and gripped the top of the couch, leaning into me.

Kaschel's mouth was centimeters away from my ear as he whispered, "Do you believe I don't know what you're trying to do?" He moved his face in front of mine. His lips pulled into a wicked grin as he tipped my chin up to meet his hypnotizing stare. "I think you've forgotten what I am. Shall I remind you, little flea?"

I lowered a brow and parted my lips. "Oh. Did I push some buttons of yours, old man?" A weak insult when he didn't look a day over thirty, but I couldn't think of anything else. When he didn't respond, I kept pushing. "Did I render you speechless, or are you just looking at my lips with such lust?"

Kaschel gripped my chin tighter and rubbed his thumb gently over my bottom lip. He inclined his head closer to mine until our lips were parallel for the second time tonight.

I couldn't break away from his intensity as he kept my chin in place.

I felt like a mouse trapped by a hungry lion, prowling, waiting for the right moment to pounce.

I swallowed, hard.

I couldn't think as the man before me smiled so devilishly my whole body wanted to cave in.

Kaschel dropped my chin and leaned back. "So, you were looking at me with desire and not the food," he chuckled with such a haughty tone that anything I felt two seconds ago vanished.

"I-I wasn't." Damn it. That wasn't convincing at all.

What the fuck, Addy? Get your shit together. Stop getting distracted by his looks.

He had nothing else going for him.

A thunderous explosion rattled the floor beneath us and an inhuman screech followed. The glasses on the bar dropped and shattered into hundreds of shards of glass as the reverberating clangor made the world mute.

26
A SACRIFICE

The thundering footfalls rang closer until Levisus came huffing out from the hallway. He leaned a hand on the wall wearing a dark cloak and what looked almost like nursing scrubs.

Levisus glanced at Kaschel with a tinge of gravity in his voice. "I need more time but I—"

"Enough. I'll handle it, but you better hurry. When one comes, they all follow." Kaschel stalked over to the door. His muscular back tensed up. He shook out one hand and put the other on his sheath, but before he opened the door, he glimpsed back at me. "Stay here and don't come out."

I jerked to my feet, ignoring his request. "I need to get Gren first."

Kaschel couldn't talk me out of it. No one could.

I couldn't leave Gren out there by himself. I would never forgive myself.

The few people I cared about always seemed to . . . No. I wasn't going to entertain a thought like that. I sure as hell wouldn't let another one I cared about slip through my fingers.

My cowardice couldn't stop me. I could retrieve Gren without falling to my knees in fear. Even if my anxiety returned the second I caught a glimpse of the creature, I just needed to call for Gren and tell him to come hide inside. Easy, peasy.

Kaschel groaned and he rubbed his temple. "Fuck. Fine but you can't waver. You grab him and you get the hell out of there."

I walked behind him, but my movement came in short spurts as my legs wobbled and threatened to give out the closer I got to our impending doom.

Kaschel grumbled at my weak attempt to get to the door. I wondered if I put a face next to the bloodcurdling screech, would I be even more terrified?

I shook my head and disregarded the cluttered mess of tension filtering through my mind and kept my focus on the door in front of us.

I gulped when Kaschel pushed it open, and Gren flapped toward us.

A beast emerged from the forest and my eyes widened in horror.

It had to be about ten feet tall with a body warped by shadows as its elongated arms with claws the size of blades dragged behind it. A disturbing smile distorted its face. Something I believed only nightmares could conjure as its crooked jaw hung loose like an unspun thread.

The beast spotted Kaschel and its mouth broadened. Its jaw cracked as it snapped together and then apart. Even its ghastly fanged teeth couldn't be concealed. They hooked outward like elephant tusks as drool poured out of its malformed mouth.

The beast shrieked again, and I almost pissed myself. Its body trudged forward, compelling the ground to tremble beneath our feet. Or maybe only my body trembled; I honestly couldn't tell.

The beast's neck craned, and another snap echoed throughout the forest. "Kaschel, you were warned, yet here you are. I can't say I'm disappointed." The beast's slimy voice slithered through the air, taunting my ears. "Imprisoning someone like you would earn me a hefty reward. I mean, just think of all the ones you threw in the Scáths who would be overjoyed to hear of your return."

Kaschel exuded so much energy and wrath it took me back as he stepped forward, unfazed by the beast's threat. "You know, I was going to pardon the others once I regained my throne, but you eradicated any chance of that. Now, I'm feeling quite blood-thirsty."

Kaschel unsheathed his sword and lunged at the beast. The clanging of metal and claws ruptured through the air as they both moved with such speed I couldn't concentrate on either one of them.

Gren perched at my side, and he tilted his head as he watched the battle unfold.

Gren looked back at me with concern. "He won't be able to defeat them all when the others arrive, but . . ."

I whipped my head down to him. "Others? Now is not the time for hesitations. Tell me, now. I don't want us to die here," I demanded, but it sounded more like a plea.

Gren huffed. "When I was interrupted, I was saying you have magic, but it's sealed away and doesn't come without a price." He hesitated again.

"Gren." I lowered my chin.

"A witch can only unlock her powers through a ritual, but dark magic is costly. The only way to gain power and a familiar is through a sacrifice. You can do both at once but it's dangerous. I can't help much as I am. After all, I'm only bound to you by an oath. And I . . . I am not whole."

I opened my mouth, attempting to make sense of his words. "Sacrifice? Dark magic? Who the fuck would I sacrifice in the middle of bumfuck nowhere? Not like I could—"

"We won't survive if you don't, but you will be bound and I promised, I . . ."

My head snapped back to the forest from the loud crash and thud.

The beast launched Kaschel against a tree and he collapsed onto the ground.

Gren turned his head to where Kaschel landed and didn't say another word about the ritual, and instead looked up at me with a darkened eye. "Get to safety."

Gren's talons grew the size of rapiers as he left my side. He didn't give me enough time to process or protest as he soared through the air and headed for the beast, slicing its back tendon as he flew past it.

Gren whipped back around and repeated the motion until a gray liquid spewed from the beast's back.

The beast hissed in pain, and right when Gren pivoted to slash him again, it snatched him midair and slammed him against the ground.

The beast picked Gren up by his wings and slowly tore them from his back.

I stood helplessly as the beast pulled Gren's ligaments apart like fleece as blood soaked his ebony feathers.

The cracks of bones assaulted my ears with each tug.

My head spun as the sounds of Gren's screams tore my heart out.

"No!" I cried, but the world stood still except for Gren's pangs of agony.

I cried out to Gren again, but as my heart hammered against my chest and chills ran down my back—I froze, my muscles quivering, refusing to move.

I couldn't stop staring as Gren's horrid scream of distress stirred another panic in me.

The beast hunched over and held Gren's now lifeless body in its claws.

I turned to Kaschel. My voice, hoarse and desperate. "Please! Do something. You have to do something!"

Kaschel appeared to have the wind knocked out of him and tried to stabilize himself. He ran his fingers through his hair. An animalistic stare—completely on edge and viciously disheveled.

Kaschel lowered his chin as the beast slinked over to his side, dropping Gren's corpse.

"You are no king of mine," the beast snarled, baring its grimy, dagger-like teeth. It tilted its head as its yellow, slanted eyes blazed with a murderous aura. "You are no FinnBheara. Look! You're helpless like a mortal. Pathetic."

Kaschel lowered his head. His face was unreadable as his alabaster hair was stained crimson from a blow he barely managed to escape. It draped over his purple eyes, and it rendered me speechless.

Kaschel coughed up a pool of blood and it gushed down his chest.

The beast cackled at the damage. "Now you look like one of your devoted followers who died without a cause."

Kaschel grunted in pain and inclined his head. His expression now held a spark of delight as he grinned. "At least my power can be restored, unlike your mangled face."

The beast shrieked and slashed its claws across Kaschel's chest.

"You won't be saying any of this when I drag you down to the Scáths where all the creatures you put away . . . anxiously await to tear you limb from limb."

Kaschel wiped his mouth and let out a dry laugh as the blood soaked his shirt. "What crawled up your ass and died?" He leaned harder against the tree and pushed himself up.

A spine-chilling howl came from the beast as it snatched Kaschel's neck and squeezed, dragging Kaschel's body up the tree bark until his feet dangled off the ground.

I watched in horror as Kaschel squirmed in the beast's grasp, desperately trying to tear its claws away from his throat, and without a second thought, I ran to Gren's side.

I cupped his limp body in my hands and brought him to my face. "You'll be okay," I whispered, choking back the sobs.

No pulse, but I wouldn't give up on Gren yet. I snatched him up and sprinted for the front door.

A zap hit my hands like lightning as it convulsed inside me.

I shrieked as the spasms tormented my lungs.

A man's voice rang in my head, louder and louder until only it occupied my mind. *Spill your blood and draw the pentagram. Drop him in and he will be anew while you will acquire what you desire. You only have to recite:* I give myself to you. Blood, bones, and all. *Now hurry.*

My body moved on its own as I glanced at Gren.

If I could save him, I could save Lucien.

Consequences be damned.

I gently set him down and brought my wrist to my mouth and bit down as hard as I could.

Blood spilled down my arm as I forced back the tears of despair.

I drew the circle first and then the star.

I picked Gren back up and placed him in the center.

I chanted under my breath, "I give myself to you, blood, bones, and all." I waited.

And waited.

I choked back the tears threatening to come back when a cacophony of pain weaved into my chest and burrowed its way into my heart.

I wailed as my body blazed like an inferno lashing at my skin and sizzling it from the inside out. A part of my soul was torn from me.

My chest, now empty and hollow.

I crumpled to the ground.

I breathed heavily, in and out, unable to move.

Pitiful thoughts entered my mind as my legs refused to cooperate. It seemed I could never be the protector.

Gren's lifeless body remained unmoving.

I bit my lip and stifled the tears back again, but they relent-lessly fell despite my attempt to subdue them.

The crackling of Gren's bones breaking and forming created a new terror in me as my breaths came out in erratic bursts.

His body transformed in front of me.

It stretched out and contorted as his claws morphed and lengthened into legs.

Feathers collected around his newly constructed back, and his talons expanded and broke into arms as his body turned . . . human.

Except for his sharp features and feral eye.

Gren laid there as a man, exposed to all the elements.

I had to blink a couple of times for it to sink in.

It was Gren. He still had his right eye and the evident scar down the other one stopping above his upper lip. He was tall and slender but still looked young and strong as his hair relaxed in waves right below his brows in the same hue as his feathers, ebony to complement his sun-kissed skin.

His eye fluttered open and it was darker than the night sky. Almost listless.

He stood up and leaned back against the tree to gain some equilibrium.

He rolled his muscular shoulders and stretched his arms in bizarre angles.

His mind looked as if occupied by a heavy fog until his eye flickered to mine.

A million thoughts ran through me. What if I summoned a demon? Were demons real? And what if a demon now possessed Gren's human body? *Did I somehow fuck up, again?*

I gawked at Gren as he stalked over to the monster—too pre-occupied with Kaschel to even notice Gren looming behind it.

Then Gren raised his hands to the beast's neck and ripped its head clean off.

A grayish blood gushed out everywhere, soaking both Kaschel's and Gren's bodies.

27
MEMORIES

Gren dropped the monster's corpse on the ground, and a clamorous thud followed.

"That would have been so much more convenient minutes ago," Kaschel growled as he fell to his feet and rubbed his bruised throat, coughing up blood.

Gren didn't respond as he turned back around. He spotted me in the dirt struggling to get my body to move.

His deadly silence made my skin crawl. My lungs collapsed with each stride he took. His forbidding aura dimmed the sky.

I wanted to stand up and run, but I also had too many questions.

Gren loomed over me with a detached stare and my breath hitched, but I couldn't utter a single word.

Gren scooped me up, and I squeaked as he guided us to the

front door.

He glanced at me, expressionless. "You're bound now."

I opened my mouth, but it just hung there with no clever retort. Gren sighed in frustration and his face clouded with indifference again.

"You're not old," I blurted out.

It wasn't the first thought to run through my mind. I had thousands upon thousands, but the idiotic ones always clawed their way to the surface and pushed the logical ones away.

Gren furrowed his dark brows in confusion as his lip twitched downward; his scar moved with it. "And?"

I mumbled a quick *nothing* under my breath. I shifted away from his grim expression to Kaschel who looked like he doused himself in a blood bath, which I guess he kind of did.

I clenched my chest as a strange emptiness ate away at me. I couldn't quite put it into words, but a numbing coldness consumed me, creating a gaping hole in my chest.

Did I lose something back there?

"We need to patch up your wrist. I think you might need stitches," Gren mumbled.

I glanced vacantly at the front door as Gren carried me inside, not really thinking much about what he said and too focused on what I had done.

"Why are you human? Are you really Gren?" I asked, still not fully believing what happened.

Gren dipped his chin down and his ebony hair draped over his scar with a sullen look. "Familiars are born with half a soul. We wander until we can find a witch who willingly gives up half . . . Your mother would be . . ." He averted his gaze and rested me on the couch, gently.

My eyes lit up, and I intently watched Gren sit on the coffee table opposite to me. "Can you speak about the past now? About my mother?"

I glossed over what Gren previously said. We would discuss it later; right now he could answer why I was thrown into this hell.

Gren kept his stare on the door, watching Kaschel stroll in behind us. "Now is not the time. We need to get to safety."

I huffed out like a child who wasn't getting their way when I knew he had a valid point. "*Soon.*" I bit down and looked away from him.

I didn't care about much in my twenty-three years, but finding out about my mother? It was something I needed to know. As much as I loathed her for abandoning me, it was like an insatiable craving I needed to feed or it would devour my whole existence.

"I will say this . . . I was content with being by your side and helping you even if you didn't remember me." Gren spoke softly as he leaned forward and brushed a strand of hair out of my face.

Gren was strangely different, and I wondered if it had anything to do with him gaining half my soul.

But that couldn't be real. Half my soul? If it was, why didn't he tell me before he suggested it?

I perked an eyebrow up when I realized what Gren had said. I couldn't remember much of my childhood except for foster care, and when I met Lucien. I remember the crows, and how they spoke to me, but I never remembered a word they said.

I hadn't found my hazy memory strange until now. It was like a vague nagging in my mind, and it only disappeared if I stopped thinking about it.

"How heartwarming, but now isn't the time to reminisce," Kaschel interrupted. "We have a hundred more bounty hunters coming our way."

Gren shot a glare at Kaschel. "That's your problem, not ours."

Kaschel clicked his tongue as he walked over to the coffee table—cool and collected, acting as if he wasn't almost choked to death.

Kaschel watched me and said, "Addy and I have an agreement, and until she fulfills her end of the bargain . . . I'm afraid she's stuck with me." Kaschel glanced back at Gren with boredom. "And it shouldn't be of any concern to her pet."

Levisus ran out of the hallway, cutting off their useless quarreling.

Levisus fixed his sights on Kaschel. "I got it, but you're not going to like where it's located." He paused and blinked a couple of times before registering Gren's presence. "Why the fuck is there a naked man sitting on my coffee table?"

"Her pet raven." Kaschel flicked his wrist in Gren's direction.

"Crow."

"Whatever."

"Stop," I snapped.

There was too much testosterone in this goddamn room.

I wanted answers. I wanted a hot shower. To wash away the dirt and grime. To find the other key and go back to living a repetitive, normal life, not listen to a bunch of men arguing like children.

I stood up and fully noticed Gren's naked body.

I turned away, ripped my cloak off, and draped it over him.

Gren tilted his head to the side as if confused by my actions, but I ignored him.

I guess our conversations could wait. We needed to leave.

"Do you perhaps have any spare clothes?"

28
VODKA, STITCHES, AND A BREWING STORM

Gren put on some of Levisus's clothes so he wasn't parading around naked—unaware that if he did, it was strange behavior.

It fit Gren's body well but looked a little lax around the shoulders. His build was thinner than that monster of a man; not that Gren was small by any means, just not as big as Levisus.

Gren stood there tugging at the collar of his gray shirt as he shimmied uncomfortably from the loose-fitting black slacks and dark cherry-wood-colored shoes.

My focus snapped back to the void in the wall as it pulsated in rhythmic waves like a heartbeat.

It occurred to me how odd it was for Levisus to have a conveniently placed escape route, but Kaschel didn't seem bothered by it. So maybe it was normal since Levisus practiced magic? Sor-

KING OF THE UNSIGHTLY

cery?

I wasn't sure what that shifty-ass man did in the safety of his room, yet I was still thankful we were leaving this god-awful place. But no matter where or what we had to walk through— shadows, portals, creepy forests, or whatnot—they all gave me the same chills nipping at my neck.

My legs moved on their own accord, and the darkness invaded every crevice of my body and propelled me forward.

My lungs constricted and I gasped for air but nothing, only the feeling of floating in space without the intense pressure of boiling, freezing, and expanding your body, leaving you unrecognizable.

Gren saw my discomfort and gently grabbed my hand. He mouthed his favorite phrase, *You have nothing to fear.*

I smiled unintentionally at him, but my comfort melted away as a disturbing thought filled my mind. The half a soul thing was maddening, but maybe there was some consolation knowing I didn't transform him into some bloodthirsty monster or demon.

The void spit me out and relaxation washed over me until I saw we were back in a forest.

And my heart sank.

I was so sick of nature at this point.

Was it impossible to drop us at a coffee shop or comfy bed? Would they force me to hike on foot for miles again?

My body crumpled inside at the mere thought of it.

I wanted to beg someone to carry me, but my pride wouldn't allow it. I had already been carried much more than I would have liked in the past twenty-four hours.

But if I was being honest, I wasn't sure how long I could last with the blisters on my heels and the throbbing pain from my wrist. Both emitted a sharp pain with every muscle I moved once the adrenaline wore off.

Kaschel chanted under his breath and the air shifted as a cool breeze caressed my body.

Thank fuck walking was out of the picture.

My eyes followed the shade from the trees balling together until a black hole appeared in front of us.

The memories of how the shadows rubbed up against my skin sent shivers down my body, and I shuddered. Was this really any better than walking?

Kaschel waved us in, and I held my breath once again and trudged through as the darkness clung to my skin like souls of the damned trying to drag me to an eternal slumber. I would have loved to take them up on that offer; sleep sounded incredible, but it was a luxury I couldn't afford.

Bile threatened to rise in my throat, and I staggered out of the shadows.

The only food I kept down this entire trip—the crusty-ass protein bar—almost spewed out my mouth.

I shot a glare at the three of them. How were they unaffected? Bastards.

When my stomach settled, I caught wind of my surroundings. We were back in Kaschel's dreadful vampiric mansion.

I sighed. It's like we took a 360. Ground zero.

How many days did I have left to get the second key? Valeria wouldn't give me much leeway; I knew that much.

Newly formed shadows shot out from the corner as Ryas transformed and strolled right up to Kaschel. Her white waves flowed with each stride.

"I have news—"

Kaschel held up his hand and it silenced her. "Take our guests to their rooms first." He looked back at Levisus. "Follow me. We have a lot to discuss. Don't we?"

Levisus eyed Ryas and me. "I would much rather follow where the fun will be held."

Ryas scrunched her face in disgust.

Kaschel clicked his tongue. "You'll have plenty of time for brothels when we retrieve my key and your brother. Unless saving him isn't vital to you anymore?" Kaschel turned away, not even bothering to hear Levisus's reply.

Levisus leaned toward me. "I'm afraid the big mean boss is asking me to work overtime. Have a good night, love." Levisus snatched my wrist and kissed my palm.

I shuddered from his warm lips pressing against my cool skin.

Ryas rolled her eyes as Levisus walked past her, winking as he hustled to get to Kaschel's side.

"Follow me." Ryas didn't give me or Gren the time of day as she walked past us, opposite to Kaschel and Levisus.

We wandered through a dark corridor with hundreds of oil paintings on the walls; they resembled a family tree spreading its branches and it looked never-ending. The more I studied the portraits, the creepier they got.

We came upon a wooden door weathered by age—dim and eerie just like the paintings.

Ryas pushed the door open and looked at Gren. "This will be your room. You'll find everything you need until morning."

"I will be staying with Addy. No reason to separate us."

Ryas lowered a brow at me, ignoring Gren. "Are all the men you brought here perverted playboys?"

"Gren's my familiar," I snapped back. For some reason I felt I needed to defend myself, but was he really *mine*?

Ryas swayed over to Gren. She looked at him. "Ah. The crow. I didn't think you would give up your soul so quickly." Ryas shrugged. "No matter. I suggest you stay in separate rooms unless you're okay with bathing with your familiar, which I guess most of your kind does."

"NO." I cleared my throat. "I mean." I glanced at Gren with a soft smile. "It will only be until morning."

Gren glared at Ryas as she beamed at him with a devilish grin. "Fine, but if you need anything . . . I'm right here."

I mouthed a *thank you* as Gren gave me a small nod and stepped through the door.

Ryas slammed it shut and turned back to me with a mischievous sparkle in her green eyes. "You seem to be some kind of supernatural dick magnet."

I choked on my spit as I forced out the words, "It's not like that with any of them."

Ryas laughed and it thundered through the vast corridor. "Sure."

I was appalled by her insinuation, but I didn't think I needed to defend myself further.

Ryas's pointy heels clicked against the floors until we stumbled upon the same room I used the day before. She pushed the door open and waved me inside.

The midnight-blue walls were oddly calming and the black spiral bed frame with pillars and intricately carved skulls and flowers protruding out of the eye sockets didn't seem to scare me anymore.

Even the mirrors on every wall except for the one with the vanity dresser made the place feel more . . . open and inviting.

I think I finally turned batshit crazy.

"It's been cleaned, and I happened to come across some old clothes I was getting rid of." She motioned her wrist toward the outfits lying on the vanity dresser beside the bed. "It's not much but it's better than the alternative."

"Thank you," I said with sincerity.

How was I so relieved to be back in this room?

Ryas coughed and shifted uncomfortably. "I assume tomorrow will be rough, so eat the food on the tray and rest because it will only get worse from here."

Without thinking, I ran up to Ryas and hugged her.

Tears trickled down my face and a small sob escaped me.

I had no clue why I was hugging her . . . maybe the sleep deprivation, the familiarity of her presence, or the tray of food.

Probably the food.

Ryas stiffened under my embrace, but I didn't care. I felt somewhat normal as I squeezed her tighter.

It became painstakingly obvious—I needed more friends.

Ryas slowly patted my head like some pet and pried my arms off her. "You're making me feel uncomfortable if this is all it takes to make you happy. So, let's not do this again. Okay?"

A pathetic *okay* left my throat as she walked out of the room leaving my thoughts to devour my wavering sanity.

I had to be starved for physical and emotional affection—and it didn't feel too great.

The bathroom door stood a few feet from me, and I wobbled into the room before witnessing the bath magically fill up with hot, steaming water.

The room had pure white marble with gold laced throughout it. The massive cast-iron tub complemented the floors as it glowed a coppery hue from the candles. A heavy contrast to the other part of the room.

I peeled the clothes off that clung to my body and submerged myself.

All the events I had gone through flashed like a cinematic movie through my closed eyelids with all the heart-pounding emotions to follow.

I didn't know how long I stayed in tub, letting all the emotions flow through me like waves crashing on the shoreline—each one hitting harder than the next.

My pruned hands rubbed against my soft skin, and I hissed when I hit my open wound on the side of the tub.

I stood up and grabbed the towel hanging on the wall, dried myself, and wrapped it around me.

The mirror caught my attention as I took in my reflection after what felt like an eternity.

I looked like a stranger. My cheeks were flushed from the steam and my wet brunette hair rested in loose waves below my chest. My blue eyes with specks of gold shimmered in the candlelight and had dark bags below them.

I sighed, ambled out of the bathroom, snatched the plate of food with my good hand, flopped myself on the bed, and started devouring the meat first and then the fruit.

A shadow shot to the corner of the room and shifted.

Did Ryas forget something? I knew for a fact she wasn't coming back for another hug.

Kaschel rose from the darkness and stalked toward me.

My gaze lowered with distrust as I studied his outfit. A loose white silk shirt and matching pants, leaving his muscles exposed when the candlelight hit him just right.

Kaschel's eyes swayed like purple flames as his damp hair draped behind him.

He pointed at me. "Let me see."

I moved my hands up to cover my exposed collarbone. "Excuse me?"

Kaschel tapped his hand impatiently. "Your wrist."

"Oh. I'm sure you could have Ryas look at it, or give me the proper supplies and I could handle it." Or anyone besides you.

Of course, Kaschel didn't listen and sat beside me. His shirt shifted and revealed his bulging pecs. So close that more of the scar peeked out, trailing down his abdomen.

I looked up at his face and he held an unreadable expression.

He was so good at masking his emotions, and it annoyed the hell out of me.

Kaschel grabbed my wrist, and I flinched. His touch, scalding hot against my skin. He glanced at me and back to my hand.

Kaschel twisted it up and inspected my wound. "You need stitches and to clean it so it doesn't get infected."

"Do you have one of those staple guns? I can do it myself," I lied. Did he really think I was going to let him stab me? Multiple times?

"If Ryas does it, you'll come out needing more, and you . . . stitching yourself? Don't make me laugh." Kaschel turned away and grabbed the bottle off the vanity dresser. "Drink this."

I looked down at the vodka, skeptically. "Do you think I look like someone who frequents a shady butcher shop for stitches, and it only takes a little bit of vodka to alleviate the pain and make me brave?"

Kaschel's deep chuckle antagonized my skin, the vibrations of his voice sent shivers through our connected hands. I sucked in a breath and avoided his detached stare.

The audacity of this man.

"I don't think you want me to answer that." Kaschel lifted the bottle and poured me a glass. "And don't worry. It's from your world. I have no reason, nor the desire, to see you drugged like before."

I knew I was anxiously staring but *that* wasn't what I was afraid of.

"What reassuring words." I groaned and looked down at his hands. "Fine." I snatched the bottle from him instead of the cup.

I lifted it to my mouth, pinched my nose, and chugged.

I gulped and wiped my mouth, making a face as the vodka burned its way down to my stomach. "Now I need something to put in my mouth." I've seen movies and I know you need something to bite down on.

I frantically looked around for something. Would a bagel work?

"Oh?" Kaschel purred.

My eyes shot back to him. "Not like that," I said, stumbling over my words.

29
A FOOL'S GAME

I held my tongue as Kaschel took the needle and thread out. My eyes squeezed shut, I attempted to think of anything but the needle piercing my skin.

My thundering pulse betrayed me and let Kaschel know how much this affected my nerves.

Something cold touched me and I flinched hard and squeaked all at once.

Then nothing.

I slowly blinked, and Kaschel perked up one eyebrow, humored by my cowardliness.

The needle was far from my skin. All he had done was disinfect the area. I laughed awkwardly and swallowed.

"Are you going to continue to squirm and make this difficult?" Kaschel asked in a low voice as he kept my hand in place.

"Probably." I wasn't going to lie again.

I loathed getting stitches, and without numbing it? Even more terrified. How did I managed to inflict this wound on myself?

Adrenaline was one hell of a drug.

I looked down at the needle, and the enormous size caught me off guard and I gasped.

The fact that it only took one look to sober me up immediately terrified the heck out of me.

"Okay. Okay. Okay. Do it. Do it now," I said before all my confidence left my body. I scrunched my face, purposely avoiding his moving hands. The needle poked through my skin, and I threw my head back. "FUCK. Couldn't you warn me?"

The needle weaved in and out of my wrist as the thread dragged behind it. My head spun as the queasiness of the needle puncturing my skin over and over again made me want to throw up or pass out, I couldn't tell which one.

Kaschel mumbled *Almost done* as he yanked on the thread.

I yelped, reacting to the tinge of pain.

I wanted to smack the living hell out of this man as his lip twitched when he finished tying the knot.

Kaschel leaned away and grabbed the gauze from the dresser, all without letting go of my hand.

"Why are you so accustomed to this? It doesn't seem typical for a royal."

He wrapped my freshly stitched skin, not lifting his concentration to meet my curious gaze. "I have many enemies who wish to see me falter. Showing weakness was a luxury I could not afford. Flaws got you killed. So, concealing injuries is mere child's play."

"Oh . . ."

"Are you feeling pity for me now, little flea? I'd have to advise you that stroking my ego would be a much more effective way into my pants. I am a fae full of vanity after all," he said mockingly as he tipped his head back; his eyes shimmered in the dim lighting as they wandered down to my lips.

"And you're deflecting." My mouth curved into a grin. "Have you become easier to read, or have you lowered your guard? Both would be gross errors on your part. You should start worrying about your lapse of judgment, old man."

"Are you threatening me?" His smile intensified, exposing his puckish disposition as he leaned closer, his chest slightly pressed against mine. His head tilted sideways as he attentively watched my lips. "How presumptive of you. Maybe . . . I find your reactions amusing." He moved his hand to my cheek, brushed my bottom lip, and placed a strand of hair behind my ear. "Do you wish to find out if I'm easy?"

I almost lost my breath when his rough hand caressed my skin but we had been here before.

He was either testing or teasing me.

He wouldn't play me for a sap again.

I turned my cheek and pried Kaschel's hand away.

We locked eyes as I leaned more into his body. "Thank you for stitching me up but"—I looked down at his full lips and lowered my head to his ear so he could feel my breath against his skin and rested one hand on his shoulder—"I think we're done here."

Kaschel didn't really want me, nor did I want him to.

He wanted to toy with me like everyone else in my life, and I was done playing the fool.

194

Two could play this dangerous game.

30
SWEET NOTHINGS

Kaschel held my stare with an impassive expression as the room reflected in his light, amethyst eyes.

He heard every thud of my heart pound violently against my chest as the room fell mute around us—except for our shallow breathing and my foolish, backstabbing heart.

When neither one of us backed down, I could have sworn time stopped.

I sucked in one traitorous breath and bit down on my bottom lip, noticing how dangerously close his were to mine.

Kaschel inclined his head as one of his hands moved closer to my hip.

I was already losing this game, and we barely started.

I almost pressed my lips to his when memories of Jared caressing my body flickered through my mind like strobe lights—*all his sweet nothings* whispered by freshly swollen lips he had stolen from another.

I was bleeding like Jared had manifested behind me and stabbed me in the back all over again—unrelenting and ruthless.

My lungs restricted as I withdrew from Kaschel's embrace and pushed myself farther away.

I opened my mouth once I caught my breath like I could explain, but the words failed me—like they always did.

It's not like Kaschel needed an explanation.

We weren't *anything* to each other, and I already said we were done here.

This was just a game of cat and mouse, and I was so desperate to not become the prey again.

God, I hated how that gremlin of a man was still taunting me even after our breakup.

I had enough.

Jared needed to vacate my mind immediately.

And I needed to move on, but I knew Kaschel wasn't the right person.

My eyes fell to his chest; I couldn't handle the intensity any longer.

Kaschel cleared his throat and ruffled his hair. "I thought it was only the men who stared down women's shirts, yet here you are, ogling me like I'm some piece of meat."

I laughed so hard I snorted and threw my hand up to cover my mouth.

I regained my self-control and looked back at Kaschel who had a playful glint as his mouth pulled up, revealing a white canine.

I shook my head. "How full of yourself can you be?"

Kaschel shrugged and each muscle in his shoulders tightened and relaxed with him. "Wouldn't you like to find out." He stood up and chanted under his breath. The shadows obeyed his command and created the gaping, black hole in the middle of the room. "We leave at dawn, so do try to rest this time . . . even if you can't get me out of your lecherous mind." Without looking back at me, he walked through it.

For some reason, his vanishing presence left a chill in the air.

I ran my fingers through my hair and sighed.

It had been a couple days since the breakup.

It was about time I slept with someone and got drunk, or both—but not in that particular order.

I took a mental note to move on once I saved Lucien, but not with some demented fae who I couldn't even read half of the time. Someone normal—not a walking, talking red flag. I already filled that slot myself.

I was glad he left. I think I would have done something I regretted.

Valeria's warning came to mind, and I hopped off the bed, grabbed my dirty clothes from the bathroom and pulled out the mirror. My fingers traced the silver thorns protruding out of the skull then slowly moved to the three golden vipers spilling out of its mouth and eye sockets.

This stupid mirror was my only bet at saving Lucien, and it was scary how I knew my odds were slim to none.

Could I save Lucien? Was he okay?

I wasn't sure, and it petrified me.

"Wipe your mouth and get changed. We're leaving in five."

Jolted awake to Ryas beside my bed, clicking a switchblade open, I rubbed my eyes and stifled back a yawn.

My eyes widened and I jerked away from the blade she held inches from my face.

"Were you planning on stabbing me if I didn't respond?" I dropped a brow.

She looked down at me like some deranged devil as her smile extended across her face, pressing the cold blade against my cheek.

I thought we grew a little closer last night; apparently not.

But it made me feel somewhat sane to know there was some-one crazier than me. I mean, I looked tame in comparison to her.

"In my defense, you were sleeping like the dead," she said with no remorse as she leaned away, sliding the sharp edge of the blade off my skin. Did she get off on tormenting people or something?

I rubbed my eyes again, stretched my legs and arms then rolled away from the center of the bed, and shot up to my feet.

I glared back at her. "I am human. We do tend to need our sleep, unlike all you psychos who thrive off . . . what . . . three, four hours?" I said mid-yawn.

"Five, and it's not that weird."

"Like I said. Psychotic."

Ryas tilted her head. "Where has my sweet, sobbing Addy gone?" Ryas batted her lashes, taunting me.

I shook my head. "To her senses."

Ryas sighed dramatically. "Boringgg." She closed the switchblade and shoved it in her pocket. "I don't trust you like Kaschel does, despite the mark, and if you so much as cross him . . . I will make you wish this was the worst of it."

The gravity in her tone was unmistakable, and my whole body shuddered in response. She meant each word, and it reminded me again—I needed to be wary of these people.

My eyes caught the all-black outfit and combat boots placed on the dresser, and I slipped them on once she stalked out of the room. Other than the pants being a little long and tight, they fit well enough.

I brushed my hair and it automatically puffed up, so I quickly pulled it into a ponytail.

Gren beamed at me as I stepped through the door. He sported a tight-fitting cream shirt and black pants with boots to match. It was an outfit more suitable for hiking than his previous one.

His wavy ebony hair unwound right above his scar; his sharp features complemented his athletic physique.

Yeah, staring at him now—I didn't think I'd ever get used to this new form.

Gren's dark eye dropped to my stitches and narrowed. "Who—I mean. I'm glad you got those taken care of." He smiled.

Gren didn't need to know Kaschel was the one who did it. Especially when I asked him to stay in a separate room. It felt like a betrayal if he found out, and I didn't want him to get the wrong idea. Not that it should matter; he didn't own me, despite having half my soul.

I looked down at my bandaged wrist. "Yeah, it doesn't hurt too much tod—"

"Move. They're waiting." Ryas shoved past us, aggravated by

our conversation.

We reluctantly trailed behind her in the endless corridor. The place looked haunted; each portrait we passed was more archaic and eerier than the last.

My sight fixed on one of a nude man underneath a waterfall at dusk with black flowy hair and crimson irises ominously following me as I scurried away from it.

My hands stuck to the sides of my pants, turning hot and sticky as I grew more anxious. I hated not knowing where it ended or what potentially awaited us.

Looking down, I fiddled with my hands when I slammed into Gren's back.

He eyed me with concern. Then he seized my hand in his and squeezed it. His cool touch calmed my jittery nerves but the feeling waned on and off until my thoughts warped to chaos.

He perked an eyebrow as he straightened himself. "I wonder how many times I have to tell you everything will be fine until you actually believe me."

My lips pulled into a thin smile. I really wanted to be stupidly optimistic, but it was easier said than done.

I didn't glance in Gren's direction and kept myself focused, fixating on how the cracks in the ceiling splintered in all directions. "Until all of this is over," I muttered, clenching one fist and hoping my restless mind would simmer down soon.

Gren chuckled. "Fair enough." His husky voice gnawed at my ears; a stark difference from his old one, and it caught me off guard.

He sounded young and charismatic. It was unsettling the more I contemplated it.

I knew nothing about Gren. *Not really.*

We trekked through another dimly lit corridor to reach a dreary room with velvet furnishing and an antique cherrywood table.

Kaschel leaned against it in all black, every muscle barely concealed by his flimsy fabric choice. His alabaster hair was pulled back in his usual low ponytail with one side tucked behind his ears. It made his fae features even more prominent.

Levisus stood next to him wearing similar attire, and it matched his darker complexion, but his presence couldn't compare to Kaschel's.

If Levisus wasn't such a filthy flirt, I might even admit he was gorgeous. He didn't seem like the type to ever drop his mask though. And from one person who resorted to sarcastic comments to avoid their issues, I could tell a mile away—he kept his true self hidden. In that regard, Levisus was an open book compared to Kaschel.

With Kaschel, I had no clue what went through his mind, and I loathed not being able to read someone.

Kaschel didn't glance in my direction once as we stood at opposite ends of the table. And I wondered if he decided to deliberately ignore my presence again.

"We don't know how long it will take, so here are your supplies," Ryas said in an intense voice as she threw a backpack at Gren, and my attention went back to her.

Gren managed to catch it with one arm.

I hadn't noticed I still held his other hand with a death grip until I pinched my nails together.

I dropped Gren's hand and glanced up at him. "I'm so sorry,

I didn't realize—"

"It's okay. Squeeze as hard as you like. It doesn't hurt."

My face scrunched in confusion. Why would I do that?

Had Gren always been this nice, or was it because of the ritual?

I took one deep breath as Kaschel's shadows balled together, and they both stepped through it without a word.

My hands trembled as Ryas shooed us in without letting me subdue my unease and followed from behind.

The dry, chilly air wailed like tormented souls as it lashed at my exposed skin, nipping at my fingertips and nose. My teeth chattered and my body shivered uncontrollably as the harsh wind whipped at my eyes, forcing them to narrow.

A heavy jacket would have been nice right about now.

Kaschel and the rest of them proceeded toward the dead pine trees all bunched together while I gaped at the mountain covered in volcanic rocks and overgrowth.

I turned to face Gren and staggered back from the sharp drop beside him. Only a few feet away from falling to our deaths. *How lovely.*

My head whipped back to Kaschel, who trudged on ahead, not giving anyone else the time of day. *He really only cared about himself.*

His gruff voice cut through the air. "The old hag had some powerful friends, so be vigilant of your surroundings."

31
THRICE A CROWD

If climbing this mountain was a race, I was in last place crawling like someone had ripped both my legs off as a cruel joke and beat me with them.

Maybe I was a tad dramatic as I propelled my legs forward despite my muscles screaming in protest. I wanted to blame my lack of endurance on the blood loss from yesterday, but I knew the truth.

Each time I stole a peek at Gren hoping he didn't see how out of breath I was, his face possessed no warmth, and I wasn't sure if the rapid gooseflesh rising on my neck came from the chill in the air or his lack of emotion. Both seemed plausible.

I tapped Gren's shoulder.

He snapped his head in my direction and dropped his chin down to meet my gaze.

Since the others were a reasonable distance away, now was the best time to question him.

"So, how about now?" I lowered a brow, curiously.

Gren tipped his head. A myriad of emotions flickered across his face, and then he avoided my stare and looked back ahead.

He knew exactly what I meant.

Gren sucked in a short breath as he tinkered with the end of his shirt. "Your mother . . . well." He wrinkled his nose. "I guess to others it looked like she ran an animal sanctuary," he said as a shaky laugh withdrew from his throat.

Without hesitation, I grabbed his wrist and gave him a reassuring nod. I hadn't taken into account his past could be traumatic . . . like mine. Was it selfish to pry for answers?

I squeezed his hand. "We can wait until we're free from"—I looked around and then back at him—"this horrible situation."

But if I was being truthful with myself, I didn't want to wait any longer.

I had been waiting my whole life, but maybe pushing for answers wasn't always the best way to go about things. Everyone could have a past they didn't want to remember. I knew that more than anyone.

I let go of his hand and twirled my thumbs as we hiked up this never-ending mountain. I almost tumbled over a couple of sharp rocks as my feet continued to drag me forward.

Kaschel and Levisus were in a deep conversation as Ryas looked incredibly bored.

My eyes lingered back to Gren.

He smiled, but his lowered chin overshadowed his false reassurance and told me he was anything but fine.

"For familiars, living without a witch or contract puts a target on our backs. If we're caught without one, we run the risk of being hunted for spells. It's how I lost my eye." He grazed his fingers across his scar, and his face clouded with dread but vanished instantaneously. "But your mother saved my brothers and me from a much worse fate, and that's when I met you." Gren trailed off as he kept his focus in front of us.

"So, she. . . she did this to me? She bound me to the key? Did she also steal my memories, or am I protecting myself and blocking out something horrible that happened when I was a child?" My voice cracked, but the wind thrashing against the hollow trees obscured it.

Gren's expression told me everything.

My hands shook, violently.

From the cold.

Or so I told myself.

What gave her the right to steal my memories from me? What gave her the right to bind me to a key that would bring me nothing but trouble?

The rage boiled within me and tainted me to my core.

I was livid.

What good would have come from any of this? What was she *thinking*?

My mind spun webs of venomous deceit until Gren gripped my shoulders, snapping me out of my spiraling mind. "All I know is she made my brothers and I swear to protect you if she didn't return. An oath formed from blood and magic. She was desperate, but she loved you. I swear."

I got lost in Gren's eye like it was a void pulling me in, nullifying all my tension.

His words indicated he cared for my mother, but all I had were tarnished memories of her leaving me behind with *them*.

I sucked in a breath.

No. It didn't matter.

I had to tell myself—it existed only in the past. And I couldn't let it control me anymore, or the fear would consume me.

I could work through this.

I was okay.

I could be strong.

No, I was a strong, capable, badass woman.

I mentally cringed at my words.

"All right, thank you for telling me," I said, jiggling the uncertainty out of my body from my fingertips to my toes. I might get some form of PTSD from all this, but trauma wasn't forcign to me. I just couldn't let it destroy me. Even if I felt wronged. No one would solve my problems. Not Lucien. Not Gren. *Only me.* I ruffled my hair out of my ponytail. It wasn't doing me any favors but whipping me in the face. "I think it's about time I get my shit together." I laughed sardonically, brushing the loose strands of hair behind my ear.

"I know it may sound redundant, but you are not alone."

"I know," I said sternly as I picked up my pace to match the others.

It's not that I didn't want to rely on others.

I wanted to. So badly. I mean, who would want to carry any type of burden all by themselves?

But was it okay to put others in harm's way for my sake? When it could mean their life hung in the balance? And could I truly trust anyone?

Gren said multiple times he was only repaying a favor for my mother. This mess had nothing to do with him. Yet I bound him to me, and he had no choice but to follow.

"Addy. You know it's okay to—"

"Shit," Ryas yelled and threw her head back.

Both Gren's and my attention shot up.

A massive obsidian rock crashed right in front of her. The clamor shook the pebbles beneath us as we all strained to stabilize ourselves.

I squinted and tried to read the white carvings on it.

Kaschel scanned the rock, and glared back at Ryas, seemingly annoyed she didn't elaborate on her remark.

"What?" Kaschel growled, peeved he even had to ask.

"It roughly says"—Ryas cleared her throat—"*A point of no return. Thrice a crowd and no delights to cast your sights. Only spilled blood will guide you. Jest in the warning and only ruin awaits you. Yours truly, R.G.*"

"You could have said once we pass this point, we won't have any of our magic." Levisus yawned. "Why say all extra stuff? Completely unnecessary." He yawned again and waved his hand dismissively at her.

Ryas looked like she wanted to jump over Kaschel and claw Levisus's face.

Kaschel spoke and it snapped Ryas out of her rage. "I loathe that trickster." He rubbed his temples.

I laughed so hard I snorted, and it echoed throughout the mountainside. And I immediately clasped my hand over my mouth.

My eyes went wide as they all looked at me like I grew a third arm. "Do you guys not see the irony? I mean, coming from a faery." Kaschel's expression darkened as the words left my lips. It made me ramble on like I could somehow save myself. "Well, aren't you a trickster yourself? I mean have you ever read the lore of your kind?" Oh my god. Smite me where I stand before I finish digging my own grave.

"No. Please continue. I would love to hear your thoughts about *faeries* through fiction," Kaschel said, his voice oozing with sarcasm.

Mortified, I ignored him entirely and waved my hand. "Regardless, we're going forward, right?" I looked at Ryas for a reply, avoiding Kaschel's murderous stare.

"Yes," Levisus answered for both of them.

"All right then. Let's stop stalling." I stepped beside the ominous rock. "Okay, before we go farther I need—"

My mouth clenched shut when my foot slipped and I plunged, slamming stomach first onto the dirt.

Air escaped my lungs as I grunted, flipped onto my back and gasped.

Staggering to my feet, I peered at the cliffside. I was only centimeters away from dropping to my death again. I sucked in a breath and waited anxiously for the others, hoping they might fall from the sky too.

I squeezed my eyes shut and counted to three like somehow it would magically change my situation.

This is fine. My hands shook with uncertainty, and in a split second a rift in the sky opened up, and a body hurled at me.

It smashed me against the ground, and my breathing hitched.

32
SPILLED BLOOD

"**Y**ou're squishing me." I wheezed, pushing Kaschel's body off me.

Kaschel stood up and dusted off his black pants and shirt without offering a helping hand. He apparently wanted to overlook the fact he launched out of the sky and pummeled me to the ground.

"Do you always jump in headfirst without thinking of the repercussions?" Kaschel growled; the frustration rolled off his tongue.

"Not always," I barked back. Yeah, I sounded like a child defending their idiotic actions, which sounded less convincing even to myself, and maybe there was some inkling of truth to what he said, but the hell if I was telling him that. I glanced behind him. "What about the others? Gren?"

Kaschel shrugged as he walked up to me and slanted his cruel eyes. "Your pet raven is of no concern to me." He paused, crouched down, and brushed some dirt off my shoulder as he leaned closer, his calloused hands teased my neck as they grazed my skin. "I think you should be more worried about yourself and the dangers awaiting us." He glowered as his cool breath sent shivers down my spine.

Unable to endure his closeness, I waved him away with my hand.

Kaschel's face reflected displeasure as he launched up and stepped over me.

My jaw clenched. Didn't he already know I was constantly worried about the keys and our situation? It occupied my mind twenty-four seven.

I took a deep breath, exhaled, and pulled myself off from the ground. Small pebbles embedded themselves onto my backside and I wiped them off and willed myself to stay calm.

"What are we supposed to do now?"

"Find the key." He grumbled and trudged on ahead, leaving me behind.

I was about to lose my shit on him.

This man tested my patience way too many times. What happened between last night and now? He was as fickle and moody as the weather here.

I groaned and stalked behind him. "No shit. I mean HOW are we going to get it? Do you have a plan that I'm unaware of? You seem to love keeping me in the dark."

"Labyrinths don't come with instruction manuals, little flea. So, the plan is, don't slow me down."

This man was really going to bring the petty Addy back to the surface.

I cleared my throat and ran my fingers through my hair. "Then can I have some form of protection? I see you're fit for battle, yet all I have to defend myself are my wits."

Kaschel stopped, grunted, and turned to me and devoured the distance between us before I could even breathe.

He towered over me with such ferocity I wanted to take back my snarky remarks—almost.

Kaschel lifted his shirt, and I peeled my eyes away. "What the heck are you doing right now?"

Kaschel scoffed and a clang of metal reverberated beside my feet, and I peeked down at a black dagger the size of my hand.

My cheeks flushed from the sudden heat. "Ah."

Kaschel lowered a brow. "I don't want you to be completely defenseless since . . . just having your wits wouldn't be your best bet at survival."

Holy fuck. He wanted to get stabbed. "You really have a way with words. Incredibly charming," I mumbled under my breath and snatched the dagger off the ground.

Kaschel's mouth tugged up, and I hated to admit it, but it was chaotically hot.

I abhorred this very moment for showing me Kaschel in such a light. He appeared incredibly attractive under the sunrays as his amethyst eyes flickered mischievously, his defined muscles even more noticeable from how the light reflected off his body. I once thought he looked the most in his element during twilight, but right now, his alabaster hair had a celestial glow, and it mesmerized me.

But I hated myself even more as his smirk turned into a full-blown smile and stirred something within me.

I slapped my cheeks to stop my thoughts from escalating.

A harsh shrill resounded off the cliffside, and then another and another.

I whipped my head to the withered trees and back to Kaschel, desperately searching for a hint of reassurance that what we heard wasn't a big deal.

Kaschel snatched my hand and hauled us deeper into the forest. My legs barely maintained the same speed with his long strides.

"Please tell me you have a better plan than just surviving," I said between breaths.

Kaschel didn't answer me for a moment, and his furrowed brows made it apparent he was calculating our chances of survival.

Kaschel spoke in a raspy voice. "Whatever they are, it sounded like a pack of them. We need to gain some distance so we don't get cornered at the edge of the cliff."

I could only nod in agreement like a bobblehead as we dodged trees, branches, and boulders.

I only caught glimpses of where I stepped as my heart thrashed against my ribcage.

Kaschel's grip tightened but it didn't bring me any relief. Instead, I dreaded the thought of the creatures catching us as sweat beaded at my brows. The frigid air flailed against my skin. The branches came alive, snagging my clothes, tearing bits and pieces off.

Crimson eyes floated in between trees and vanished.

A scream bubbled up my throat, but I was so out of breath and could only force a few words out. "I saw"—I sucked in the air again, and it grazed my throat like pins and needles as it punctured my lungs—"something."

Kaschel snapped his head to the side and turned us in the opposite direction. "Jump."

I almost didn't register his words in time to leap over the fallen tree before us.

Another sharp howl echoed through the forest, and a blur plowed and snapped branches from the side as it closed the distance between us.

My jaw dropped in horror. I hoped to fucking god Kaschel had a plan.

I slammed against his back. "Why are we stopping?!" I pushed myself off him, and my eyes widened in disbelief.

We were back where we started.

We couldn't run or hide.

We had to face whatever creature that came after us head-on.

My whole body trembled and a realization hit me.

Kaschel didn't have his abilities, and I was practically useless.

I opened my mouth to speak, but Kaschel shoved me to the side with so much force I went tumbling.

A bloody howl pierced my ears again, and I landed on my stomach. A loud *Ooof* escaped me as my head bounced off the rocky ground.

A vociferous thud followed, and I pressed myself off the dirt, but the world spun around me.

My vision came into focus as I picked myself up.

I gaped as the mutated gray wolf launched itself at Kaschel.

The wolf bared its fangs, and its spiked horns spiraled out of its skull—dangerously close to puncturing Kaschel's throat.

It enveloped itself in a red mist and drove Kaschel closer to the edge.

I stood there frozen, unable to move my body as I gawked at its colossal size that was comparable to an overgrown grizzly.

The wolf lunged at Kaschel again and dug its claws into his back, and Kaschel groaned out in agony as it brought him to his knees.

I panicked.

What could I possibly do? Poke it with this tiny dagger?

Run?

The dagger wouldn't even pierce through its fur, and I couldn't risk running since others were silently watching us from the forest.

And I would never survive on my own.

The wolf howled again, and Kaschel crumpled to the ground as it hovered over him. Drool poured from its malformed mouth, hitting Kaschel's neck and making a low hissing sound each time a droplet fell onto his skin.

Kaschel clenched his jaw as he wrestled to get the wolf's claws off of him.

But the wolf overwhelmed Kaschel, edging him off the cliff. It snarled and lunged at his neck.

My heart hammered harder against my chest as adrenaline took over my limbs and propelled me forward.

I grabbed the nearest rock and sprinted to Kaschel's side.

Without thinking, I smashed the rock against the wolf's skull.

And I smashed and smashed, screaming as spraying blood obstructed my vision.

It toppled over him and slid down the mountainside.

I inhaled and exhaled heavily as the silence rang in my ears.

I glanced down at Kaschel who breathed just as erratically. A wild look unraveled on his face as he stared back at me.

The wolf tore Kaschel's shirt in half and drenched him in blood, but I couldn't tell if the blood was his or the wolf's.

I held the rock to my chest as my uneven breaths exacerbated my unhinged appearance.

I threw my head back and laughed.

I mean, I fucking laughed like some deranged psychopath—not someone who had just murdered something.

My feet were at Kaschel's side as I tilted my chin to meet his confused expression. He narrowed his eyes and mine sparkled back with mayhem as a wicked grin stretched my cheeks.

I had never been one to filter myself, and I said the first thought that crossed my mind, "You know, you really are too weak to be this pretentious."

33
PALPITATIONS

The rock slipped through my fingers. "Oh, shit." It nailed Kaschel in the chest. We both gasped simultaneously but for extremely different reasons. He groaned and turned to his side, and I panicked as I crouched down beside him. "I'm so sorry. Let me help—"

Kaschel tossed a hand up and staggered to his feet as the rock thudded loudly on the ground, creating a small dust cloud around it. He wobbled for a few steps before he straightened his stance.

I stood up and eyed him cautiously.

His hair was in disarray, and his lowered gaze made him look gruff and dangerous in a hot kind of—I slapped my cheeks. Girl, it was not the time to be drooling over someone who just got mauled.

Why did my mind think now was a sensible time to head

straight for the gutter? He almost died! What was wrong with me? Was I really depraved or what?

Kaschel cleared his throat, and my attention went back to him. "You've done plenty, but I could have done without the boulder to the chest. If you had any animosity toward me . . . you could have waited until I was more conscious."

I grimaced at how banged up he appeared. His clothes were tattered and stained crimson. His bare chest was exposed, and the evident slash marks on his shirt hung on by the sheer willpower of two very thin strands of fabric.

"I swear it wasn't—I mean . . . let me help you walk," I said in a hushed tone like if I spoke any louder he would crumble to the ground.

Kaschel pursed his lips. "Pity is the last thing I want or *need* from you. Now move. We need to get out of here and try to get out of this loop."

I was baffled by how collected Kaschel behaved despite what happened.

I panicked and pointed to Kaschel's chest as blood squirted out of his open wounds. "How could you be fine when you're gushing blood?!"

Kaschel sighed and flicked my forehead. "This place can nullify magic, but it can't take away what I am. Have you forgotten?" he asked, enunciating the word *forgotten* a little more aggressively than I would have liked.

I mean, I saved him. A little gratitude wouldn't kill him. "Whatever. Just know that if you pass out on me . . . I'm leaving your ass behind."

Kaschel's deep chuckle tickled my ears as he wiped his bloody hands on his pants. "Shall it go both ways then?"

"Of course," I bluffed, and Kaschel's face told me he saw right through me.

Kaschel's lips twitched into a half-smirk, and he chuckled again. It was low and throaty and tantalized every crevice of my body.

Wait, what? *No.* I sucked in a breath and Kaschel perked up an eyebrow playfully—like he heard every indecent thought crossing my mind.

My cheeks burned red, and I looked away.

"All right then. Both ways it is," Kaschel teased, still grinning as his lively eyes didn't falter like mine.

How did Kaschel have so much energy? He acted entirely too energetic for a man gushing blood.

I wobbled as the dirt rumbled beneath us and the forest shifted. Our world crashed down, tore apart, and came back together.

The shades of dead branches laced and weaved together, stitching new life, and we, the outsiders, watched it all unfold.

Everything transformed in the blink of an eye—like some sick individual threw us into a video game, advancing us to the next level.

We weren't on a mountain or in a shivered-up forest. We were in some humid jungle teeming with life. Freshly fallen rain and soil caressed my nostrils as the birds chirping softened against the abrasive creatures screeching.

"Blood is guiding us. I guess we have more to look forward to," Kaschel said, snapping me out of my daze.

"Kill or be killed. Cool."

So whoever made this labyrinth was a sadist. Noted.

Kaschel scanned our surroundings and fixed his stare back on me. "It's not that simple and we need to find a place to rest. I need time to heal."

"Where could we possibly rest in a place like this?"

"Not sure."

"Great," I quipped.

Kaschel stepped through the shrubs and eluded all the liana vines crawling from each tree while I tried not to trip over the roots sprouting from the ground.

Sweat dripped from my neck as the blazing sun dipped down allowing the moon to ascend as we stumbled upon a grove with a remote waterfall. It seemed entirely too good to be true as the moonlight reflected off the stagnant water.

Yet the stillness in the air couldn't stifle the tremors of my pulse.

Kaschel bent down and his shoulder blades flexed and moved as he rinsed his hands, sending a catalyst of ringlets onto the water.

Kaschel placed his hand on his zipper and peeled his pants off.

I swallowed, hard, wiping my clammy hands on my jeans. "What are you doing?"

Kaschel didn't spare me a glance as he stood there exposed; his tight backside blinded me.

"What? Have you never seen the male physique before?" Kaschel remained serious as he dipped himself in, scrubbing the dirt and grime off his clothes. He titled his chin and looked back at me, his sharp eyes devouring mine. "If there's another monster tracking us, we need to get the blood off." It was a calculated thought, logical even, but I still didn't want to strip down to nothing. "I have no urge to look in your direction if that's what you're thinking," Kaschel clipped, not caring to elaborate.

I wanted to be offended, but the dry, crusted blood in my hair and clothes stiffened up and scratched against my skin.

I peeked at Kaschel who rinsed the remaining blood off his chest wounds, and I saw they already started to stitch back together.

I sighed. *He was right.* I leaned down, took my boots off and then my clothes, dipping myself in the water.

The abrupt coldness stole all my warmth and gooseflesh sheathed my body.

A shaky breath escaped my mouth, and I submerged myself.

My teeth chattered uncontrollably as I popped up and rinsed the remaining blood off my clothes.

I wondered if the best way to die was from hypothermia or getting mauled by a beast. *I think hypothermia wins.* Shuffling out of the water, I struggled to put my wet clothes back on as they stuck to my skin like a second layer.

Kaschel rose from the water, and he resembled a god ascending his throne. His white hair matched the moon's luminance. His ripped chest muscles and arms on display, showing no remnants of blood.

I turned my body before I allowed myself to look any lower.

If Kaschel caught me ogling him again I would never hear the end of it. It would be like screaming he won this twisted game of cat and mouse.

And I *hated* losing.

I shifted my body away and compelled all the indecent thoughts to disappear. "Can you see anything with that *faery* vision of yours? I assume you have better eyesight than me," I teased, but it came off quick and curt.

Kaschel shook his wet, long hair, and it dripped down his back to the dimples on his—no. Damn it, Addy. Stop.

I pinched my arm and refused to falter by his lack of apparel.

"Even after a near-death experience, you still have a mouth on you. I'm amazed. Truly." Kaschel didn't say another word as he clothed himself and walked toward the waterfall.

"I think you were the one who almost died, not me."

Why did I feel the need to clarify myself again? Did I subconsciously want to push his buttons?

Kaschel huffed but didn't respond, and I followed behind him. We slid past the cascading water; it splattered against the rocky floor, and we proceeded to go deeper into the night. The farther we went, the more it reeked of moss and dew. An oddly refreshing mixture.

"Stay here. I'll be right back."

"Excuse me?" I squeaked out, unable to hide my nerves.

"You murdered a beast in cold blood. Brutally, I might add. You'll be fine for a few moments without me."

It was a fluke. We had no idea for certain I could attempt the same thing twice, but I let my overwhelming pride win and flicked my wrist for him to leave. "Fine. *Go.*"

Shrouded in darkness when his light hair left the cave, the only comfort I found was the faint splashing of water against the rocks.

I swore an eternity came and went before Kaschel returned. His vibrant presence lit up the gloomy tunnel.

"Miss me?" Kaschel dropped an assortment of logs and

branches beside me.

So Kaschel went out to gather wood for a fire.

A spark ignited and it erupted into flames. The heat instantaneously blazed against my skin. It crackled and hissed, illuminating Kaschel's sharp jawline.

I raised my hands up as the fire warmed my fingertips. "Your *glamour* has always been lackluster so it's nice to see you're at least good for something, if not for protection, then as a portable heater." I perked up a brow in Kaschel's direction.

Kaschel lifted his gaze from the fire, and his alluring eyes danced wildly with the flames, staring into me.

"Are you trying to bait me, little flea? I can assure you, I'm good for more than mere parlor tricks and heat." Kaschel dipped his head to the side and smirked.

Kaschel's toned body and bare chest glistened from the rising flames. And I wouldn't deny myself any longer the chance to take in his exquisite build.

Checking him out wasn't a *sin*. I could indulge in his beauty a little.

"I find that hard to believe considering your bad track record. I did save you after all." Oh my god. What was I doing? We could be attacked at any moment, yet my mouth wanted to move on its own and see how far I could press him.

Kaschel suddenly crouched in front of me, and I jerked backward, making him smile more.

His face dimmed as he faced away from the flames. "Are you wishing to find out how useful I can be? Honestly, it would be a pity if you were all bark and no bite *again*."

I tilted my head and laughed as Kaschel studied my features.

He searched for something in my eyes, but I doubted he would find what he was looking for.

"I don't think I'm the one who's been all talk." Yeah, I was unhinged, but did I care at this point in my life?

No.

Was I tempting the devil?

Absolutely.

Would I hate myself once I came to my senses?

Of course.

But . . . I loved to gamble even with what little odds I had of winning, so fuck it.

If Kaschel thought he could keep toying with me . . . He was dead wrong.

One kiss. One kiss and I would be over it. And my thoughts of him would cease to exist.

Before Kaschel retorted, I grabbed him by the hand and pulled him close.

He lost his footing and fell into me, his knee between my thighs and his hands at my side, dangerously near my hips.

Briefly shocked, Kaschel inclined his head, and I matched his movement, parting my lips.

And I kissed him. I mean, I fucking kissed him.

I leaned into his body, amazed at how mine curved perfectly into his. He let out an unstable moan as our tongues met, and I pressed my lips hardest against his like I'd starve without them.

Kaschel flinched, and I panicked from his hesitancy.

Rejection wasn't something I could handle. *Not right now.*

I pulled away, but Kaschel squeezed his hand on my lower back and pulled me in. "Did I say you could move?" he growled and stole the distance between us, brushing his thumb over my bottom lip.

"I shouldn't have . . ." I trailed off as I put my hand to his chest, hoping to gather enough time to clear my thoughts.

But I was thawing from his firm grip—hot and embarrassed—I tried to retreat farther away before his shameless stare depleted all my worries.

I had no fucking clue what possessed me.

"Don't," Kaschel whispered and kissed me like he'd go feral if I left his side.

My body melted and froze, and melted again as Kaschel bit my lower lip and cupped my cheeks. My body liquefied from his touch as his hands moved slowly down my back to my hips.

I pushed on Kaschel's chest again, breaking our contact. My voice came out breathless and uneven. "I still find you incredibly arrogant."

Kaschel's deep chuckle sent goose bumps down my legs as his lip twitched at my words. "You think I care?" He seized my chin and lifted my face so our lips were parallel again.

He caressed my cheek before letting go and my insides burst with excitement as his hand glided down my side. His touch was soft but steady as it moved to my inner thigh. He teased me with his thumb, gently rubbing it in a circular motion.

God, I really hated his smirk too.

I hated this man, but I also wanted him back on my lips, consuming them. I was a fucking contradiction, but I didn't care. As much as I hated him, I wanted him more, and I yearned for him to want me just as badly.

My lips were centimeters from his as I breathed in. "This

doesn't change anything."

He laughed and it was low and vibrated against my bottom lip as his maddening touch made me ache for more.

"So this is what you've been doing? Fucking around with some guy?" a voice asked with such a sharp tongue it pierced through my heart.

I *knew* that voice, but it didn't sound like him. It wasn't sweet or radiating warmth and kindness.

It was cold, bitter, and full of resentment.

But it was still *his* voice.

I pushed myself away from Kaschel, and my soul shattered when Lucien emerged from the darkness.

34
GOOD FELLOW

I released my breath as my heart flailed violently against my chest.

Lucien stood there with his hands shoved into his jean pockets.

He wasn't wearing his usual clothes—not his grimy trucker hat to cover his blond waves and not the black joggers I never caught him dead without.

Instead, Lucien wore a gray collared shirt, and it hugged his muscular back and arms, purposely flaunting the physique he cultivated from countless hours spent at the gym.

Lucien pinched his lips into a grimace as he studied Kaschel by my side.

The dark shadow cast over his face gave him a calculating and vicious appearance. A stark difference from the expression he always greeted me with; I almost succumbed to his darkness.

His gold-speckled eyes shifted away from Kaschel and pointed all their hostility toward me. It was like he lodged a knife into my very existence with a mere glance.

My vision tunneled in as Lucien stalked closer. Each step—predatorial—sent shivers down my spine as my breathing came out in sharp and unstable spurts.

Lucien's footfalls echoed off the cave walls, and my concentration faded.

My gaze flickered to Kaschel, but he froze in place with a deadpan look.

Had time stopped for Lucien and me? But it wasn't *really* him. It couldn't be *him*.

I blinked, and we were back in his apartment.

My temple throbbed, and I winced in agony as it thundered against my skull—until the pain blinded me.

A chill in the air caressed my skin, and I quivered.

I rubbed my pulsing temple harder, trying to recollect what I was doing before this, but a heavy fog funneled into my mind, and I couldn't for the life of me remember why I was at Lucien's house.

What *was* I doing here again?

I snapped back to it, and Lucien towered over me—pinning me against his sofa. "Addy, are you okay?" he asked in a hushed tone like he would shatter me if he spoke half an octave higher.

I lifted my head and stared back at him. I clenched my chest from an intense throb, gasping for air. My body was drowning, and my lungs filled up with water each time I tried to recall the previous day.

God, why did my chest hurt so much, and why did I feel so devastated as Lucien watched me with his honey-colored eyes and pouty lips?

I rubbed my temples again and memories flashed in my mind. *Of Gren. Running for my life. Hades Cliff.*

I cleared my throat and wiped my sweaty palms on my jeans. "Wow. How much did I drink last night?" I let out a shaky laugh—a little unnerved by his proximity. "Where's Lynne? Did you just get off work?" I scooted more onto the couch cushions hoping they would gobble me whole and save me from his chaotic temperament.

Lucien's silence ate away at me. He was never quiet unless I had done something seriously stupid—which was entirely possible since I couldn't remember a damn thing.

Lucien leaned his head to the side and scanned my body. Shackled by his gaze, I boiled from within as his cold stare moved back to me—searching or waiting for me to speak. But paralysis overtook me as if he had cast me under a spell.

Lucien clicked his tongue and brushed a brunette strand of hair out of my face. "We broke up," he replied, short and right to the point.

I gulped.

My eyes narrowed, recalling our previous conversation. "Are you fucking with me because of what I said to you earlier about not brushing my teeth? You know, I was joking about the kissing part too." I laughed, and it came out high-pitched and squeaky.

Lucien's face relaxed from my words, and he gave me that boyish grin; the one where his stupid dimple sprung out, and without fail—my worries dissolved. "Now, why would I be teasing you?" He lowered a brow. "That doesn't sound like me at all."

Lucien moved his hands to my waist, and my breathing hitched.

He had to be fucking with me. I knew how much he loved teasing me ever since we were kids.

I turned my face slightly, but I still felt his eyes burning a hole through my skull like if he blinked or looked away, I would disappear from his line of sight forever.

"I-I don't think you're in your right mind," I stuttered as he leaned closer to me. "You're heartbroken and need to process your emotions. I get it. Honestly. More than anyone actually."

Lucien paused, threw his head back, and chuckled, soft and humorless. "Addy." He clicked his tongue again. "You really are something else. You know?" He lifted his hand from the couch and raised my chin. He moved his rough hand against my skin, cupping my cheek. "You have always been so clueless. It worries me since I thought I had been clear enough."

"What are you talking about?"

Lucien leaned into me until his lips were aligned with mine; I could feel his breath with each word he whispered, "There's only so many signals I can send you before I get discouraged."

I opened my mouth but the throbbing in my temple resurfaced and intensified.

I winced in pain as an aggressive knock on the door jolted me from a slouched to upright position.

35
A WAGER MALICE
AND MISCHIEF

The door rattled from the forceful pounding on the other side. A gust of wildflowers and dew fused with musk assaulted my nostrils and they flared out.

My eyes darted back to Lucien. "Are you going to get that?" I asked and scrunched my face, confused by his hesitancy. When he didn't budge a muscle, I pressed him further. "What if it's Lynne wanting to talk?"

Lucien scoffed and flicked the tip of my nose. "You should be more concerned about me, not the door."

I flinched, crinkled my nose, and I flicked his nose back.

Lucien was caught off guard, and I crossed my arms and raised a brow. "Don't flick me. I'm not your dog," I huffed, annoyed by his strange behavior.

Lucien grinned without an ounce of sweetness in his face. His stance was calculating and ruthless. "You could be," he hummed as he twirled a lock of my hair.

My body shuddered from his empty words.

Did I hear him correctly? "I could . . . what?"

Lucien laughed and shoved me further into the couch and sat beside me.

The atmosphere was off, or maybe Lucien was off. I mean, why would he say something so . . . *unsettling*?

I gulped at the realization of what he meant.

I eyed Lucien, slightly guarded. "Leave your fetishes for your next girlfriend." I squinted and scanned him over again; his eyes were more animated than before. "Are you on drugs? Honestly, I thought I would be the one more likely to be tripping, but who knows." I shrugged, and I sank more into the couch to evade his touch. "Maybe you're testing the waters."

Lucien traced his fingertips on my knee and I retreated inward, but he snatched my waist and pulled me close.

My stomach lurched, and I wanted to vomit or pass out. God, why did I feel this way? *And why couldn't I remember anything?*

The side of Lucien's body was firmly pressed against mine as his head rested on my shoulder. "Why are you so nervous? Testing the water is only natural after all," he murmured into my neck.

His voice was smooth and seductive as he ran a hand down my spine. With the other one, he pinched my cheeks and turned my head to face him.

I froze from shock.

From how forward Lucien was.

From how his body mashed against mine and how close our lips were to touching.

Each breath he took tickled my skin and sent gooseflesh down my body.

Lucien didn't sound like himself. He was as dense as a rock. He *would* never . . . not after all these years.

"You're . . . this isn't like you."

"How so?" Lucien let go of my cheeks and nuzzled his nose into my neck.

His soft lips brushed against my skin, but it felt rough and devoid of any real tenderness.

Chills rose all over my body as I tried to push Lucien back. "This isn't right," I said, a little more assertively.

The pounding on the door amplified with my throbbing temple as if they were in sync—both lashing out at me.

Lucien dug his nails into my back, and I cried out in pain as they punctured my skin. The warmth of the blood soaking my shirt quickly turned cold. I slammed my hands hard against his chest, desperate to push him off.

I lifted my chin and met his glowing eyes.

"How inconsiderate of you . . . even when I have been so attentive." Lucien's voice was laced with so much hostility as he squeezed his nails deeper into my ribs.

The pain spread through my body as if he dipped his nails in poison to ravage my mobility. "What the fuck are you?"

The smell of nectar became so strong it turned repugnant— until a heavy stench of moss and honey overtook my senses.

The knocking on the door wouldn't let up as the fierce pulsing muddled my concentration.

All my memories flooded back in ripples of agony.

Lucien flared his nostrils in annoyance and snapped his fingers.

The whole room warped and melted away along with his hair, face, and clothes as if someone doused him in acid and his skin dissolved off his bones.

Lucien morphed in front of me.

His deep red hair draped down to the ground as the floor spun and turned to stone. His blazing gold eyes twisted into an animalistic crimson as he emitted pure chaos from his body pulsating in red waves.

The man dressed in a metal-gray garb, concealing his body, but his bestial features couldn't be hidden. His thick black claws tore open my skin as he yanked them out.

I winced from the throbbing and anxiously looked around as Lucien's place transformed into a throne room with corpses adorned with rubies and diamonds impaled on the walls.

A pack of shadow-like creatures materialized by the man's side—morphing into short and round beings, baring their twisted, sharp fangs as their deep red eyes swallowed the darkness around them.

My vision landed on Kaschel who stood behind a glass-like barrier, smashing his fists against it.

My attention darted back to the creatures before me.

"Call me Fell," the man quipped, stroking the fox fur draped over him as his red eyes shone brighter than the creatures behind him.

Kaschel's hands and ankles were cuffed and chained, but I couldn't see where they trailed off to.

And the man had dodged my question—not that I could force him to answer and tell me what he was—when he held all the cards.

The man, Fell, craned his head at an unnatural angle as he pouted at me. "I blame it on that pesky Unseelie. Ruining a perfectly good show for himself. It would have been so entertaining to see his reaction. Don't you think so?" he huffed and rested one hand on his cheek. "I wanted to fool around a little more." He stalked over to a throne made of bones and jewels and plopped himself down. "So, what do you think you can offer me? You don't look like you have much except for the key in your pocket but I'm assuming you came all this way for the other one."

How did he know it was in my pocket?

I shuddered at the thought of the man coming any closer to me.

And what could I possibly offer him in exchange for the other key? I had nothing except for the clothes on my back and they weren't even mine!

Faes loved to bargain . . . Right? "A favor."

Fell slammed his hands down on his throne and his laughter filled the cave.

Fell's face twisted as his grin stretched all the way to his sharp cheekbones. His pearly white teeth were just as luminous as his bestial features. "Now why would I want a *favor?* People have come here offering me immeasurable treasures and entertainment, yet you come here with nothing and expect me to hand over what you desire? A foolish little witch." He nodded at the horde of creatures behind him, and they screeched in unison.

My ears couldn't handle the sheer volume, and I threw my hands up to cover my ears.

But silence fell as if I half imagined the noise.

The creatures didn't flinch or move. Not even another screech or snarl.

I cautiously uncuffed my ears and glared back at Fell.

This fae was delusional, and that meant he was even more dangerous.

"How about the Unseelie? I have a bone to pick with him, or should I be asking him what he has to *offer*?"

"No!"

God, Kaschel was right about me. I never thought about the repercussions of my actions.

"No?" Fell's playful tone turned venomous. "How about a wager? If you win, you get the key. *Simple*."

"And if I lose?"

Fell smiled, and it curled up to his feral eyes. "You become a part of my collection." He waved his hand toward his mounted *trophies* on the walls.

36
MURK AND RIPPLES

"Okay," I agreed, mid-panic.

I mean, what other options did we have?

"It's a deal." Fell clapped his hands, and it resounded off the walls.

With one blink, he launched me into an arena.

The rusted walls shot up for miles, dyed with gruesome scars of past battles. A crowd magically materialized—their cheers and chants made the bloodstained walls convulse.

Death lingered in the air, and one emotion resonated deep within me.

Dread.

Fell's voice echoed around us, but he remained hidden. "Should you fight the beasts behind the wall, or should I have you learn the true meaning of *fear*?"

I stepped back, my heart palpitated as Fell's words slithered across my skin.

A deep sigh encircled me. "You're taking too long. I'll make the decision for you." Fell hummed and its rhythmic patterns sounded like a clock ticking. He spoke again and it cut through the stadium. "If you reach the end, you succeed, but I have to warn you. My last participants didn't survive long," he sang out, his voice full of delight. "Good luck."

Roots broke loose from the soil, throwing me off balance.

They stitched together, creating mountainous walls, and enclosed me on all sides except for two.

Kaschel dropped next to me and rose to his feet. He looked entirely too good for the shit we just went through.

"What the hell did you agree to?" he snarled, cutting his words short. "You never make a deal with a fae, let alone the king of tricksters. *Fuck*." His jaw clenched and his neck muscles strained in response.

"Do you even hear the hypocrisy in what you said?!" I shot a glare at him. "And that man had shadow creatures behind him. Aren't shadows supposed to be your thing since you . . . I don't know . . . control them?!"

Kaschel's scowl darkened, and a flicker of an emotion I hadn't seen before crossed his face.

Was he . . . *pouting*? At a time like this?

"They are not mine to control." Kaschel huffed.

Shadow daddy, my ass. Levisus lied.

Massive metal doors slammed in front of the pathways—symbols burned and etched into both.

One door had a realistic grieving face with vibrant eyes, and its mouth was full of fangs. It looked like the embodiment of two conflicting emotions.

The other mask emitted a malevolent aura with its serpent-like eyes and tongue split in two as it hung out of its mouth.

I gulped. Did we really have to choose?

I couldn't read the chicken scratch symbols on it. So, how would we know which door was right?

I glanced back at Kaschel, hoping he looked more confident than I felt.

"If we split—"

My heart hammered violently as those words left his lips. "Fuck no. Have you never seen a horror movie?!" I looked at him with incredulity. "You never split up, and I'd be the first to die." I mumbled the last part.

"Movies are not real life." He creased his brows like I was the idiot here and not him.

"No. It's crazy. It seems like you quit thinking altogether." I enunciated the word *you*.

"If you long to be by my side that badly, you just had to say so, little flea," Kaschel said in a condescending tone as he stepped closer to the metal doors.

For real? "Sure. You figured me out." I rolled my eyes. "Strap me to your chest, baby. I can't stand being away from you."

His cool and collected attitude pissed me off. How could he be so . . . *insufferable*? Didn't he just say I royally fucked up our situation?

Kaschel ignored my remark and muttered under his breath. "I think it doesn't matter what path we take, there will be hardships regardless. Some will be worse than the others."

I leaned closer to the masks, analyzing them a little more carefully.

If we chose the vicious looking one, would it be too obvious we hoped it would be the opposite? Or do we need to take the one sporting two emotions, hoping our initial instinct was incorrect?

Oh my god, I had no clue.

Kaschel pressed his hand on my shoulder, and I jerked forward.

He lowered his gaze to me as I squeezed my hand to my chest to catch my breath.

"Calm yourself. You don't need to work that little brain so hard. We'll take the double-edged sword one. I'm guessing it could have two paths within it, and one will be the right choice."

Kaschel didn't have to elaborate to get his point across. I knew what he meant; if we chose the wrong path, we were done for.

But if he thought insulting me and reassuring me would help—it didn't.

My anxiety went through the roof now. "Fine, but you go first." I pointed at the door, ushering him forward.

I had no shame anymore. Not after all the hell I had gone through in the last forty-eight hours.

Kaschel shook his head and walked past me. "How thoughtful of you." He emptied a dry laugh from his throat.

"Well, this knight in shining armor can only save the princess so many times before their luck starts to run out," I said half-mockingly.

I called him a princess and useless. My mouth had a mind of its own, and it really wanted to throw hands at the worst times.

Kaschel smirked, and it was wickedly delicious as his face shimmered in excitement like it could devour me with just a glance. "You seem in high spirits despite your insipid decision-making skills."

Kaschel didn't utter another word and pried open the two-faced door and walked through as I followed behind him into the night.

I stepped forward and my foot sank; half-submerged in murky water, I faintly caught glimpses of Kaschel's back as he disappeared into the dark. The water thickened and I scrambled to match his speed.

Kaschel grunted, stopped, and turned back around. He appeared as a silhouette against the dim light until he closed the distance between us; his amethyst eyes radiated before me.

I didn't notice Kaschel's movement as he snatched my hand and dragged me behind him.

But I didn't complain or comment.

I knew with one misstep we could get separated, and I had no clue what awaited us.

Kaschel held my hand tightly in his—his rough skin against mine as I squeezed his in response—and my fears slowly melted away.

I didn't know if he heard my heartbeat settle and pick back up again as he squeezed my hand in return, or if he allowed his face to relax in the darkness, revealing his true desires.

But I wanted to know. I *craved* to know.

To see what he hid beneath that mask of his.

Was he ever genuine?

Was I?

A small splash rippled through the water, meters away from us.

Kaschel's grip tightened, and he gained momentum as I pushed myself to maintain the same speed.

37
SCARS AND RUIN

The thing about fear is it's irrational, shows itself at the worst times, and I couldn't always control it, no matter how many fucked up situations I had already been through—like now. Something slithered up my leg and bit me, and I latched onto Kaschel's back like a piranha jolting out of the water ready to take a chunk out of his ass.

"What are you doing?" Kaschel asked, confusion laced in his voice.

My face was smashed against his upper back, but I didn't need to see him to know what expression he wore.

His eyebrows had to be lowered; his mouth was probably slightly open like he wanted to say more but decided against it.

I didn't lift my head as my arms wrapped around his neck and my legs locked around his bare abdomen.

"My body aches, and I thought it was about time you did something useful," I lied through my teeth.

I was too embarrassed to say something brushed against me and bit me. I had no clue if it might come back for another taste, and I sure as hell wasn't stepping back down to find out.

But I was so far from okay: fatigued, delusional, hungry, and *fearful* of what might happen next. *Of the psychotic witch trying to torment me. Of the red moon. Of what lurked in the darkness.* Of pretty much everything that happened to me up until this point.

I was human. I couldn't magically get over it. I needed time to digest.

I needed stability. I needed a goddamn therapist.

God, I wished this nightmare would end. And I could wake up in my apartment, snuggled under my comforter. Safe and warm.

I apparently wanted a lot of things I couldn't have, and I never thought I would miss my shitty apartment, yet I did—immensely.

All the pressure had hit me like someone dropped a heavy anvil on my back and told me to run with it when all I craved was to bury my face into my bed—but I couldn't.

Instead, I carried on trudging through some creepy swamp land because some demented fae seemed to have way too much power and wished to play a twisted game with people's lives like we were his chess pieces—and he could easily take us out if he pleased and start over with the next sorry saps coming his way.

"I'm not sure I said you could ride me, but I'm not entirely against it."

I choked on my own spit as his words registered in my mind

and took me out of my thoughts.

Kaschel chuckled, and the low vibrations of his voice rippled through his body and tickled my chest.

"I'm glad you can make jokes at a time like this," I mumbled. My cheeks were on fire. I didn't want to think about *that*, at a time like *this*. We could die, yet he teased me again like he had no cares in the world when he literally called me stupid two seconds ago. He was unpredictable and annoying. "I mean, you can never be serious, can you?"

"Oh, that's rich coming from you. Now shall I continue carrying my chivalrous little flea? This princess is growing quite weary."

"Stop mocking me," I murmured against his shoulder blade.

"Ah, is my gallant flea finally comprehending things? How rare."

I laughed involuntarily and shook my head. "You're so annoying."

"I prefer quick-witted and dastardly arousing." He hummed, and I felt every vibration swell through his throat as he squeezed my thighs, bringing my body closer to his back.

I hated to admit it, but his ridiculous words relieved some of my uncertainty.

A smile crept across my face and all the tension drained from my body.

I cleared my throat and changed the subject. "I have no idea what to expect. Do you think it's another creature?" I asked, whispering the last part.

Kaschel chuckled again, and it stirred my heart and made it flip. "Why do you sound so nervous? Just do the same as before. You seem stronger now somehow, but there's a strange magic pulsing through your veins so I can't say for certain if it's for the best." Kaschel's voice turned icy as he dropped me.

I barely managed to catch myself and glared at him. "*Really?*"

"You should keep your wits about you and the dagger accessible. You never know when something might happen."

"Sure, super easy."

So he refused to have a normal conversation with me. And what strange magic?

"It's called multitasking, a skill you seem to lack," he said, curtly.

Holy shit. This stupidly hot capricious man had me burning with rage. How could he be so fickle? Could I believe anything he said, or was he saying things to humor himself and pass the time?

"Adeline Rose Winters. Do you need to be cleansed again?" a woman's voice buzzed from behind me.

I shuddered.

No. No. It wasn't her. I was hallucinating like before.

It couldn't be her. No, I knew it wasn't her.

This was Fell's plan.

I still couldn't breathe; it was like someone had pried open my ribcage and viciously played operator with my lungs, hitting all the sides as they plucked my insides out.

My chest tightened and my heartbeat lashed against my ribs and shook my resolve.

I couldn't stop myself from twisting my body to see if Fell decided to play tricks on me again.

I gulped hard as Mrs. Kelley crawled out of the murky water resembling a ghoul rising up to haunt the living. She craned her head, and it cracked and snapped back in place.

My breathing hitched again, and I clenched my nails into my chest. My breaths came in short and uncontrolled shots, like daggers digging into my throat.

"I can't do this. Not now." I gasped and shook my head, but she wouldn't disappear.

Kaschel grabbed my shoulders and squeezed. "What's wrong?"

My concentration warped, and my hands trembled relentlessly even with his firm grip grounding me.

Kaschel's voice gradually drowned out until he faded into the night, and the darkness swallowed us both.

A similar smell of mildew and bleach caressed my nostrils.

The clanking of metal chains resounded off the wooden floors as the coldness seeped into my bare legs. My shallow breathing was inaudible as footfalls rang from above.

38
FRAGMENTS

Step. *Clank*. Step. *Clank*. Step. *Clank*.

Mrs. Kelley rounded the corner, and my eyes widened. My body shook, and I fidgeted with my fingers until I couldn't take it.

I scratched and scraped; my nails dug into the floors, splinters impaling my fingertips as her clicking heels became unbearable.

Her blue eyes pierced the superficial light and shone like hell flames in the basement.

The place I so adamantly tried to forget.

That I desperately wanted to burn from my memories.

I thought I pushed them so far down I couldn't remember, yet here I was reliving it like I turned sixteen again.

One treacherous breath escaped me as her pungent vanilla fragrance mixed with cigarettes wafted into the room and turned my stomach inside out.

Her bobbed brown hair with streaks of gray bounced as she swayed closer to my side—not a single strand falling out of place, just as I remembered.

Mrs. Kelley clicked her tongue and arched her over-plucked brow. "You've been telling the neighbors of your sight again. Haven't you? Tsk-tsk. You know what this means, don't you?" she asked in a hushed tone, delicate and hollow against my ears.

I could never find the courage to confront her—not even now.

I turned away and lowered my head, avoiding her hostile stare.

In my mind, I screamed over and over again; she couldn't really be in front of me. It was a cruel trick. It would end eventually.

Mrs. Kelley drifted to my side and her red heels pointed in my direction. She crouched down and pinched my cheeks with her fake nails, drilling them into my soft skin.

She forced me to look into her dead eyes; her crow's feet even more pronounced as her leather skin sagged from all the hours she spent in the tanning bed.

She was too real and too close.

I squeezed my eyes shut and hoped my surroundings reverted back to the swamp.

Cautiously, I opened them, and she remained above me.

She pinched my cheeks harder from my lack of resistance. "Now you choose to act like a corpse? Are you mute now too?" she snipped. It was sharp and piercing, lashing at my skin.

She dropped her hand from my cheeks and stalked over to the plastic off-white table. She nabbed the leather rope and snapped it against the wooden floors.

I flinched from the cracking noise assaulting my ears.

Her eager eyes bore into mine as they sparkled with anticipation. "How many lashes will he accept as your repentance? Ten? Twenty? Or a hundred this time?" she mused, stroking the rope in her hand.

"Please make th-th-this stop." I scraped my fingernails against the wood.

I wasn't sure who I begged. If anyone could hear me. If Fell hid somewhere, relishing in my deepest nightmares.

My mind spun and unwound like thread. Losing all my sanity as she crept closer with the whip dragging behind her.

I had no time to consider my options for escaping, and the only blaring choice I could think of was Kaschel's dagger.

She walked past me, and without hesitation, I lunged at her.

I stabbed her side, but no blood came out.

Nothing.

I stumbled back from shock.

She turned back to face me, an evil glint revolving in her irises as she smiled and tipped her head. "A hundred it is." She snapped the whip again, and it cut through the calmness of the air.

My heart dropped and accelerated, hammering vehemently. My muscles liquefied as I clawed at my throat for air.

My vision tunneled as the whip slid behind me, and the dirty walls of the basement edged closer, imprisoning me.

I counted to five.

To ten.

To twenty before the first lash hit against me and shredded the back of my shirt.

I screamed in agony as the pain shot in waves throughout my body.

I thrashed against the chains, but my legs refused to respond.

The tears surged down my cheeks, and I choked on my breaths between each strike.

I wailed out again when the whip smacked my spine. I lost count as my skin went raw, and I barricaded myself within preserving what little sanity I had left.

I looked outward of my body, as if an outsider, witnessing myself chained against the floors.

A stranger to my futile howls of despair as Mrs. Kelley cackled at my pangs of suffering.

Time fell still or was forever moving, or maybe I couldn't stop spinning.

I didn't know how many more lashes it took for me to crumple to the ground, my cheek smashed against the floor facing the stairs. Until I contained nothing but emptiness.

My body could only handle so much before my eyes flickered open and closed.

I about lost it when reverberating footsteps came from above.

Was it *Fell* coming to finish the last fifty?

Tears pooled down my cheeks as a hint of a white blur shifted past me.

A heavy thud and warm blood pooled by my legs.

Someone stroked my forehead, and I dared steal a peek.

Kaschel crowded my vision and crouched beside me, his rough hands gently touched my legs, and I shrank further into the floors.

He busted the chains off my legs and hands; his delicate touch abandoned my skin, and I exhaled.

Unable to hold his gaze, I looked away and muttered, "It

didn't work." I stifled back a sob attempting to flee my mouth. "The dagger." I pushed myself to sound strong and put together, but my voice cracked and revealed my shattered self.

Kaschel didn't respond and snatched me from the ground, cradling me in his arms.

All the emotions I thought I could hold in poured out of me. My sobs turned into dry heaves as everything went mute. Kaschel carried me as if he could strip away all my sorrows.

He witnessed the room. The chill to the air. The lacerations across my back.

The scars.

"It's over." Kaschel finally spoke as he ran his fingers through my hair and instead of soothing me, I ugly cried harder into him.

I snuggled my face deeper into his chest, fully taking in his masculine scent of spice and earth.

"How did you get out?" I asked, my voice a delicate whisper.

My quivering body eased into his, and the drone of his heartbeat hypnotized me.

Kaschel pressed his forehead to mine. "I have been broken and molded back together more times than I can count." Kaschel didn't elaborate on what happened to him when we were apart, and I didn't think I needed to push him further.

Instead, I nodded my head as his warmth sent sunlight through me, clearing out the raging storm in my body.

I lifted my chin, and our eyes met.

Kaschel maintained his vacant expression. I couldn't tell what crossed his mind or what he thought of me now.

But I knew he finally caught a glimpse of the real me. The one I thought I could hide.

All the blemishes, imperfections, and trauma.

Everything I kept locked away so no one would know how truly damaged I was—laid bare in front of him.

39
DESIRE

Kaschel swerved and dodged trees as the air whipped around us. I buried my face farther into his chest as the cold air assaulted my shivering body.

I didn't know how long Kaschel ran as he carried me in his arms—but he never pressed me further, and after some time had passed, my stomach wrenched my insides.

The silence could only alleviate my mind for so long before I went stir-crazy.

We had an elephant in the room, yet he decided for the both of us to turn a blind eye and not address it?

Did he have nothing to say to me?

I was calmed by it at first, but after the prolonged silence, how could he not care?

Did I want him to care?

Was I too quick to let him sweep me off my feet?

Kaschel couldn't be Fell, but I still had to check.

"Are you real?" I asked, only realizing how stupid I sounded after the words left my mouth.

My paranoia was justifiable, though.

Kaschel narrowed his eyes and wrinkled his nose. "Do you want to continue groping me, or shall I stab myself a couple of times to satisfy your curiosity?"

"Maybe once or twice." I avoided his heated stare and sucked in a breath. "The stabbing," I clarified. "Not the groping."

Kaschel chuckled, and it echoed throughout the swamp.

The condensation thickened the air as the red maple trees surrounded us.

I wriggled as Kaschel held my body close. Even as I moved in his arms, he carefully avoided touching the throbbing wounds plaguing my backside.

The affliction against my skin tormented me as I shifted restlessly.

I sighed. I was being ridiculous. I knew that already, so why couldn't I stop myself?

"All right. Can you walk?"

I manifested all my confidence, but it still came out abrupt and squeaky. "Yes."

I avoided his complacently smug face, cleared my throat, and tapped my fingertips against my thighs.

Kaschel smiled and softly rested me next to a patch of white flowers that had spiked up, attempting to reach the sun despite their disadvantage of being enveloped in shadows.

I glanced back at Kaschel and watched him intently. He

reached into his back pocket, took out a switchblade, and clicked it open.

Kaschel kept his focus on the blade, shifting his stance to give me a better view of his forearm.

Kaschel's rugged voice stroked every inch of my body as he spoke. "My father was a Seelie. He was meant to be pure and of sound resolve." He paused and brought the blade to his arm and pressed it into his skin. Blood trickled out as he locked eyes with me. "When he had my brother, it was painstakingly obvious we were opposites in every way imaginable. The sun and the moon. Grabiel was light, and I was the shroud of darkness contaminating their divinity." Kaschel laughed, and it was deep and titillating as the blood dripped from his arm to the ground.

I drew in a breath, and I sat there mute as Kaschel spoke again, hanging on every syllable like he sang a hypnotic hymn, enchanting me with every word. "My father cheated on his queen, and I, the byproduct of his adulterated obsessions. My brother . . . well he was supposed to take the throne, but my uncle got him before his coronation." Kaschel let out another shaky laugh as he shook his head.

Kaschel closed his switchblade, put it back in his pocket, and ruffled his hair. "And what better way to gain the throne than blame the bastard? My uncle framed me for treason so he could ascend in my place. I mean, who would dare want the king of the Seelie moving through shadows? Condemned souls?"

Kaschel revealed a sliver of himself, and it didn't even scratch the surface. "Is that why you're so desperate to find the keys, so you could become the king of the Seelie?" I whispered.

I was so afraid if I spoke any louder, he would change the

subject and leave me in the dark again.

"I am no lightbringer, little flea. Nor does fauna rise in my wake." Kaschel stalked toward me and lowered his eyes as he towered above me, his stare intensifying as his lip tugged into an indelible smirk. "It trembles and convulses, repulsed by my wicked nature. I am darkness and depravity who brings only destruction and chaos. The Unseelie. Soiled, immoral—a fae of lust and terror—a fae constructed in my mother's image. The Seelie crown was never meant for me."

"So you were never a king?" I wasn't sure why I kept asking questions.

I wasn't sure why I hung on every word he said, or why I was so desperate to know more.

But I craved it more than anything.

Kaschel shrugged, and his face relaxed. "I was, but the politics between courts is always such a mess, and my uncle made sure to see me banished even when I was chosen for another crown." His chin dipped down, and his face carried an emotion I couldn't decipher. "So, what I'm trying to say is . . . I know what it's like to be betrayed by someone who was meant to protect you. By someone who was meant to foster your ambitions. Not someone who took pleasure in crushing them."

My heart stirred feverishly by his words, and I wasn't sure if I wanted to cry or if I yearned for a hug or *more*.

Out of everyone who filtered in and out of my life—why was it only him who understood me . . . *who saw the real me?*

40
GREED OR SORROW

Kaschel was an enigma I couldn't quite figure out. One minute he was cold and distant, and the next, he said all the right things to make my heart pound just as furiously as when we were in danger.

It was unsettling.

I wanted to pressure him for more information about his life—and his past—but I also knew we were at a dead end.

Nothing could go any further between us. We kissed by mistake. The heat of the moment and nothing more.

So why was it seared into my memory and playing on repeat at a time like this?

I couldn't afford to go soft, not now. I still had so much to finish—like saving Lucien.

We were no more than a few lustful glances and rising heat.

And the heat between us would simmer down eventually, and I wouldn't think twice about him after that.

Not his amethyst eyes seizing my world with just a glance. Not his charismatic smile sending shivers down my body when he revealed a hint of amusement. Not his alabaster hair that had grown on me; I wasn't sure when it happened or if I had always found it captivating.

Now I longed to trace his scar with my fingertips from his bottom lip to his chest without scaring him away. What were the stories behind each one marking his immaculate body? When did he get them? And why did he have fresh lacerations?

Why didn't I notice them before?

I knew how I should and shouldn't feel.

So why was he dangerously close to my lips, and why did I have the urge to taste them again?

With everything I knew, why couldn't I resist his lowered gaze roaming all over my body?

His bare chest was exposed and in front of me. I craved to feel his warmth pressed against me. To consume me.

I wanted to be consumed.

To have the chance to forget all my sorrows and worries as we explored every inch of each other, indulging in our carnal appetites. But the nagging in my mind wouldn't allow me to fully give in to him.

So what if he had shown me a fraction of who he was? It didn't mean I knew him or should trust him.

But if we kissed again, would I hate myself more for the inevitable? Would we be a passing flame burning brightly but fading out just as quickly?

Was I only lonely and desperate for company? *Was he as damaged as me but . . . better at hiding it?* They do say birds of a feather flock together.

Kaschel brushed my hair behind my ear and cupped my cheek. I drew in a breath and melted into his hand.

He stroked his thumb under my jaw as his restless stare set me ablaze.

Kaschel's rough voice caressed every part of my body as he whispered, "Are you okay now?"

I let out a dry laugh. "How many times are you going to ask me?"

"Until you mean it."

"Okay, okay. I'm fine. I'm good." God, he was being too gentle. *Too caring.*

Kaschel had to stop, or I would start to believe the sincerity in his tone and the hunger in his eyes.

He was tempting me to shatter all the walls I built around myself just so I could get one more kiss.

Kaschel was an error in my system I couldn't clear out. No matter how many times I told myself his affection wasn't real, my body still reacted to his touch, *his voice*, and the vast emotions churning in his vibrant eyes as he waited with bated breath to taste me.

I lifted my chin as Kaschel grazed his thumb over my bottom lip.

We looked at each other, both of us too stubborn to make a move.

Kaschel relinquished his pride and pressed his lips to mine. His gentle touch turned desperate.

Desperate to be closer, craving more and more.

My icy heart thawed from each stroke of his hands against my skin as they explored my body and skimmed past my hips, resting below the sides of my ribcage.

We greedily consumed one another as each touch and gasp for air exhilarated us.

He nibbled on my bottom lip and ecstasy shot through me as I brushed my fingertips across his shoulders and moved them slowly down his firm back, tracing over every muscle and raised scar along the way.

I pulled away from him, but not because I wanted to.

I wanted him so badly, but what I wanted and needed were two separate matters.

We didn't have time to drown our sorrows. We had to worry about making it out of here alive.

Kaschel didn't say anything as we let the silence eat away at us.

It's like Kaschel already knew what crossed my mind, and his mask concealed his emotions again.

Any tenderness I saw, or believed I saw, vanished.

🌙

The magenta night embellished the sky with flecks of gold as the vine walls closed in on us—until we walked a path leading in only one direction.

We didn't talk about what had happened, and I was fine with that. Relieved even. It would only unnecessarily complicate things, and my life was already complicated enough.

So we concentrated on what was ahead since with one wrong

step the possibility of getting impaled by arrows or falling to our deaths was extremely high.

The soil beneath us shifted and contorted to the will of its creator. I almost fell multiple times, but Kaschel snatched my waist before I plummeted to the bottom.

My adrenaline wore off, and the agonizing pain returned tenfold.

My legs screamed as my back stung with each gust of wind. I wasn't sure how much longer I could last in this state.

"Did you feel that?" Kaschel scanned the area.

"Feel what?" I scrunched my face, unsure of what he heard or saw.

"The trembling of the ground? It's getting closer."

I sure as hell didn't feel the ground moving beneath us, no more than usual.

"I think you might be—" I glanced behind us and gasped in horror. "Holy fuck."

41
TREACHERY

swarm of gigantic centipede corpses crawled toward us. At least they looked like centipedes as they desperately piled over each other, crashing and cramming themselves against the ground and walls.

They ravenously surged and screeched collectively as a thick slimy fluid poured out of their disfigured mouths.

Kaschel stood there stunned like me. "What is wrong with this psycho?!" I screamed as the corpses scurried closer to us, accelerating their speed with each unbearable shriek.

"Archaic magic abides by no laws!" Kaschel yelled out like I would somehow understand his words as he snatched my hand and hauled me behind him.

We fled until the walls shifted closer together.

It was like everything in this crazy world wanted to squeeze the life out of us.

Our pathway started to barricade us in, becoming smaller and smaller until we had to flee by crawling on all fours.

My breaths were shallow as the cramped space had my head spinning. I felt more claustrophobic as the spiked thorns on the vine walls dug into my sides and shoulders.

I was so thankful Kaschel let me go first, but a horrid thought entered my mind. *What if they reached us and snatched Kaschel and dragged him away?*

What if I was next?

The vines convulsed around my shoulders, and I lost confidence by the second.

A dim light shone from a distance, and I hoped to god it led out of this monster-ridden labyrinth.

I couldn't deal with this shit anymore.

I reached the end, stood up, and peeked back at Kaschel who was right behind me.

He rubbed his temples and sighed.

The same doors from the beginning of this hell loop.

But this time the massive metal doors had different symbols burned and etched into them, and now, I could understand it.

The grieving-face door with a mouth full of fangs suspended before us. The words under it written in silver. *Still or be steel. Both weep for cordial affairs. Rust will be anew if you seek the truth. One for two, ruin awaits if uncertainty brews.* I looked at the other door with the mask, serpent-like eyes, and the dangling tongue split in half. *Two hearts, one beats, and the other pumps. Two of one, desire for none. Let it be known one bleeds and the other sows.*

What the hell does that even mean?

On the verge of hyperventilating, I peeked over my shoulder, and the centipedes increased their speed, burrowing faster.

Kaschel unsheathed his sword and sliced the ones shoveling their way out of the tunnel, lunging at us.

Kaschel split them in half one by one as a green substance oozed and sizzled out of them.

A heavy rancid smell permeated the air with each killing blow Kaschel landed.

"Choose one, and I'll be right behind you!" Kaschel swung his sword again and again.

Another one hissed as it squeezed its appalling body through the hole before Kaschel decapitated it.

I panicked as I looked at him and back at the two doors.

The first one seemed like the only option with a somewhat promising outcome if I understood it correctly. *Right?*

I pushed open the grieving-masked door and prayed for the first time in my life to not let it be another trap.

Kaschel stumbled in after me as the room we left filled to the brim with centipedes.

I slammed the door shut behind us and huffed for air.

Kaschel was drenched in the neon green slime while I only had little bits of it spattered on my clothes.

A slow clap came from above.

It evolved, louder and faster.

I glanced all around us, and the sky melted away and morphed back into Fell's throne room.

Fell looked the same, lounging lazily on his throne of bones and jewels with his horde of creatures craning their necks behind him. "You guys are quite the entertaining pair," he said, and it made my whole body convulse.

Fell glided to our side.

Fell seized my chin with his claws and tilted it so fast, he caught me off guard. "What a treat. You chose the same door as Larisa."

My eyes widened. "What do you mean?"

Fell shrugged.

Kaschel snatched Fell's hand that touched my chin. "Enough games. We did what you asked."

"Hmm. She did." Fell inclined his head as he inspected Kaschel with vexation. Fell clicked his tongue. "A bet is a bet." He snapped his fingers, and the silver key in the shape of a hexagon with an engraved crescent moon manifested in front of us, floating in the air. "Now, Adeline. Will you make the same mistake your mother did?" Fell's toothy grin devoured his whole face, revealing his wickedly sharp teeth. "Take what you desire, but you must leave something of the same weight in stature."

"That wasn't the deal."

"Oh, child. I said you get your prize if you win. *Did I not?*"

I glanced back at Kaschel, but I couldn't read his expression. It was strategically hidden—all his emotions carefully stored behind a tough front.

I held eye contact with Kaschel as I spoke. "As I said before, I don't know what I could offer."

"Not what. *Who.*"

My heart thrashed against my chest as my pulse went wild. "What? No. He's not mine to give," I choked out.

"Are you certain?" Fell hummed as he twirled a lock of my brunette hair. "I see the only one who holds power is *you.*" His voice turned to venom as he yanked my hair by my roots and pulled my face inches from his fangs. My eyes flickered to Kaschel, but he was unmoving. "Is your resolve strong as steel, or will you falter because of one insignificant *fae*?" Fell asked and his words rattled me to my core.

"I can't. I can't have someone trapped for a decision I made." I tried to say it with confidence, but it was weak and barely audible.

"Take the key and run, Adeline. I won't say it again," Fell whispered into my ear. His hot breath burned against my neck, and I recoiled in disgust. "Or neither of you are leaving my prison."

A whirlwind of emotions filtered into my body as I snatched the key without thinking.

Fell broke into a manic fit of laughter, and it bellowed throughout the throne room. "Cold-hearted just like Larisa too. You truly are your mother's daughter."

"What do you mean? What do you know about my mother?" I could barely hear my voice as the pounding of my heart deafened his cruel taunts.

"Who else begged me to hide the key? She sacrificed so much and now, it's all for nothing. Who knew her blood would be the one to ruin all her hard work! I mean, the only one who could take it from me is someone of kin. But what are the odds *you* found *me*?"

So my mother had been here, but why did she give the key to some monster like him?

I was about to speak again when the ground beneath me shifted and crumpled inward.

I caught a glimpse of Gren and the others from below.

I glanced back at Kaschel. I opened my mouth like I could say something, but I couldn't articulate the right words as he snapped out of whatever trance Fell had cast on him. His face was riddled with confusion until his eyes landed on the key in my hand.

Kaschel's expression twisted into pure enmity as the radiating fury engulfed him.

A sharp pang in my chest cemented itself within me. I clenched my heart like it would suppress the pain, but it only made it worse.

I didn't owe Kaschel my loyalty.

I didn't owe him anything, but my chest still constricted as I watched the rage swallow him.

I wished Kaschel screamed or shouted, or at least told me how vile I was. I could handle the yelling and name-calling—but not the silence.

And nothing could have prepared me for what came next.

Kaschel's demeanor turned placid as the vines snatched and crawled up all his limbs and slammed him against the wall with all skeletons adorned in diamonds and rubies, positioning him as the centerpiece.

Kaschel hung there like a spectacle for all to witness.

"Wait!" I cried out.

I didn't truly grapple with what I had done to him until it was too late—until everything slipped through my fingers and faded from view as I fell through the floor, and dropped to the front entrance of where it all began.

42
A BREWING STORM

I wasn't prepared. *Not now* and especially not when that crucial moment came, and I desperately needed to stay level-headed. Someone's life hung in the balance, and I was the puppeteer who held all the strings. Maybe I could have saved Kaschel but instead, I cut all his lines and let him take the fall.

I made a judgment call where I knew no matter what route I took the outcome would never be in my favor, yet I couldn't help but be repulsed by my actions.

Now I had to live with myself for what I had done.

"Where is he?" Ryas asked, concern leaking from her voice. When I stood there silent, I could see the wheels turning in her mind as she pursed her lips. "Where is Kaschel?" she asked again with more malice.

Levisus stepped closer to Ryas's side. His deep purple eyes harbored a despondency in them as he ruffled his short silver hair. He was a wreck, a stark difference from when I first met him.

Levisus lowered his dark brows as he placed a hand on Ryas's shoulder. "Hey, calm down. There has to be a solid explanation. Right?" He glanced in my direction, and all I could do was stare blankly at him.

Levisus was acting sensible, and I honestly didn't think he could be anything other than an overly flirtatious playboy.

Ryas huffed in aggravation as she crossed her arms.

Before I could say anything, Gren stepped in front of me and blocked them from prying any further. His obsidian hair reflected the sun's brilliance—and I lost it as an ache gradually gnawed at my insides and twisted my stomach until I felt nothing but a numbing sensation.

I buried my face into his shirt hoping to feel something, anything but it was only cold and relentless.

And just when I thought I was in control of all my emotions, Gren wrapped his strong arms around me and patted my head, and I lost all control.

He didn't utter a single word as I unleashed all my miseries on him.

He squeezed me tight, and I nestled my head more into his chest. I couldn't form a coherent sentence or answer. It was like every time I tried, my throat constricted.

And I couldn't face Ryas or Levisus in this state.

Not now. Not when it was all too fresh.

Levisus lost any chance of setting his brother free, and I had no idea how far Ryas's connection to Kaschel went or *how deep*.

All I knew was I was no better than Jared.

No better than the killer of the mangled corpse we saw in the cabin. No better than the witches stalking and tormenting me.

No better than the trickster bastard himself.

I played into his trap. Hook, line, and sinker.

I might as well have taken Kaschel's sword out of its sheath and stabbed him in the back with it.

Again and again and again.

My mind twisted what I did, attempting to justify it, like sacrificing someone else was forgivable. *You barely knew Kaschel. You had no other choice. Kaschel wouldn't have given you the keys if you asked. Lucien was waiting for you. Have you forgotten? You still needed to save him.*

My lungs revolted against me, and I gasped in between my cries of pain.

A pity party for one when I knew better. I *knew* crying wouldn't solve any of my problems.

It wouldn't reverse my despicable choices, and it wouldn't bring Kaschel or Lucien back.

I squeezed Gren harder and tried to calm down and think of my next course of action. My face was red and puffy as I wiped the tears staining my cheeks.

Gren's body tensed as I broke away from him. His dark brows creased as he fiddled with the seams on the bottom of his gray shirt.

He looked distraught.

A zap shot through my wrist and shifted to my fingertips.

I looked down at my hand, and the mark Kaschel gave me flared like a flame, the crescent moon glowing silver until a searing sensation assaulted my skin. I winced and threw my hand behind my back, afraid Levisus and Ryas would understand what it meant.

I stood on my tiptoes and whispered into Gren's ear, "We need to leave. *Now*." I leaned back, and he straightened his posture and unwound the tension in his body.

Now his face held a determined glint.

Gren nodded and before I could tell him what I was thinking, he said, "Hold tight."

He scooped me off my feet and ran for the cliff. I squeaked as he propelled us off the edge.

I squeezed my eyes shut, waiting for the inevitable plunge to our death. If he could morph back, how would he carry my weight?

Seconds passed, and the wind whipped around us.

I blinked, and Gren's hair rippled in waves as his matching massive crow wings carried us through the sky. His iridescent feathers shimmered a deep violet when the sun touched them.

I didn't know how long we soared through the sky, but the cool air lashing at my wounds didn't do anything except make me quiver in agony.

Gren dipped down, and I clenched my nails into his arms.

It took everything in me not to scream as the ground closed in on us.

A soft thud vibrated off the earth as Gren landed us near a gas station with a Motel Five right behind it.

A familiar aura hung around and it bore a striking resemblance to my apartment complex. All the people hovering by their rusted and chipped-paint vehicles dealing who knows what from the trunks was an uncanny parallel.

"We're far enough, and the wind should mask our scent."

"You don't think they're right behind us?" I asked in a hushed tone.

Gren held an empty gaze, and I wasn't sure what he thought.

He sighed. "No. I think they have more important things to worry about."

Kaschel. *Yes.* Why would they come after us when they have no idea what happened to him?

"You're right." I groaned. I flipped my phone out and the date read Wednesday, October 29th. I snapped my head back to Gren. "We were trapped for three days?"

I didn't notice until now the dirt clinging to Gren's shirt and pants, his look of exhaustion, and the heavy bags under his dark eyes.

Gren shifted uncomfortably. "Yeah, and the fact I couldn't get through the barrier . . . and I had to wait while you were trapped somewhere with . . . *him*." He cleared his throat. "The only thing that kept me sane was the fact I knew you were still alive because . . . I was still here." Gren beamed.

I returned his smile, but it was forced, and I probably looked exactly like the three-day-old roadkill a few steps away from us.

I held my phone tightly in my hand and choked on my spit, fully aware of how close we were to facing Valeria.

My hands trembled at the horrifying realization. "It's . . . the red moon tomorrow."

"We can't go in unprepared."

I ran my chipped nails and raw fingertips through my hair as I tapped my foot. "I know. You need to teach me something, anything."

Gren shook out his hands, bent down, and snatched a couple of leaves.

I eyed him with concern and curiosity. "What are you doing?"

Gren shifted his free hand over the leaves, and a swirl of black mist devoured them and quickly evaporated and left dollars in the palm of his hand.

"You need food and rest before we do anything. You look awful."

A loud chuckle erupted from my throat.

Of course, I looked like shit. Who wouldn't after everything I went through? "Thanks, but I'm fine. We have to keep going. I need to prepare." I shoved Gren's chest to make him move, but he stood there, unbudging.

I huffed in frustration.

"No. You're exhausted, wounded, and emotional. You need rest." Gren shifted his feet and shoved the money into his back pocket. "And are you certain you have to do what Valeria says?"

My focus went back to Gren.

How could he say something like that? After everything I have done? I couldn't fold and throw in the towel now.

"I can't let them torture Lucien. He's the only family I have, and he wouldn't be in this mess if . . . if he didn't know me." Another unstable laugh fled my mouth, and I shook out my hands and pressed my pointer finger to his chest. "I've already done horrible things I can't take back. I need to see this through. He needs me." I swung around and choked back the sobs threatening to spill out of my throat, but I couldn't calm down.

Gren's words ignited a fury within me. It pulsated in violet waves like an electric current shooting through my veins.

Blood flooded my vision as an intense anger shattered me from within. It churned and fed all the rotten emotions I buried, flailing back alive against my skin with thousands of needles puncturing me all at once.

My flesh burned from the inside out as the needles burrowed deeper.

I screamed out in agony as all my bleak emotions came alive, sinking their venomous fangs into me and cementing themselves into my flesh and bones. The crescent mark on my hand pulsated violently as I tossed my head back.

I was rotting from within as the pangs of brutality radiated through me, convulsing inside me like a deadly storm raging on until my vision went black.

The energy traveled up my throat and through both my arms and legs as if coerced out of me, and my body lightened under the release.

My eyes fluttered open, and Gren squeezed me into a hug, my arms frozen at my sides.

His firm body against mine—strong and determined.

Gren pulled away and spoke, but I couldn't hear a goddamn thing as my body crumpled under the weight of gravity, and I lost all the strength to stand.

Gren caught me before my knees slammed against the asphalt.

I wanted to push Gren away and ask him what the fuck was happening, but my eyes rolled back, and all I could do was let the beckoning darkness swallow me whole.

43
IN SPITE AND ANGUISH

Startled awake from an intense throbbing against my skull, I rubbed my face and scanned the room. The dim lighting produced a clean look, but the black gunk at the top of the cream walls stuck out. Most likely from chain smoking since a strong odor of cigarettes plagued the motel room, presumably from its last hundred occupants.

I wanted to recoil inward from the putrid smell and vacate this place, but my whole body ached so badly I could hardly move.

I struggled to get myself in a sitting position as I glanced down at the firm mattress with its cheap floral-designed comforter draped over me; a stained mahogany nightstand sat beside it with my phone on top.

My eyes glided over to the bay view window behind a circular table with one chair pulled out. A thick layer of dust rested on the plastic blinds. Only a minuscule amount of light filtered through them, but I could still catch glimpses of dirt particles floating in the air from each ray creeping in.

I snatched my phone, but I had no messages from Lucien despite finally having service.

So they took him.

My chest tightened as if someone pinned me down and compressed my lungs. My breaths intensified as each bit of air left my throat.

Faint footsteps grew closer from outside.

Someone stopped at the other side of the door and fiddled with the handle.

Tremors bombarded my nerves as apprehension clouded my mind.

I panicked and launched out of bed. I snagged the burnt orange lamp, yanked it out of its plug, and moved behind the door.

I couldn't guarantee it was Gren. From what I learned up to this point, I had to be cautious.

The door clicked open as a shadow engulfed the room.

I raised the lamp over my head and swung at the ebony waves bouncing past me.

Almost scraping the side of Gren's face with the lamp, I sighed and slid against the wall, crumpling to the ground.

God, I was so paranoid.

Gren held a brown bag in his hand with a pool of grease soaking the bottom.

So he left to get food.

Gren turned away from the bed and his eye landed on me—on the ground, clenching the lamp against my chest.

Gren scrunched his eyebrows together and crouched by my side. "Are you all right?"

"Fuck no. Not being in control was . . . terrifying," I confessed, and I couldn't believe I let those words spill out of my mouth. I cleared my throat, placed the lamp next to me, and pointed at the brown bag Gren held. "I'm famished. Is that what I think it is?"

Gren opened and closed his mouth like he had no idea what he should address first.

He stood up, walked over to the wobbly table, and set the food on it.

He took a seat and stared at me with the same blank expression, and he shook his head. "Come eat. I know it's been a while."

He tore open the bag and set a flimsily wrapped burger opposite to him.

He peeled his open and started eating.

Gren sat, silent, and I knew he was the quiet type, but this felt different. *Strange.*

I rose from my feet, walked over to the table, and plopped down beside him. "What happened?" Gren didn't say a word, and I pushed him further. "I mean, how did you stop me?" I looked up from my burger, anticipating an answer, but he stayed tight-lipped.

Gren finished his food, wiped his hands on the napkin beside it, and glowered at me. A mixture of anger and something else I couldn't pinpoint.

Gren averted his glare and rubbed the back of his neck as he slouched more into the chair. "You lost control." He licked his lips as he took a deep breath. His darkened gaze refused to meet me. "So, I absorbed your magic until you were able to calm down."

I eyed him. "Did something else happen?"

Gren appeared shocked for a brief moment and concealed his emotions again. "Not particularly."

Gren was hiding something, but if I kept pressing him now, I knew he would never tell me.

It had to be on his time. He would trust me, eventually. Or so I kept telling myself.

I threw my head back and rubbed the sides of my face. I was so exhausted from these games. "All right, I trust you."

A flicker of dismay enveloped Gren's face before he started talking again. "Do you want to shower?"

"Only if you come with me," I teased him.

I tried to lighten the mood, but it turned sour on my tongue, and I felt like a creep.

God, why did I always have to joke around at the worst times?

Gren only leaned his head. "I'm not entirely familiar with the customs of how humans bathe, but if you need my help, I'll do my best." He blinked at me with a trusting sparkle in his eyes as the joke went way over his head.

I snorted so loud I shocked myself and gave Gren a weak smile. "I was only teasing. I didn't mean it."

Gren sighed again. "You're as odd as I remember."

I scoffed. "Are you saying I was a weird little girl?" I tried to decipher if he was messing around or if he truly meant it.

Gren's frown told me he meant every word. "Extremely."

I laughed again. "Says the talking bird that turned human."

"But I'm not human or a bird."

KING OF THE UNSIGHTLY

"You know what I mean."

My body eased as I relaxed into the chair, but my mind wouldn't let go of the cluttered thoughts, and I wished to silence them somehow.

Gren raised a brow, and his dark eye bore into me. "Go shower, and I will teach you what I know from the days I spent living with you and your mother."

My eyebrow perked up in excitement. "You mean it?"

"What would I gain from lying, Adeline?"

44
FOREBODING TIES

The dirt and grime rolled off my body and swirled around the shower drain until it fell through.

I didn't know how long I stared—or how long I stayed in a fetal position in the shower—as the steam suffocated the cramped bathroom, but it was oddly comforting.

What would it take to break me until there was no return? Wondering when or how it would happen was always a thought that heckled me . . . until now.

Here I was—shattered into a million pieces and I would have a hell of a time putting myself back together. I was more likely to cut myself on the shrapnel than become whole again.

So I buried my unwanted feelings as before, digging a metaphorical hole in my mind and barricading the worthless emotions in a coffin as I stood above it—shoveling the dirt on top until I suffocated the noise and their ruthless taunts.

I couldn't let their constant pestering stop me from pushing forward.

Right now, I had to think about my main objectives—learn magic, save Lucien, and trick the bitch, Valeria. All within a twenty-four-hour period. Doable . . . *I fucking hoped.*

The small white towel hanging on the wall at least looked like they washed it with bleach or took it to the dry cleaners, so I grabbed it and dried myself off.

I wiped the mirror with it and saw my god-awful reflection staring back at me.

I slept, but I still had bags under my eyes, and if anyone decided to look at me for longer than a second, they would see what a wreck I was.

My brown hair felt thinner than my patience from all the stress-induced shit I went through. Luckily, I didn't look malnourished too.

I turned away from the mirror and slid the new clothes Gren bought from the tourist shop down the road. But they were no better than my previous outfits. A small cotton-candy-blue shirt with a mermaid on it and black letters read *Siren's Cove*, and a pair of cargo pants to match.

I groaned. Would I ever be able to wear a normal outfit again?

The shirt fit like a crop top, and the baggy cargo pants rested right below my hips. I felt like I was thrown into the early 2000s with this fashion disaster.

I didn't give myself another glance as I stepped out of the bathroom. Steam followed me out as I saw Gren still sitting at the table with his arms crossed, gazing at the slightly closed blinds.

For a second, I could have sworn his eye flickered a deep gold when the light hit it, but it vanished just as quickly and went back to its dark hue.

Gren's eye fell on me, and his unreadable expression clouded with so many emotions, unlike his typical vacant look.

It left me feeling skeptical of what truly went through his mind.

"Do you feel better?" Gren asked.

His tanned complexion was a contrast against the cream walls. He stood out even more with his sharp features and toned arms. By society's standards, he looked like a painting come to life with his slender build and striking jawline, and the scar down his left eyelid trailing all the way to his jaw.

It was still weird to see Gren like this. It made me miss when he gave me reassuring pats on the back as a somewhat cute bird. Like an emotional support animal, but now I wouldn't dare call him that.

"A bit." I walked over to the table. "But it's time. No excuses." I leaned down, smacked one hand on the table in front of Gren, and gave him my best I-mean-business face. "And I won't take no for an answer."

Did I have to be this straightforward and aggressive? Did crows have some weird power dynamic where I had to assert my dominance before I got my way? Gren always disappeared, and I couldn't let him weasel his way out of teaching me.

Gren looked at me with a hint of amusement; his upper lip moved, and it made him look dark and suggestive.

No, I had to be imagining things.

Was this the first time I witnessed Gren genuinely smile?

Gren stood up and he skimmed me over.

His voice felt deep and earnest as he spoke. "Okay, but it's going to hurt like the first time."

"What?"

Gren smirked, and I looked away to regain my thoughts.

"Place your hands on mine." Gren reached out, his palms facing up. I did exactly as he asked, and he continued. "Now, breathe in and out, and try to imagine yourself pushing the energy through your chest to your fingertips."

I eyed him with suspicion but listened and inhaled and exhaled slowly.

But no energy flowed through me. The only thing within my chest was a gnawing pain.

I jerked my hands away. "This weird breathing exercise isn't working." I crossed my arms like a child. I felt ridiculous, but I didn't have the luxury of time to be bad at this.

I uncrossed my arms and loosened the tension in my body, shaking my hands.

Gren ran his fingers through his ebony hair and let out a dry laugh. "Trust me, okay? Try it again." He kept his hands in place, waiting for me to reach out. "You know, your mother was from a coven that didn't need to use their grimoires to cast magic, and you clearly have the same talent. So, humor me, and try it again."

It's like Gren knew my weakness.

When he talked about my mother, as much as I resented her . . . I craved to know more. *Who was she? What was she like?* Even if she stole all my memories. I had a familiar ache I couldn't free myself of.

"I'm just impatient. So, don't worry. I'll keep trying even if my eyes bleed again."

"No, we can't have you exhausted before the gathering. I'm going to grab us some more food."

"Can you get some ice cream? Rocky road?"

I had been craving ice cream all damn week, and by god I was going to eat my comfort food before I had to throw myself in further danger.

Gren chuckled, low and pleasing against my ears. "Sure thing. I'll be right back."

45
RED MOON

I clenched my hands into fists, attempting to clear my chaotic mind but to no avail. I took another deep breath and released all the pressure in my body.

A spark ignited within me as I willed it to move through my arms and to my fingertips.

A violet light shot out of my hands and settled back down as it hissed like a flame underneath the red moonlight.

The pulsing magic on my pointer finger looked like fire, but the blazing inferno didn't consume me. Instead, a warmth blanketed me.

I actually did it! But what did Gren say I had to do again? I pointed my finger at the rusted black car in front of our motel room with a can of soda on its hood and imagined myself propelling the can forward, but only a small spark flickered at my fingertip and vanished.

I pointed my finger again for shits and giggles after thousands of failed attempts, but it was more like a flick of the wrist.

A violent lightning bolt shot out of my hand and collided with the car.

A rumbling clamor enveloped the whole parking lot as I stumbled to the ground and landed ass first.

The blaring noise set all the car alarms off, and they hollered in unison as steam rose from where I struck the car.

I shuffled to my feet, scurried back into the motel room, and slammed the door behind me.

I sighed and shook out the last remaining spark on my pointer finger.

The violet energy swirled in the air, disappearing into the dark.

Honestly, why couldn't my magic be the color of the sky or swamp green or—*anything other than purple?*

I hated how it reminded me of Kaschel's hypnotic gaze. It's like every time I used it thoughts of him plagued my mind.

I slapped my cheeks and pushed all the useless thoughts of him away.

Now was not the time to think about that man.

I popped open a blind and a swarm of people filtered into the parking lot—glancing around—confused as to why someone's car got struck by lightning when the night sky glowed with all the constellations, not a cloud in sight.

Thankfully, no one witnessed me cast magic.

I really didn't have the time to bring any unwanted attention to myself. But I also didn't think I could create much damage. I thought I would barely move the can, let alone flatten half the car.

My fingers tapped nervously on the table, and I groaned as I watched all the people curiously talking among each other, asking if anyone saw what happened.

I peeked at the alarm clock next to the nightstand, and it read 11:30, so close to midnight.

I rubbed the nape of my neck, trying to relieve the pressure. All the stress finally caught up to me and ate away at my body with each passing second.

The red moon ominously shined down on me with peeks of crimson light filtering through the dusty room.

My anxiety skyrocketed, and I tapped the heels of my boots on the floor.

What was taking Gren so long? I had been waiting for him all day. I didn't want the ice cream anymore. I needed a drink or five.

The door handle jiggled before Gren cracked the door open and slid inside.

He lowered his brow with a slight smirk. "Did you have a vendetta against someone? Their poor car was demolished." He popped open a blind, whistled, and looked back at me. "That hard-working civilian probably lost everything."

I rolled my eyes. When did Gren ever joke around?

"I'm sure the only important thing they lost was some spare change and fast-food wrappers." I straightened my posture. "It's almost time."

Gren nodded his head, mechanically. "I know."

I frowned. I wanted to believe this would be the hardest part, but life loved to throw curveballs excessively at my face, so I highly doubted it.

"Okay," I said weakly.

"If anything feels off, I will stall them long enough for you and Lucien to run away."

I raised my head; the confusion furrowed into my brows as a hint of anger swirled in my irises. "No. I would never leave you."

"Are you worried about me?"

"Of course!"

Gren snatched the two keys from my palm and leaned so close I could see the swarm of emotions flicker like stars in his eye. "You really shouldn't."

Gren's reply stunned me.

What did he mean? I thought we were in this together!

I placed my hand on his firm shoulder. "Why?"

Gren's expression turned sour as he looked away. "I have half your soul. That's more than I deserve. So please, don't sacrifice for someone else's sake again." He smiled brightly, and if I was an outsider looking from afar at our conversation, I would have thought his expression was from pure joy.

But I knew that wasn't the case. If he thought his hollow look would calm my nerves . . . He was dead wrong.

I squeezed Gren's shoulder.

I couldn't always be the one losing someone, but for now I indulged Gren and told him what he wanted to hear. "All right, I promise."

My face tightened with the same smile he gave me. A smile layered with a multitude of emotions where if he wanted to reveal the truth hidden behind it, he needed to peel the deceptive layers away, one by one.

"Good. Now, are you ready?"

I laughed, and it was dry and bitter against my tongue. "As ready as I'll ever be, I guess."

The mirror was placed in my pocket when I pulled it out and traced the silver thorns wrapped around the skull, and gently moved my fingertips against the three golden vipers spilling out of its mouth and eyes.

I squeezed the mirror in my palm and expelled all the air filling my lungs.

The vipers came alive and wrapped around my arms, and before I reacted, they sank their fangs into my flesh. The room spun around me as Gren snatched my hand before I fell backward.

"You have the keys, right?"

Gren patted his pockets anxiously and searched.

His face twisted with worry, and his lips moved, but I couldn't hear a sound as darkness shot out of my fingertips and surrounded every inch of the room until it devoured us.

46
TAUNTING ADELINE

The darkness dissipated into the night sky and forced us out. The world spiraled in hues of cerulean blue as a heavy fog crawled in.

An audible thud echoed throughout the surrounding forest as we dropped to the ground.

Somehow, Gren wrapped his arms around me and pivoted us so I landed on his chest instead of the damp soil.

My vision refocused, and my jaw dropped.

I knew exactly where we were, but why here? If those bastards were always this close, why didn't they come for me sooner? Was it really because of some barrier?

We were right outside of Deanville in the cemetery next to Hades Cliff where marbled tombstones encircled us as we sat on a freshly dug grave.

"Addy, please remove your knee," Gren groaned, breathlessly.

I glanced down as I pushed myself off his chest and removed my knee from his nether regions. "Fuck, shit. I'm so sorry. I didn't mean to knee you in the balls." I cleared my throat. "Do you even have balls? I mean, what? Are you okay?" I rambled, grimacing at the word vomit I spewed, eying him in mortification.

Gren laughed, but it was strained—probably because I just squished the hell out of his grapes.

"You're so crass. You know?" He shook his head, and his ebony waves shifted with him.

Gren grabbed my waist and plopped me beside him like I weighed less than a feather.

I had forgotten how strong Gren became and how he decapitated a monster like it was nothing. It sent shivers down my spine, but it still reassured me to know I could count on his strength.

My attention went back to Gren, about to defend myself and ask about the keys, when the crunching of leaves from behind us ignited my fight-or-flight instinct, and I shot to my feet. Gren rose from the ground after me, and we both surveyed the area.

The area was alarmingly quiet even for a cemetery as my eyes roamed to each pristine gravestone encompassing us. Only one had a death date with no name or birth. Which was abnormal since gravestones were fucking expensive.

A soft whistle caressed my ears, and my body revolted against it.

I scanned the cemetery again, but the thick fog obstructed my vision, and I couldn't see anything farther than five feet in front of me.

Whoever the person was, they were whistling an unearthly

tune triggering gooseflesh to creep up my arms and legs.

Like a relentless wraith patronizing the living, Valeria emerged from the fog. She looked surprisingly normal again and not like some distorted nightmare. Her lips were stained red, and her black dress hugged all her curves and rippled against her bare legs with each step she took. Even in the dead of night, she was a rich contrast against the white marble graves.

Valeria parted her ruby lips, and her voice slithered through the air. "You already replaced him, and with your familiar no less." She cackled as she snapped her neck to the side. "And here I thought I was the heartless one."

I didn't give in to her obvious taunt and kept my mind focused on our objective. "We have what you want. Where's Lucien?" I asked, gritting my teeth.

If Valeria believed she could play more mind games on me, she was sorely mistaken.

She snapped her nails, and within the blink of an eye she disappeared.

I panicked and whipped my head around, desperate to find her.

Valeria materialized beside Gren, stroking his cheek with her long and bony fingers. "Not bad for your first one, but he's still so young and inexperienced. And it seems you forget they're wild and need to be tamed."

Gren couldn't move, but his jaw clenched tightly.

I wasn't sure if she cast a spell without us noticing, or if she was just that powerful.

Both frightened me immensely.

I shook out the tension in my hands and met her amused

KING OF THE UNSIGHTLY

gaze.

I needed to stay level-headed. Our lives were on the line.

"You seem to have a problem with touching people without their permission." I snatched her hand and pried it off Gren's cheek. "And when I have Lucien, I will give you the keys," I said, hoping I sounded more assertive than I felt.

"So possessive; just like your mother. Oh, how it takes me back to our little quarrels." She sighed and shook my hand off her wrist. "I guess now is not the time to reminisce. Follow me. *They're waiting.*"

If one more person told me *that*, I was going to scream with frustration. I never in my life wanted to go around stabbing people as much as I did right now.

How could everyone know my mother except for *me*?

Valeria snapped her fingers again, and Gren relaxed under the releasing pressure.

He moved with so much speed he nabbed her off balance.

Gren snatched Valeria's throat and raised her off the ground. "Tell me why I shouldn't snap your neck right now," he growled, lowering his brows as his features turned animalistic.

Gren looked feral as black mist pulsated around him.

Valeria's mouth stretched across her face as she let out an insidious laugh.

She didn't respond to Gren and instead, looked through him to me. "You should have a tighter leash on your familiar. Or are you a fan of gentle training? Whatever it is, I should warn you. The things he does behind your back are quite serious."

What did she mean? Was she trying to pit us against each other?

Gren squeezed Valeria's neck tighter as her feet dangled off the ground. She dug her needle-like nails into Gren's forearm, but her smile never faltered.

For a split second, I wanted Gren to finish the job.

My mind screamed to kill her.

To kill her now, and I would be free.

But I couldn't let them harm Lucien.

I gripped Gren's shoulder and looked at him with a grimace. "Please."

Gren's face softened, and he dropped Valeria to the ground.

Valeria caught herself and rubbed the deep purple bruises already forming around her neck.

She didn't utter another word as she turned her back to us and walked deeper into the haze, signaling us to follow.

47
SING FOR ME

An enormous white granite mausoleum with four thick pillars loomed over us. Each one had a distinct design carved into it. One covered in thorns. The next had blooming lilies. The other two had the moon and stars at the top with bodies piled at the bottom; it resembled a mountain desperate to reach the heavens. A work of art cut into four parts, telling a hauntingly vivid story of longing and death.

Valeria dragged the black granite door open, and it scraped against the concrete floor.

She tilted her head and beamed at me, acting like some valiant chauffeur, but she looked more like the ferryman, Charon, escorting us across the River Styx after we paid our dues.

"Enter," Valeria said, delicately waving us in.

I gulped and jiggled the tension out of my hands.

My heart pounded against my ribcage like the last remnants of my soul didn't even want to be here either and were desperate to flee my body.

I tried to calm my nerves as I stood in front of the ominous entrance.

My eyes flickered back to Gren, who paled as he scrunched his nose, yet he still took my hand and squeezed it longer than usual before letting go.

I gave him a thin smile, and we walked past her.

I *knew* Gren was by my side, but it didn't make me feel any less nervous as I picked at the drying scabs on my fingertips.

Could we really escape unharmed if it was a trap?

A nagging thought told me even if I could do a little magic, it didn't mean I could go up against an unknown entity who had been tracking me for god knows how long.

A casket with the same engraving as the pillars caught my eye, and it made the hallway appear more menacing as moisture permeated the air.

My body tensed and I barely stopped myself from having a full-on panic attack—only the sound of water dripping from the ceiling alleviated my nerves.

My legs took another treacherous step in the eerily lit hallway, and the granite walls warped and melted like acid as the air around me turned thicker than the swap I trudged in with Kaschel. The resemblance it had to his shadows was uncanny as it wrapped around my body and filled my lungs.

Each step pierced the soles of my feet and shot agonizing ripples throughout my legs.

The hallway ended with another black granite door, and it

automatically swung open when it detected our presence.

I hesitated for a split second before walking through, and a woman in a gunmetal-gray suit and shoulder-length, salt-and-pepper hair stood there, arms relaxed. Her sharp brows harshened her expression; her yellow eyes blazed in the dim light, revealing her monstrous nature.

She wasn't what I expected.

She looked like some big-shot CEO, yet she was here in some rich dead guy's mausoleum—if we were still in the mausoleum. I doubted it.

Valeria stalked past me and kneeled before the woman.

Valeria inclined her head, as if waiting for something.

The woman's soft voice cut through the room; my skin crawled as it slithered across my flesh. "Next time, don't stray away from what I assigned you. I mean, what made you think you could wield her grimoire?"

Valeria rose to her feet. Her eyes were desperate for forgiveness. An expression I had never seen on her before.

Pure terror.

Bile rose in my throat, threatening to eject across the floor when I couldn't stop the tremble in my hands.

Valeria lifted her chin, catching the woman's agitated gaze. "I thought it would help us—"

"Don't." The woman held her hand up, and it hypnotized Valeria. The woman gently caressed Valeria's neck and brushed a strand of blonde hair behind her ear. "My ambitious Valeria," she hummed as she stroked Valeria's cheek. Valeria leaned in, completely enamored by her touch. The woman clicked her tongue. "Lynne, take her away and make sure she repents for her misplaced avarice."

A familiar petite woman with long, dirty blonde hair emerged from the shadows. Her blazing eyes turned pitch-black matching Valeria's as she snatched her by the hair.

Lynne wrapped one tiny hand around Valeria's neck and before Valeria could defend herself, Lynne twisted it.

A snap resounded in the room, and Valeria collapsed onto the ground, limp.

"I hate when they don't listen and become thirsty for more than they deserve. Don't you agree?"

I stood there gaping at Valeria's lifeless body as Gren took a step forward, responding to my shock, and attempted to shield me from any potential harm. A kind but unnecessary gesture. I didn't need anyone getting injured for my sake.

The woman shivered in revulsion as she stepped over Valeria's corpse and strolled over to my side.

Lynne winked and gave me a small wave as she dragged Valeria by her leg and disappeared into the dark hallway.

The woman dusted her hands off on her suit like she had touched something revolting when she didn't even lift a finger.

The woman finally spoke again, and all the hair on my body rose, but her focus went to Gren. "Did you do as I asked?"

Gren took another step forward, blocking the woman from getting any closer and nodded his head.

The woman laughed, hollow and abrasive against my ears.

My mouth hung open as I stood there dumbfounded.

I had to be hearing things. This wasn't what we discussed.

My words were barely audible even to me. "What is she talking about?" When Gren didn't respond, and the silence in the air was so palpable I could taste it, I asked Gren louder and more forcefully, "Did you plan this from the beginning?"

Gren didn't glance my way and spoke to the woman in front of us. "The blood ritual is almost complete as requested. She is tethered, you just need to finish the last part."

"Good. Then I shall keep my promise to you."

"Thank you." Gren bowed.

"You may go." The woman flicked her wrist.

Gren stepped away but I snatched his hand. "*Gren.*" My voice cracked. "Were you the one who spoke to me? The ritual? *How could you?*" I looked into his eyes, hoping to see any emotion, any hint of truth.

But his vexed complexion held no lingering tenderness. *So it was him.* He was the one who said those words to me?

Gren pried my hand off him. "Don't act so pathetic, Addy. It doesn't suit you."

My heart dropped, and I fell to my knees as I watched Gren disappear from my view.

A deep pit formed in my stomach, and I tried to make sense of everything around me. Gren couldn't do this. Not after everything we had been through.

Anger boiled through me like molten lava, fueling me to continue.

The woman pointed at me, and my knees slammed hard onto the ground. She flicked her wrist and sent me flying to the other side of the room.

I collided with a wall, creating several cracks in the hard stone. I gasped for air, coughing up blood.

I cried out in agony as a sharp pain stabbed at my side with each breath.

Fuck. I thought they were after the keys, not me. And I thought Gren was on my side too. How many times was I going to let people fool me? *I misplaced my trust, again.*

I inhaled, and the piercing pain made me scream out as it sobered me enough to witness the woman prowling toward me.

"I'm sorry, I'm feeling a little hostile since your mother hid you from me when all I wanted to do was cultivate your powers. Welcome to the Winters family, my sweet Adeline. Your grandmother has missed you dearly." She brushed the back of her hand on my cheek, and I flinched. "Please call me Ingrid for now since we're not on familiar terms yet."

My heart slowed as her words crawled against my skin. No way she couldn't . . . no.

My only family was Lucien.

I blinked away the tears and forced the words out. "Let Lucien go."

The woman, Ingrid, laughed and it sent me over the edge. I called on my magic—from my chest to my fingers—but every time I tried, something blocked it.

Ingrid's mouth curled, immoral and slimy—like a businesswoman swindling me for everything I had—not a grandmother who reunited with her long-lost granddaughter.

Ingrid took a deep breath and lifted my chin with her pointer finger. Her sharp fingernail dug into my skin.

Her smirk spread and her magic released my body, and I slackened as the pressure left me. "My daughter created a potent witch." She snapped his fingers, and I fell to the floor.

Lynne reappeared from the hallway with Lucien chained,

dragging him behind her. His light hair ruffled as dirt clung to the same clothes I last saw him in. His face was gaunt and covered in deep purple bruises.

I shot to my feet and ran past Lynne and kneeled beside Lucien.

"What happened?" The tears stung and blurred my vision as he looked at me with indifference.

I cupped his jaw, but Lucien didn't move or flinch from my touch.

"What did you do to him?" I seethed, clenching my other hand into a tight fist as I stared at Lynne.

She chuckled, haughty and full of pleasure. "He should be fine in a day or two. Probably."

My attention snapped back to Ingrid, who dared to call herself my family, as her temperament turned wrathful. "I'm feeling generous since my daughter's debt is now cast upon you. So, don't test my patience with all your useless whining. I hated it when Lasira did it."

Ingrid materialized in front of me and tapped my forehead. She snatched my arm and traced her black nail along my skin. She pressed down on a vein and punctured my flesh.

Ingrid moved so quickly I had no time to react.

I recoiled from the tinge of discomfort and jerked away, but she had a strength I couldn't match.

My struggle made her mouth warp into a devious grin as she brought her hand to her lips.

She bit down and stretched out her hand and dropped her blood onto the floor. A ring cast in blue flames encircled us.

I yanked and pulled, but I still couldn't budge. "Let go!" My head spun as a force entered my body and clouded my senses.

"You should be more careful with how you talk. We will be in the presence of a *sin*."

"Wh-wh-what?" I thrashed harder against the force attempting to occupy my mind, but it was cruel and persistent.

Ingrid groaned in irritation. "A witch is only as strong as the demon they sign with, and you have always been *his*. Had she taught you nothing?"

"She . . ." I opened my mouth, but I couldn't get any more words out.

"Of course she didn't." Ingrid chuckled. "She betrayed us and well, I guess you know how great it worked out for her." She shook her head. "My poor little girl." She sighed but it held no maternal affection. "I will say, she did a remarkable job at hiding you until now." She snapped her fingers, and Lynne dropped Lucien to the ground.

My focus shifted to his lifeless eyes. "Are you okay?" I asked, waiting for a response.

I was hoping to catch a flicker of life, but Lucien stayed mute, knees pressed to the cold floor.

I fought back tears as fury burrowed deep within my chest.

Ingrid's grip tightened on my wrist as she studied the mark on it. She leaned forward, frowning as she traced Kaschel's mark on the back of my hand.

"You stupid girl. Do you know what you've done? How angry this will make him?" Ingrid yanked me behind her and chucked me to the ground at Lynne's heels and clapped her hands. The blue flames extinguished in the blink of an eye. "Take them downstairs, *immediately*. We need to gather the others and find a way to get rid of him."

48
RUN, LITTLE FLEA, RUN

The cold and damp room held little to no light, and instead, I was swathed in darkness, and it distorted how time moved around me. I could have been trapped here for days . . . weeks . . . or *months*.

I wasn't certain of anything anymore.

Maybe my stay here numbed me, or maybe . . . the betrayal, the grief, and Lucien's odd behavior—or lack thereof—was nothing more than a fleeting memory now.

I exhaled and wiped the dirt and grime from my hands onto my worn-out pants and glared at the rusted bars in front of me as two guards stood watch. It's like they thought I would be able to bend the metal and escape.

I wasn't superhuman. It seemed a tad excessive, and Ingrid had already made it painstakingly clear the cell was warded against magic.

I still tested the theory out over and over again until my fingers went raw.

I wasn't even given a bed or blanket, but I didn't think she cared if my stay here was comfortable or not.

What psychotic lady treats her granddaughter like this?

I scooted closer to the stone wall and wrapped my arms around my knees and pulled them closer to my body.

I tipped my head to the side to check on Lucien, who was staring blankly—a common behavior from him.

The only passing pleasure I found in this hellhole was catcalling the guards, hoping I would get a reaction out of Lucien.

"Hey. HEY." I could hear the guards grumble in annoyance as my voice pierced their eardrums.

It made my lip twitch in amusement.

I stood and sauntered over to the bars and clasped my hands tightly around them. I dipped my head to the side and batted my eyes.

I probably looked like some dirty gremlin, but it only made it more satisfying to see how uncomfortable they appeared.

"Are you a sorcerer?" I paused and saw both guards' faces turn pale. "Because I'm cast under your spell." I glanced back, but the only response I got from Lucien was him turning his head to the side—refusing to look at me.

So I pushed the guards again. "Are you a demon?" I reached out a hand and caressed the closest guard's shoulder. "Because I can feel how hot you are from here."

The guard stumbled forward, shuddered from my touch, and gave me the most disgusted face I had ever seen in my life.

I tried to hold in my laughter as I clasped my hands over my mouth.

My sanity left me a couple thousand marks-on-the-wall ago.

It also didn't help that the only pickup lines I could think of were ones from my T-shirt collection. Maybe Lucien needed me to use new material since he had seen me wear those shirts countless times in the past.

I glanced at the guards and noticed they both sported similar expressions of anguish.

Was I hallucinating? Why did I feel like the guards saw me as some creepy old witch from a fairy tale who came to poison a princess, and they saw themselves as the damsels?

It was almost laughable how much they abhorred my presence. I mean, weren't they some witch's minions? Yet, they were more terrified of me than I was of them, like they knew something I didn't.

It made me curious.

I could hear the guards' hushed squabbling, but their whispers were so loud I could make out every word spilling out of their mouths.

"Switch me places."

"No way."

"Come on."

"No."

"Then make her stop. She's been at it for weeks."

"How do you expect me to do that? Kill her? She would disembowel us if we so much as touch her."

"Ugh."

I turned away, not caring to listen to their useless bickering, and looked back at Lucien in the cell next to me.

He didn't even budge.

I grunted, half tempted to rip my hair out in defeat. "Oh, come on. You definitely would have laughed at it before." I so badly wanted to see his dimpled smile again instead of this barely walking corpse.

"How can you be so optimistic at a time like this?" Lucien asked as his light eyes fell onto me, and my jaw dropped.

I ran to the other side of the cell.

My eyes widened with anticipation. "You finally spoke." My voice came out high-pitched and squeaky and I cleared my throat. "I had been talking to myself so much I thought I was going crazy." I squeezed his hand through the metal bars. Lucien was back. I fought back happy tears and took a deep breath. "And you think me catcalling the guards is me being optimistic?" I lowered a brow.

"No, it's you refusing to feel anything and trying to use humor as a defense mechanism," Lucien muttered; his gravelly voice was solemn, but his face stayed emotionless.

I opened and closed my mouth.

He wasn't wrong.

I brushed my fingers through my tangled hair and watched his expression darken as he tightened his square jaw.

We held eye contact, and I decided to ignore his previous remark. "Are you okay?" I positioned my hand on his forehead.

Lucien felt unusually hot.

"I will be when we get out of here." He pried my hand off him, and a sudden tinge of pain cemented itself within me.

He was so cold and distant.

I had never witnessed this side of Lucien. "I'm sorry." I looked away from him. "You wouldn't be in this mess if it wasn't for me." I choked on the last word but forced back the tears and smiled weakly at him. "I will fix this."

Lucien stayed silent, and I yearned for him to hug me and say he had missed me.

That he was glad to see me.

And if he had to choose anyone to be in a situation like this—he would choose me. Each time.

But he didn't say anything.

A deep ache burrowed into my chest as my heart pulsed erratically. And no matter how many deep breaths I took, it was there, pounding rapidly until I felt like I was going to explode.

A myriad of emotions flickered across Lucien's face like he wanted to say something but couldn't.

I was about to speak to him when a bloodcurdling scream reverberated against the stone walls, and a hot liquid sprayed against my back, soaking my clothes.

The look of horror was written all over Lucien's face as he pressed himself away from me and leaned against the opposite wall.

My breathing turned shallow as my body spun around on its own volition to witness what—or who—was behind me.

I stood there horrified.

My eyes had to be deceiving me.

It couldn't be him. "Kaschel?" I whispered as I gaped at the towering man before me soaked in the blood of the guards.

Their mangled corpses lay crooked and bent on the floor.

"I should have known there would be no other place for a

little flea but in a dungeon rotting away in filth with the rats and mites."

"What. How." I stumbled over my words, too aghast to speak clearly.

Kaschel inclined his head and chuckled; it was throaty and menacing as it echoed throughout the empty corridor. "I had told you once before I had schemes you were unaware of."

Kaschel wrapped his strong hands around the bars and the shadows crawled from his body and swallowed everything in sight except for the small corner of the room he forced me into.

Now there was nothing between us. Nothing to stop him from doing whatever he had come here to do.

Kaschel stalked toward me and snatched my wrist. "My little insurance plan paid off." He kissed the back of my hand; the crescent moon radiated silver, expelling all the shadows away.

A loud hissing assaulted my ears, and I involuntarily puked my guts out as I fell to my knees.

My world spiraled, and I couldn't stop hyperventilating as my erratic breathing felt like knives against my throat.

Kaschel's amethyst eyes outshone the light, and it revealed his wicked nature as he crouched in front of me.

Kaschel tipped his head down, and his alabaster hair moved with him. "I keep my promises, *unlike you.* Now hurry. Your friend doesn't look so great." Kaschel clicked his tongue and turned his back to me. "And don't worry, your punishment will come later."

A black hole materialized in the corridor, and he walked out of the cell and vanished into the abyss.

I stumbled to my feet and snagged the key off the guard's mutilated body. The key soaked in blood, I fiddled with the lock on Lucien's cell until it clicked open.

I ran to his side and collapsed next to him, but he wasn't moving, lifeless again.

I grabbed his cheeks and squeezed. "We need to go now!"

Lucien's head flopped forward, his arms dangled to my sides, and he fell into me; no matter how much I squeezed—he didn't move.

Why wasn't he moving?!

I cried out in agony and wrapped my arms around him, hoping to god he would open his eyes.

This was all a nightmare.

And I would wake up in my bed in a cold sweat knowing none of this was real.

But it was.

And I could feel all my rage and grief surge through me at once.

My magic cracked and hissed as it engulfed the cells and hall, spreading like wildfire.

I screamed as pangs of anger splintered within me.

All other emotions were swallowed by the violet light thrumming inside my chest.

As the discomfort settled down, I got to my feet and grabbed Lucien by the legs and struggled to drag him behind me. He was still limp on the cold ground as the violet waves lashed at everything around me except for him.

I couldn't feel my soul any longer. My chest was hollowed out and emptied. All the pain twisted me into a broken marionette doll with only one emotion.

Rage, and it made me *hungry.*

Hungry for power. For revenge against all who tormented me. For answers.

And somehow, I knew what I needed to do: get Lucien medical attention and find the creepy witch lady who warned me from the beginning.

Want to know when the next installment of Tempting Trickery will be released? Teasers? Sign up for Belle Briar's newsletter here.

BELLE BRIAR resides in Northern California with her supportive husband and their feral little boy. When she's not writing or drinking coffee, she's wrangling her toddler and trying to convince him vegetables are yummy, and jumping off the couch onto the hardwood floor is a no-no.

Publishing her first series, Tempting Trickery, Belle always loved reading lore about the fae as a young girl, and she always hoped one day she might run into a broody but handsome fae who would sweep her off her feet. Sorry, husband(don't worry, he understands).

Milton Keynes UK
Ingram Content Group UK Ltd.
UKHW031950281024
450365UK00008B/419